TO DISCOVER MORE AND GET A **FREE** COPY OF THE SHORT STORY PREQUEL TO THE AMAZON BESTSELLING COMING OF AGE FANTASY **TIMOTHY SCOTT: SHADOW ISLAND** HEAD OVER TO:

TOBEY-ALEXANDER.COM

GET YOUR EXCLUSIVE PREQUEL SHORT STORY AND STAY UP TO DATE ON EXCITING NEW PROJECTS FROM THE AUTHOR.

Dedicated to any of my multiple personalities, they make these adventures all the more real although, in truth, this is dedicated to all those who believe in me when I don't. You know who you are.

DARK CURSES
ICEMAN

TOBEY ALEXANDER

PROLOGUE
5,000 YEARS AGO
CHALCOLITHIC PERIOD – EUROPEAN CONTINENT

SNOW was being whipped in every direction by the buffeting wind. The cold season had settled in and it was not a time to be out and exposed. Between the breaks in the tumultuous snowstorm the distant ice-capped mountains could be seen, but between those moments there was nothing but white.

Deep in the heart of what would become known as modern Italy, a solitary figure appeared in the fog of dancing snowflakes. A man dressed in sewn leather clothes staggered through the storm. His bear-pelt hat threatened to whip from his head in the wind, and the pieces of hide he had fashioned into a coat kept as much of him as warm as possible. Nursing his right hand, the man staggered across the soft snow and inspected the bloodstained cloth wrapped around his palm.

The cold was bitter and although he hugged the pelt of fur tight to his chest, he could not hold back the bitter sting against his exposed flesh. Eyes wide with panic he looked around in desperation. He knew he was being hunted. Adjusting the makeshift bandage on his hand, droplets of blood stained the snow as an enraged voice carried in the wind.

Spinning around, the man looked for any sign of the voice. Shielding his eyes against the snowflakes that whipped past his face he saw a silhouette in the distance. His heart sank as he watched the silhouette be joined by a second and third. He had hoped the storm would disorientate his pursuers, venturing this far into the glacier was risky even on a cloudless day but now, consumed by desperation, it was a gamble that was not paying off.

Cursing, the man pulled the cloth tight around the jagged wound on his right palm and secured it in place. Wincing against the pain, he took a moment to compose himself before turning his back on the approaching silhouettes and venturing deeper into the snowstorm.

Moving at such a slow pace, his heart raged in his chest. The leather boots on his feet sank into the snow as he trudged deep into the storm. Feeling the snow flake inside the boots, he ignored the piercing cold and pressed on as the voices grew closer behind him.

Taking another step he felt the snow swallow his feet but, unlike before, his foot did not find solid ground beneath the deep snow. Putting all his weight onto his front leg, it overcame him with fear as the ground swallowed him.

The man felt himself slip through the snow as he fought to find a handhold in the sea of powdery snow. As a sharp pain erupted in his side, he found the momentum of his fall halted. Pressing his hands into the snow, he felt relief as his hands found the concealed rock buried beneath the surface.

Unbeknownst to him, the rock had been his saving grace. Where he had trodden, there had been nothing but compacted snow and ice that had buckled the moment he had pressed his weight against it. A short way ahead of him the ice had crumbled to reveal a vertical drop of more than a hundred feet. The rock that had stopped his descent had been the jagged edge of an enormous fissure in the mountainside he was now daring to cross.

The voices, muffled by the whipping wind, drew closer and he knew he was done for. Try as he might the snow had collapsed in around him and he was stuck between the rock and certain death with the fall that faced him. Craning his neck to look for his pursuers, he saw their silhouettes much closer than he had expected.

With no other choice, the man scooped the snow from the ground around him and piled it up and around his exposed neck and head. Knowing his makeshift camouflage was less than ideal, he scooped the last handfuls of powdered snow over his head as the first of the hunting party emerged from the storm and into view.

Holding his breath, the man kept still beneath his concealment and prayed. Desperate to escape the clutches of the three men, he listened but could hear nothing but the crunching of ice somewhere beneath him. Fighting to calm his racing heart and ragged breaths, time felt endless as he waited.

There was no way to know how long it had been or how far the other men had gone. As his disguise failed him, the warmth of his breath melting the layer of snow in front of his face, he decided to move.

Half expecting to find the tip of a copper spear pointed at him, it relieved him to see the last of the three men disappear back the way they had come. It had only been a few moments, but it had been long enough for the hunting trio to discover the sheer drop a little way beyond the man's concealment. Satisfied there was no sign of their prey, they had regrouped themselves and traced back the way they had come.

The man was not so fortunate. Still buried to his chest in the snow, the only thing keeping him in place was the rock that bit into his skin as he fidgeted. The only purchase he had beneath the snow came from him pushing himself up with his hands. Try as he might the strength in his injured hand was of little use and his arm collapsed with pain each time he tried to push himself up.

Grunting and heaving, he fought to keep his voice low but felt jolts of pain with each attempt to climb free of his confinement. As his fingers sank into the snow, he felt his body drop a little lower until his feet, he could tell, were floating above nothing but air.

Desperation saved him, fuelled by his desire to escape he found purchase beneath the surface and dragged himself free. Heaving with all his strength, the tied bandage broke free as he pulled himself up and back onto more stable ground. Crawling away from the hole that had almost been his doom, the man left a trail of blood behind him until he collapsed gasping onto his back.

As he lay on the floor looking up, the wind eased a little and the snowstorm's ferocity dwindled. Calming his ragged breaths, he saw a break in the clouds and the crystal-blue sky high above him. Admiring the majesty and beauty as the storm faded away, he felt a sense of peacefulness and calm.

All that changed as raised voices broke the sudden silence.

Sitting bolt upright, he turned to see the three hunters running through the snow toward him. Each man was armed with a metal-tipped spear as they spied their prey.

Faces contorted with anger and determination, they moved with laboured grace through the deep snow, their weapons pointed towards him as they moved.

Forgetting the beauty of the serine blue sky that peaked through the heavy clouds, the man righted himself and made his attempt to run.

Unarmed as he was he was already at a disadvantage. Fleeing into the mountains he had had no time to arm himself and had only the clothes on his back as he left the screams of his village behind him. Seeing an outcrop of rock ahead, he steered his course towards them and hoped to reach them before the first of the hunters reached him.

Dragging himself behind the shelter of rock, the first of the three hunters had pulled away from the others in the party and rounded the bluff seconds behind the man. It had been enough time to snatch a jagged rock from the ground as he had disappeared from view. The hunter, rounding the corner, was surprised to find his prey pressed against the face of stone. There was little time to react as the man drove the sharp stone down onto the top of his opponent's head.

As the surprised hunter's legs buckled beneath him, the snow was dashed with fresh blood from the vicious wound the rock had caused. Cracking the man's skull, he flailed on the ground as the crimson blood seeped from the gash that stretched from his forehead to the crown of his head.

Dropping the bloodstained rock to the floor, the hunted man ripped a copper-headed axe from the other man's back and staggered away from the twitching body. The once peaceful mountains and virgin snow were now stained with blood and corrupted by desperation.

Armed with the axe, the hunted man staggered away as the other two from the hunting party burst around the outcrop of rock. The first crashed into the body of their injured companion, sending him sprawling to the floor. The other looked on in horror at the bloodied body of his friend.

In a tongue long forgotten, the enraged hunter cast a torrent of abuse towards the fleeing man and set off in pursuit. Fuelled by rage and anger, the other man closed the distance on his prey faster than he had expected.

Turning, the man felt a wave of terror as the second hunter dived through the air; spear raised out in front of him and attacked. More by luck than skill, the man stumbled to the side as the tip of the spear sliced through the air and buried into the ground where he had been stood.

With no time to react, he felt a powerful fist smash into the side of his face as the hunter lashed out. In their native tongue, a dialect long forgotten to history, the hunter offered the man one last chance to surrender.

'You are no warrior, you are a medicine man.' The hunter snarled as he watched his prey fumble with the axe. 'Your people wait for you.'

'No.' Was his only defiant reply as he smashed the axe out towards the other man.

'You will pay for what you've done.' The other barked as he cast aside the poorly aimed attack. 'Blood stains your hands.'

There was no need for more words as the two men fought in the snowy clearing. Immersed in the battle the hunted man had forgotten about the third in the hunting party. Transfixed on his opponent, he did not see the third man scramble up the face of rocks and take a vantage point above the clearing as the two men fought and parried.

The hunted man knew he was out-skilled by the other

man as he felt the sharpened metal-tip of the spear scrape across his skin. Recoiling from the bite of metal he staggered away, but it was too late.

The finishing blow came not from the man's spear, instead he felt himself thrown forward to the floor by a heavy blow from behind. The third man, taking advantage of his high-ground position, had knocked an arrow into the bow across his body and loosed an arrow at his prey.

His aim had been true as the arrow arced through the air and buried itself in the hunted man's armpit. Although a distance shot, the arrow-tip coming to rest in bone, the power had been enough to knock him from his feet. Sprawled face-down in the snow, the hunted man coughed a mouthful of blood onto the floor beneath him. 'You will pay for what you have done.' The spear-wielding hunter growled as the man rolled onto his side to look up at him.

There was a look of defiance on the injured man's face, something the other had not expected to see. It was the same look the man maintained as the hunter reached down and snatched the arrow from his armpit.

Watching the pool of blood spread around the man's body, there was no need to offer a final blow as he watched the man's skin turn pale as death took him. As the warm blood melted the snow around his body, the older man glared up at the hunter.

His last words were weak, hissed between pursed lips, but their message was clear.
'I do not die this day,' the life in his eyes fading as he spoke, 'I am to be reborn, a true-'

The sentence remained unfinished as the man took one last breath.

CHAPTER ONE

APRIL 1941
LONDON

STANLEY Grand was tired, and yet the
Luftwaffe's nightly bombardment would not let him sleep.
Crammed with his family in the Anderson Shelter, nobody
was sleeping, least of all Stanley in the damp-smelling
shelter. At twenty-seven he was still young in his father's
eyes and although his return from the front line had been
sooner than they had expected, they had welcomed him
home a hero.

Not that he felt one, deep down he felt a failure.
Nursing the scar on his collarbone, the dampness
aggravated his still healing wound as he closed his eyes
and thought about his time in France. The pound and thud
of the falling bombs felt all too familiar as he closed his

eyes and allowed himself to remember the past.

Serving his country, enlisting in the Army to serve King and country had been a proud moment for him. Dressed in his uniform, he remembered the look of pride on his parent's face as he had boarded the train. He had left a young hero, destined for noble things in the heat of battle and yet now he was nothing more than another injured soldier.

It had been during an assault of a small outlying village that a German sniper had loosed a single round and stole his hope of glory from him. Laid on the cold, damp floor he had feared the worst as his sergeant had exposed the wound on his left shoulder.

'Am I going to die?' He had stammered as the soldier searched for an exit hole.

It felt ridiculous as he looked back, an inexperienced young man caked in blood and mud, almost crying in fear. The embarrassment built up inside him as an explosion somewhere nearby rocked the Anderson Shelter and snatched him back from his melancholy.

'Buggers are getting closer!' His father groaned as he rolled over on the uncomfortable bed to peer out of the narrow opening above the shelter's door. 'If Jerry's smashed my windows there'll be hell to pay ain't that right Stanley?'

'What?' Stanley groaned as he rolled to look at his dad. 'Oh, yeah, hell to pay.'

'What's wrong son?' His dad pressed as Stanley adjusted himself on the bed against a jolt of pain from his arm.

'Nothing.'

'Oh come on boy, quit your mood and remember your mother and I are glad you're back.'

'I know.' Stanley sighed, fighting the urge to tell his dad to be quiet.

'That's right Stanley, all a mother wants is her children to be safe.'

There was little use in arguing or trying to explain the sense of disappointment he felt, instead he offered a forced smile and laid himself back on the makeshift bed to try to sleep. Staring up at the corrugated ceiling, he longed to be back with his friends, away from the powerlessness he now felt as the Germans once again bombarded London with an onslaught of bombs.

As the echoes of explosions and wail of the sirens faded, Stanley found enough peace to drift into an uneasy sleep filled with vivid dreams of his time on the front line. His dreams were less flights of fancy and imagination and more like the haunted dreams and nightmares of his memories.

Morning came and with it the smell of burning wood was the first thing that Stanley recognised as he woke. Looking around the shelter, it surprised him to find he was alone in the subterranean shelter. Brushing off a layer of dirt and dust from his chest, he sat up and wiped the sleep from his eyes.

Taking a moment to compose himself, he brushed himself down and emerged into the early morning sunshine that bathed the back garden of his family home. Being spring there was still a chill in the air and he felt it as he stepped onto the lawn and looked towards the end townhouse he called home.

'Glad to see you're awake.' His dad called from the back door across the small yard at the back of the house. 'Only one window gone, could have been worse.'

Taking a moment, Stanley looked down the length of the street and at the houses connected to his own. At the far end of the row he saw the Jones' house had not been so lucky. The collapsed roof still smouldered, and he saw that the complete side wall had collapsed during the midnight air raid.

'Are they all right?' Stanley asked as he stepped over the debris that littered the back garden.

'What's that?'

'The Jones', are they ok?' Stanley pointed to the destroyed house down the street.

'I think so,' his dad replied as he moved back into the kitchen. 'Your mum's gone down to see if there's anything we can do to help. Go and give her a hand.'

Too old to fight, Stanley's father had regretted not being able to serve alongside his son when the call had been made for volunteers. Although he had served in the Great War, there was still a sense of duty in his father, but the fact was he was too old made it impossible.

It had not stopped George Grand making his impact on the home front, having him home for the air raid was a rare event as he was normally out doing what he could to help others during the raids. Watching his father through the taped kitchen window, Stanley could not deny the role model his father was to him. He respected him far more than he would ever let on, but he also understood the frustration and helplessness his father felt. It was a feeling he was all too familiar with himself.

Sighing, Stanley loosened off his tight left shoulder and walked along the back of the row of houses towards the smouldering wreck of the Jones'. As he walked through the alley to the street, he could hear the familiar chatter of voices that accompanied the morning after a heavy bombardment from the Germans.

Emerging onto the street, it always saddened him how battered and forlorn London looked. The street he remembered playing on as a child was now a mix of debris and shattered glass. Buildings looked like rows of crumbling teeth with many houses standing as shells with roofs and walls missing.

As he walked towards the smouldering wreckage of the latest victim of the blitzkrieg, he caught sight of the portly Mrs Jones sat on a pile of bricks on the far side of the road. Her face was caked with dirt and soot and she sat with a confused expression on her round face as she watched the plumes of smoke clambering skyward where her roof had once been.

'Are you ok Mrs Jones?' Stanley asked as he walked across the cobbled street to his neighbour.

As if disturbed from a daydream, the old woman turned her attention and smiled up at him. Her wayward grey hair stuck out in many directions and the glasses she wore around her neck were cracked and broken. She had always been a jovial spirit, a kind old woman who had offered the local children sweets and treats as they walked past her door. Now, however, she looked broken at seeing her beloved home destroyed.

'Oh, Stanley,' she wept, tears tracing through the soot on her cheeks. 'What have they done to my house? Eric would be furious if he were still here.'

Eric, her husband, had died before the war had begun and had left Mrs Jones on her own. It had done nothing to dampen her jovial spirits and her smile, yet now she seemed broken by the relentlessness of the war. Awash with sympathy for the kind old woman, Stanley offered her a hand and helped her from her perch on the pile of rubble.

'Come on Mrs Jones, let's get you a cup of tea while mum and the others find some of your things.'

'You are a splendid boy Stanley,' she murmured as they walked along the street leaving the smouldering ruins behind them. 'I remember when you were a young lad, always saved extra treats for you.'

She patted his cheek with affection as he guided her back home and through the front door.

Helping her into his father's seat by the cracked living room window, Stanley took another look at the war-torn street outside. London felt nothing like the city he remembered. Even though the destruction he could see was only limited to his own street, he knew there were countless other families feeling the same waves of loss and confusion.

Although everyone pulled together, brought together by the community spirit of a nation under attack, it still felt a lonely place. As he looked down the street, his father's hand on his shoulder made him jump.
'We will need some milk if you're going to invite all the neighbours for tea.' His father feigned annoyance, but the coy smile gave him away. 'Get yourself to the shop and see if you can't get some powdered milk before she drinks it all will you son?'

His dad handed him the tattered ration book and returned his attention to the overweight Mrs Jones who now occupied his chair. Thankful for the distraction Stanley grabbed his coat from behind the front door and stuffed the ration book in his trouser pocket.

Eager to see beyond his own street's destruction overnight, filled with a strange sense of curiosity, Stanley took the long way and to avoid being accosted by his mother. Turning away from Mrs Jones' house, he sauntered along the street and out to join the expected lines of shoppers who had risen early to fetch their daily rations.

It was not a morbid curiosity that consumed him but more intrigue to see the damage left behind from the night's bombing. Secured in the shelter behind the house, he had listened to the familiar whistle and silence as the German Luftwaffe loosed their torrent of bombs down on the city below. Having heard the relentless symphony of whistles and explosions, Stanley was curious to see what was left of London in the bombing's wake.

As he reached the end of the street Stanley took a moment to take in the view in front of him. As his street sat on a hill, he had an impressive view of London. Plumes of smoke billowed into the sky from various buildings as far as the eye could see. Barrage balloons wafted in the wind and the entire city looked battered.

The thing that caught Stanley's attention was a thick column of smoke coming from the magnificent structure of Westminster Abbey. Forgetting his task to get milk and rations, an insatiable curiosity washed over him as he heard the roar of sirens carry in the air from the direction of the Abbey.

Fuelled by his almost childish desire to see what had happened, Stanley broke into a jog and descended the sweeping hill, keeping the black cloud of smoke in his sights as he navigated the streets towards Westminster.

CHAPTER TWO

WESTMINSTER Abbey stood, a spectacular feat of architecture. The gothic spires clambering skyward seemed less ornate in the wake of the night's bombings. Shrapnel had scarred the high-pitched tile roof and the outside walls, normally smooth and clean, were covered in damage from shrapnel and debris.

What fires had burned had been extinguished and, as Stanley arrived, the beacon of smoke had almost disappeared. Slowing his pace so as not to draw unnecessary scorn or attention from the tired faces, Stanley walked along Tothill Street with the enormous twin spires dominating the view ahead of him.

Even from a distance he could make out portions of the impressive arched window had been damaged in the blast and his attention was fixed on the building as someone bumped into him. Turning his attention to the sudden interruption, he looked down at a soot-stained young boy.

'Watch where you're going!' Stanley snapped at the boy who hugged his arms around his chest.

The boy had a head of blonde hair that almost looked grey beneath the layer of dust and soot that covered it. His eyes were wide as he looked up at Stanley and offered little in the way of apology. About to offer the boy a telling off a sudden commotion at the end of the street stole Stanley's attention enough for the boy to make good his escape as he sprinted off back the direction Stanley had come.

'Bloody kids, he should be an evacuee.' Stanley scoffed as he looked to a gathering of people at the bottom of the road.

Reaching the junction of Victoria Street, he could finally see the source of the raised voices. A handful of people were crowded around a tired and irritable police constable. Stood with his arms stretched wide, the officer looked less than impressed with the dozen onlookers that crowded around him to peer at the damage to the infamous Abbey.

'Listen here love,' the officer barked at a middle-aged woman who tried to peer around him. 'Get yourself back home and let us get on with what we need to. It don't help having you lot interfering and getting in the way.'

A handful of auxiliary fire-fighters tidied up their hoses behind the policeman and navigated themselves with caution around a jagged hole in the ground at the foundations of the wall. Whatever bomb had caused the enormous crater had been lucky not to bring the entire wall tumbling down. Keeping his distance from the gathered crowd and the irritable officer, Stanley tried to make sense of the hole in the ground.

The hole sat at the base of the old castle-like battlements on the right-hand side of the Abbey. Judging by the raggedness of the crater, Stanley could see the exposed foundations of the stone wall and it sent a chill down his spine.

'Move along now son,' a second officer instructed as he moved past Stanley.

'Sorry.'

Not wanting to feel even more out-of-place Stanley walked past the dispersing group of neighbourly women and passed along the side of the battlement wall. He realised, as he walked along the side of the impressive stone wall, how much the structure had taken. With no real clue how old the walls were, he suspected it was not the first time they had been ravaged and damaged in warfare. Considering a bomb had exploded less than a handful of feet away from it, the only scars were superficial and the wall had remained standing.

Moving around the magnificent Abbey building, Stanley made it onto Abingdon Street and found another, less sizeable crater on the grass between the Abbey and St Margaret's Church. Westminster Hall had remained untouched during the raid and, looking at the concentration of damage, the focus had been on the iconic structures in the capital that night.

Unlike the damage on the far side of the Abbey, the smaller hole was of less interest to the passing public. The uneven crater sat between the two buildings and, awash with curiosity, Stanley chanced a look into the jagged hole in the ground.

Passing through the twisted iron gates, distorted by the blast of the falling bomb, he skirted around a fallen tree. Splinters of wood stood grotesque from the ground where the explosion had torn the tree in half, sending its upper branches tumbling to the ground. As he lifted himself over the fallen tree, he felt a tug as his coat caught on a snapped branch.

Trying his best to go unnoticed by the milling pedestrians along the street, knowing his actions would end up in scorn and disapproval from any onlookers, he tugged at his coat to break free. The branch would not give and it took a handful of rough tugs as he balanced over the fallen trunk before the broken branch gave in.

Caught by surprise, balanced straddling the fallen tree trunk, the sudden release sent Stanley tumbling backwards across the grass. Unseen by anyone, he dropped to the floor and rolled back to the edge of the second crater in the ground.

The momentum of his fall was enough to send him tumbling downwards and into the mouth of the hole. Scrambling for a handhold as he fell, there were only thin roots to slow his descent into the dark unknown beneath the ground. Feeling the weak roots snap as he grabbed them, he tried to relax himself for the expected collision with a solid floor, however far down that may be.

The solid floor welcomed him with a thud and sent the air spewing from his lungs. Landing on his back, Stanley looked up at the hole in the ground and the cloudy sky high above. Much to his relief he had not fallen far and as he fought to recover from the winding, he realised he had fallen far enough to leave the soil lip of the hole out of his reach.

Not wanting to move, fearing he had aggravated the injury to his shoulder, he stayed laid on the icy floor for a few minutes trying to think of a way out of his sudden predicament. Short of shouting for help, a less than appealing prospect as he suspected nobody would hear him, he would have to find his own way out.

Taking control of his laboured breaths, Stanley fumbled through his pocket until he found an old battered lighter. Pulling it free, he opened the lid and sparked the flint. The flame lived only for a second with his first attempt, but it was enough to bathe the subterranean room in a moment of light. As Stanley teased the flame to life, he allowed his eyes to adjust and took in his curious surroundings.

Much to his surprise, he lay in a narrow underground tunnel. The floor was made of smooth stone and the walls arched up to where the bomb had torn through the vaulted ceiling. Sitting up, Stanley cast the lighter around until he had seen enough.

In one direction the tunnel stretched off into the darkness, no signs of life or light. In the opposite direction, a short distance away, Stanley looked at a wooden door that sat ajar. Awash with renewed curiosity, Stanley rose from the floor and attempted to brush what dirt he could from his clothes.

Looking around, there was nothing he could use as torchlight as he felt the heat of the flickering flame on his thumb. Moving towards the door, it surprised him to find it undamaged and open wide enough for him to squeeze himself through. The door looked medieval, thick wood, and iron rivets gave it the appearance of a substantial barricade. Pressing his hand against the door, he tried to push it open wider but it would not move.

Inspecting the face of the door a wooden plaque caught his attention. Etched into the wooden plaque was a curious image that felt familiar. What appeared to be a religious figure stood in the centre of a large circle. The figure held a cross in its right hand with a halo emanating from its head. In the flickering light Stanley struggled to read the letters etched on the inside of the circle around the figure.

Struggling to make out the finer details, he turned his

attention to the door and pressed himself through the narrow opening between the door and the stone frame. Passing the lighter into the room beyond, Stanley squeeze through and entered a sizeable chamber that looked like a museum.

Curious items stood in glass cases and on ornate shelves and stretched the length of the underground room. Moving to the nearest of the glass cabinets, he looked at a curious skull encased beneath the glass. Although it looked familiar, like something from a bull or horse with wide nostrils and side-facing eyeholes, it made no sense to be contained within such a case.

Overcome with an insatiable sense of curiosity at the room of hidden treasures, Stanley walked deeper into the room and admired the strange collection of items around him. There was everything he could imagine scattered around. Unopened chests were piled high with their contents, he presumed, written in Latin on labels mounted beneath them.

Some words he recognised, but mostly the contents of the boxes were a mystery. As he brushed his hand across the dusty surface of one box he was frozen with fright as the sound of falling stone echoed from the corridor outside the room.

Holding his breath, Stanley extinguished the flame and inched with caution back to the open door. Peeking through the narrow gap, he allowed his eyes to adjust to the light that spewed in from the hole he had fallen down. Half expecting to find some curious curator or guard, he was relieved to find the corridor was still empty.

Knowing he was on borrowed time and in a place he should not be, Stanley thought it best to find a way out before someone caught him. Although he longed to know what was in the room, the hairs on the back of his neck told him it was time to go and he was already pushing it too far staying inside the room.

Squeezing back through the narrow opening he stood back up in the corridor and inched back towards the floor where he had landed as he had tumbled through the crater. As he stepped into the pool of light from the surface, he froze on the spot as a voice called out from the mouth of the crater above him.

'Hey, you!' The woman's voice echoed along the corridor and he snatched his gaze up in fright. 'What are you doing down there?'

Stanley covered his eyes against the harshness of the daylight and saw a youthful woman his own age peering over the lip of the hole. A tin Brodie helmet with a cream W stencilled on the front sat on her head as she fought to keep it in place while peering down the hole.

'What are you doing down there?' Her voice was stern yet laced with concern.

'I fell down when I was…' He trailed off thinking of a way to not sound foolish.

'I'm guessing your friends thought it funny to leave you down here?' She scorned.

'Friends?'

'Seems they pulled the rope away and left you down there on your own.'

As she answered she tossed a coil of rope down into the hole for Stanley to use.

'You've got me mistaken,' Stanley protested as he pulled himself back up to the surface. 'I fell down, I wasn't here with anybody I promise.'

'Likely story,' the woman groaned as she helped him back up. 'Just so happens there's a rope tied to the tree then?'

Stanley was about to answer when another voice stole both their attention.

'You two stay where you are! What are you doing there?'

Both Stanley and the mysterious Air Warden turned as the frustrated policeman Stanley had seen berating the crowd stalked across the grass towards them.

'Great!' The woman groaned as he marched towards them.

CHAPTER THREE

BOTH of them felt the frustration of the police constable as he glared down at them. Panting from the sudden run across the uneven ground and scramble over the tree, he now towered over them with his notebook in hand.

'And just what were you doing down there?' The constable asked as he pointed his pencil at Stanley.

'I fell.'

'Likely story.' It was clear he was unconvinced and as he dusted himself off Stanley could feel both the woman and the policeman watching him.

'I swear officer, I came for a look around when I know I shouldn't but it was a total accident.' Stanley continued to protest. 'If it wasn't for her I'd be stuck down there still.'

'Ah, so you were with this young man were you?'

The policeman rounded on the woman, who cast Stanley a disapproving glare. Removing her helmet, she tucked it beneath her arm and explained.

'I was passing by when I saw something out of place, I decided to take a look and found him down the hole. I couldn't just leave him now, could I?'

Stanley admired her tenacity. She spoke with a confidence that surprised him, her words were respectful yet it was clear she was not afraid to speak for herself.

'Right,' the officer interrupted and placed the tip of his pencil onto his notebook. 'I've heard just about enough of you pair. Names, please?'

Stanley was about to protest, but the woman stopped him and offered the constable her details.

'Hazel Johnson, I'm an Air Warden.' She tapped the helmet beneath her arm, but the officer wasn't looking.

'And you?' He levelled his gaze at Stanley.

'Stanley Grand, but I promise she was only helping me.'

The officer silenced Stanley and took the rest of their details. Once they had given the policeman, their full details they were allowed on their way, but not after he had given them a stern warning. As they walked back through the bent gate at the side of St Margaret's church, Stanley very much felt like he had his tail between his legs.

'Well thank you for that Stanley Grand!' Hazel snapped as they reached the road. 'I could have done without that after the night I've just had.'

'Look,' Stanley stopped in his tracks and turned to face her.

It was the first time Stanley took in her appearance apart from the fleeting glance he had from the bottom of the hole. Although she looked tired, and her clothes were covered in dust, she was striking. Her auburn hair was tied in a bun at the back of her head and what little makeup she had on accentuated her features. What stole his attention was her emerald green eyes that now bore into him as she waited for him to continue speaking.

To look at her it was hard to guess her age but Stanley, in his mind, wouldn't have put her much older than himself.

'I didn't mean to get you involved, I promise it was just a series of unfortunate events that led to me being down there.'

'Honestly,' she snapped in frustration, 'I don't care. I want to get home and get to bed. Messing around dragging you out of a hole wasn't on my list of cares today.'

She took a step back and turned to storm away from Stanley. Seizing his chance and feeling overcome with guilt at having her crossing the irritable policeman's path, he grabbed her arm and stopped her in her tracks.

'Listen, I feel bad and would like to make it up to you.'

'I'm not interested.'

'A coffee, something to say sorry for getting you in bother?'

'Stanley, someone your age should fight for our country and not be messing around in churchyards poking his nose where it doesn't belong. I've had my fill of people that can't be bothered to do their part so no, I don't want your apology.'

Stunned into silence her words felt like a punch in the stomach and before he could find the words to answer she had stepped away and stormed off leaving him stood alone on the pavement. Intentional or not, her words had cut through him like a knife and it was hard for him to hold back tears as he watched her disappear into the crowds of pedestrians.

Doing his best to compose himself, Stanley turned in the opposite direction and made his way to Lambeth Bridge. Avoiding the main flow of people, he walked with his hands stuffed in his pockets and head hanging low.

The events of the last hour were forgotten against the crushing feeling of disappointment he felt.

Reaching the bridge he found his way down to the banks of the Thames and took a seat by the station of the bridge. Away from prying eyes and casual glances, Stanley allowed himself to cry as he buried his head into his hands.

He remained there for most of the morning, unseen by the Londoners as he stared into the rippling water of the river. The reflection of the city was distorted, and it reflected how he felt inside. Somehow since coming back from the front line he had felt broken and incomplete. Not a day passed when he did not think about the crack and thump of the round being fired that stole his chance of glory.

Thinking back to the small French village, Stanley could remember the events like it was yesterday. The trees were barren; winter had long since stripped the leaves from the branches. Patches of snow still covered the floor, and they were passing through another unoccupied village in the search for a platoon of German soldiers they had been hunting for.

The first shot had sent them all running for cover, but Stanley had missed the first gunshot. As ever his mind had been ironically wandering to his family and home and it wasn't until the familiar voice of his sergeant bellowed for him to "MOVE" that he snapped back to where he was.

By then it had been too late, the sniper concealed in the old village church tower had adjusted his sights and fired his second round, the one that had tore through Stanley's left shoulder. By blind luck the bullet had missed his lungs and heart, but the pain had been enough to convince him he would die.

As Stanley recalled the echoing sound of the gunshot,

something on the bridge above created a similar sound and he jumped back from his melancholy daydream with his heart racing. Looking around it took a moment to bring his thoughts back from the battleground, but he felt relief when the sound of the river returned to his senses.

Realising his parents would be worried, Stanley climbed his way back to the bridge and made his way back home. As he passed by the small local store he realised he had forgotten to get the rations and knew by now, there would be little left worth queuing for. Resigning himself to the fact he would face an onslaught of annoyance from his parents, he made his way home.

The fact the sun had dipped back towards the horizon told him he had been on the riverbanks longer than he had thought. It wasn't uncommon, since returning home, for him to lose track of time when his mind wandered back. It wasn't something he could share with anyone else and the only time he had tried to speak to his father about his feelings he had been shot down in flames.
'You're a hero to us son.' His dad had tried to comfort, but it wasn't what he needed to hear.

With his hands buried in his pocket he turned back onto his street and was relieved to see the hive of activity around Mrs Jones' house had lessened. Trudging up the cobbled street, Stanley kept his gaze low and offered his neighbours muffled greetings as he made his way to the front door.
'Mum? Dad?' He quizzed as he stepped through the door and removed his coat. 'Anyone home?'

Looking around Stanley could see his father had repaired the cracked glass with more tape in the front window but the living room was empty. The seat Mrs Jones had sat in was covered in crumbs and as he looked around, he heard voices in the back of the house.

'Mum?' He pressed as he made his way into the kitchen. 'Where's Mrs Jones gone?'

Stanley wanted to ask more questions, but the well-dressed stranger clad in a brown suit stole his attention. The man fell silent as Stanley walked into the kitchen to find both his parents talking to the stranger, both sharing the same concerned look.

'Stanley Grand?' The man asked as he pulled a notebook from his pocket.

The first thing Stanley noted was the man's distinct Irish accent. He was Stanley's senior by ten or more years and wore a pair of narrow spectacles on the bridge of his nose. As the man leafed through the pages, he waited for Stanley to answer.

'Don't just stand there like a fool, Stanley.' His father snapped, the irritation in his voice catching Stanley by surprise.

'Would I be right in saying you gave your details to a colleague of mine this morning?'

The question confused Stanley, and it took a moment for him to process what the man was asking of him.

'I'm sorry, who are you?' Stanley pressed, a sense of nervousness washing over him.

'Detective Inspector Damien Kelly, Metropolitan Police.' The Inspector removed his warrant card and flashed it at Stanley, who paid it no attention. 'So, as I was saying, is it right you provided your details to one of my constable's earlier this morning?'

Feeling both his parents staring at him, he struggled to meet their gaze as he answered the Inspector's questions.

'Yes, that's right.' Stanley's nervousness was palpable as he felt his hands shaking. 'It was all a misunderstanding though, I was only-'

Inspector Kelly raised his hand, pencil pinched

between his fingers and silenced Stanley as he fumbled to explain what had happened.

'Better save that for the station,' Inspector Kelly sighed. 'I'm arresting you on suspicion of burglary, young man.'

Stanley longed for the ground to swallow him whole and was dumbstruck as the Inspector slipped a pair of chain-link handcuffs onto his wrists. Feeling the cold metal against his skin brought him back as he watched his mother bury her head into his father's shoulder.

'It's not what it looks like.' Stanley protested, eyes wide as his mother wept.

'I think you should listen to the Inspector and not saying anything else or end up upsetting your mother.'

Led by the Inspector, Stanley was grateful they escorted him out through the back garden to the alleyway behind the house. Instead of being paraded in handcuffs through the street, it relieved him to find the black Wolseley Police car idling in the alleyway. The same constable he had given his details to was sat waiting behind the wheel.

'If you wouldn't mind getting in?' The Inspector opened the door, and Stanley slipped into the back of the imposing car.

The last thing he saw was his father's disappointed expression as they drove him off along the alleyway at the back of the house. Right then Stanley would have done anything to be back on the damp front line.

CHAPTER FOUR

THE King's Head pub had long since closed. Someone had covered the windows in sheets of wood and the building stood an empty shell of its former self. The landlord had left to fight and nobody had wanted to take over in his absence.

Although a small portion of the roof showed signs of damaged, the guttering having been destroyed in an air raid; the building stood proud and mostly intact. It was almost a symbol of defiance against the onslaught of the German bombing raids.

Such a sizeable building was too good to waste and as young Owen made his way into the old beer garden, he imagined what it had been like before the war.

Owen should have been evacuated long ago, the city was no place for an eleven-year-old boy, but it was his home. Instead of boarding the train, he had scurried away and disappeared into the crowds. Wandering the streets, he had been offered a home in the abandoned public house.

'Please tell me you've got something for me?' An adult voice startled him as he moved around the back of the pub.

Owen was still dressed in the same clothes he had been when he had bumped into Stanley on Tothill Street. Although most of the dust had fallen from his hair, he was still a dirty sight to behold. Skin marked with dirt and debris, he scanned around until he found the source of the voice perched on an upturned milk churn.

'I think I got what you wanted.' Owen answered as he moved to the man.

Colin had taken Owen, and others, under his wing. Seeing opportunity and promise in the services of his *Hidden Boys,* he could make a very lucrative living on the black market in London. A greasy man, Colin was not the person you wanted to cross and Owen knew that.

That morning, after spending the night in the pub's cellar as their makeshift air raid shelter, Colin had woken Owen and given him a task. Never one to miss an opportunity, it always surprised Owen how much the Hidden Boys' leader knew about what was happening.

'I need you to go with some of the other boys and get me something,' Colin had explained as Owen had wiped the sleep from his eyes. 'You can take any of the other boys with you but I want it to be you who gets it for me.'

'Why me?'

'Because I trust you the most.'

Colin was an expert at grooming people to do what he wanted. Owen's diminutive size and flexibility were just the tools he would need, and he knew just what to say to have the boy pandering to please him.

'Can I get more sleep first?' He had asked and

immediately regretted it.

'Maybe I should choose one of the other boys,' Colin had manipulated. 'Someone who isn't more bothered about sleep than finding us the money for our next meal.'

'I didn't mean that.' Owen had protested, now very much awake.

'Do you think it's easy feeding you and all my boys?' Colin pressed, knowing the guilt tactic worked best on Owen. 'I can't exactly walk into the stores with a ration card and collect our supplies, you know that. Everything we have I have to pay more for, all of this is black market and costs more than it should.'

'I know, I'm sorry.'

Colin had given Owen his task and within the hour, without breakfast, Owen and two other Hidden Boys left the pub heading to the bomb site at Westminster Abbey.

'So, come on then, where is it?' Colin pressed as Owen joined him on the makeshift stool.

Colin watched as Owen reached into his ill-fitting jacket and removed a wooden box from beneath the fabric. The ornate carved box looked oversized in the boy's hand as Colin waited for Owen to pass it to him.

'Are you sure this is the right one?' There was a sense of nervousness in Colin's voice.

'It's the only one that looked the way you described.' Owen replied as he handed over the box. 'A wooden box with three skulls carved on the front, in the open mouth of each skull there are symbols of fire, water and wind.'

Colin listened to Owen as he admired the curious trinket. Just as the boy described, Colin admired the craftsmanship and artwork etched into the wooden lid of the box. Three skulls did sit next to one another on the top and letters in a language he did not recognise were etched around the edges.

'What is it?'

Colin seemed transfixed by the box as he admired every side. Much to Owen's surprise the lid had been secured with nothing more than a latch and a piece of rope tied through the loop to stop the lid from opening.

'Did you open it?' Colin asked as he looked at the underside of the box.

'No,' Owen defended. 'There wasn't time, it was kind of scary down there and I wanted to be out as quick as I could.'

'Were there other things down there?'

Colin's curiosity had piqued, and he returned to look at the grubby boy. Although he was expecting handsome payment for this curious wooden box, if there was a chance of more treasures in the underground room then it was an opportunity he would look to seize upon.

'There were loads of things,' Owen mused. 'Skulls in cases, boxes and lots of weird stuff. I didn't touch any of it, the place felt like it was haunted.'

'Don't be daft, Owen.' Colin laughed. 'It's just a room beneath a church, nothing more. I think we may have to pay another visit and see what else is in there.'

Owen was not looking forward to that prospect. Having ventured, as Colin had instructed, alone into the gloomy chamber beneath the ragged crater, he had felt a coldness he could not shake. There was something about the hidden room that had unnerved Owen and he was in no rush to go back down again.

'There were lots of people, the police were trying to keep people back on the other side.'

'Were you seen?' Colin's temper rose a little. 'Did anyone see you coming out?'

'No.'

'Are you sure?'

'There was nobody around, the police were busy keeping the old women back on the other side.'

'The man who asked for this was very particular that nobody should realise it was gone. He made me promise to send my best boy to do the job, that's why I chose you.'

The moment of frustration passed and Colin returned to stroking Owen's ego just enough to keep the boy obedient. Running his fingers through his greasy black hair, Colin waited for a moment as he realised he would soon meet with the mysterious man who had tasked him with retrieving the box.

'Get yourself something to eat.' Colin smiled and motioned towards the empty pub. 'I'll get this to where it needs to be.'

Rising from his perch, Colin stepped across to Owen and ruffled the young boy's hair. With a warm smile Colin stuffed the box into his own jacket and walked out of the overgrown beer garden. Casting a look behind as he emerged out onto the street, he was pleased to see Owen was pulling aside the wood that covered the old back door and returning to the sanctuary he had created.

Leaving the pub behind, Colin made his way along the street and marvelled at what he had created.

Since the war had begun, he had done all he could to avoid enlisting. The day he had refused his own family had kicked him from the house. Labelling him a disgrace, they weren't surprised by his selfish choices. Colin had always been that way, always teetering on the wrong side of the law with fingers in pies his family could never dream of.

As he saw it, Colin was better placed taking full advantage of what war-torn London offered him. With so many men his own age off fighting the war, they left him to do what he did best. Finding his own niche little place it did not take long for Colin to be the familiar face for the locals, a man who could get some of the comforts many missed.

The boys he had taken under his wing were a necessary evil. As an only child, Colin did not understand brotherly bonds. To him, the boys were the means to an end. By having them working for him he could act even more in the shadows and, most important for him, away from the attention of the law.

Children, as Colin had learned, were very good at camouflaging. Even though most children had been shipped to the countryside as evacuees, those that remained could move around almost unseen. Everyone was so preoccupied with the war effort that a child meandering the streets could almost move around unnoticed.

As they spent more time with him, however, Colin was feeling some care for them. That was a surprise to him, especially Owen who had been the first to join his little posse. Owen reminded him of a boy from his old neighbourhood, but he knew at some point this would all come tumbling down and it would force him to leave them behind and start afresh somewhere else.
'Colin!' A voice interrupted his thoughts as he walked along the pavement. 'Colin, have you got a minute?'

Turning to look at the source of the voice he saw a youthful woman jogging across the road towards him. Even without speaking, Colin felt his cheeks flush as the golden-haired woman ran across to him. Her name was Sandra, and he had taken a shine to her the moment they had met. He knew she was besotted by her fiancé who was off fighting in the Royal Air Force, but he couldn't help but feel there was something there.

As she stepped up to him Colin straightened his collar

and stood a little taller.

'Hi,' he offered with a sheepish smile. 'What can I do for you?'

'I've been looking for you all day,' she answered in an excited voice.

'Well you've not been looking hard enough.' Colin answered with a playful wink.

'Have you heard?'

'Heard what?'

'The boys are coming home on furlough, I will see Freddie next week isn't that amazing?'

Colin's heart sank as Sandra spun around in excitement. The prospect of seeing her fiancé had brought a fresh shine to her already captivating eyes. The desire to impress and look good for Sandra evaporated and was replaced with an undeniable frustration.

'Yeah,' he conceded after she had finished her gleeful dance. 'That sounds great.'

'I was hoping you'd be able to help me get some things together to welcome him back.'

'I'm not sure, things are tight at the minute.'

'Oh please!' She interrupted and grabbed his hands.

Despite his annoyance, the softness of her skin against his hand melted his coldness for a second. Fluttering her eyelids did the trick enough and once again he replaced the boyish smile. He was about to speak when the echoing toll of Big Ben carried in the air.

'Bugger!' He exclaimed and looked down the road.

'What's wrong?'

'I am supposed to be meeting someone and I'm going to be late.' Colin pulled his hands free. 'Grab me tomorrow Sandra and we will sort something out. I promise.'

Before the startled woman could offer anything else, Colin sprinted off down the street. Tonight's meeting, with the man who had requested the box, was not one he wanted to miss.

Too much was riding on it to mess it up now.

CHAPTER FIVE

STANLEY remembered the last time he had been inside a police station as a child on a school trip. Never in his life had he crossed the law enough to warrant time in a cell. Being his first time it was as a surprise how cramped the room was behind the reinforced cell door.

Stanley was feeling the closeness of the surrounding bricks when the moody Detective Inspector invited him out for, as he put it, a chat. Following the Inspector along the corridors and to a small office, Stanley took a seat behind the desk and waited.

It felt like being back at school as Inspector Kelly dropped into a creaking wooden chair behind a well-used desk. Tossing the crumpled notepad to the tabletop, he said nothing and looked across at Stanley.

'I'm no burglar.' Stanley blurted, feeling uncomfortable with the intensity of the other man's stare. 'I know I shouldn't have been down there but I took nothing I promise.'

Inspector Kelly said nothing; he sat back in the chair and allowed Stanley to speak.

'I saw the smoke from home, I was supposed to be getting rations you see as Mrs Jones' house was bombed last night and she needed some tea. Dad wasn't too happy I invited her in, but he'd never turn her away, he's good like that.' Stanley missed the wry grin on the policeman's face as he continued to blurt out every last piece of information. 'While I was walking down the hill, I saw the smoke from Westminster and wanted to look. I know I shouldn't have, but I was curious and only wanted to see what damage there was. When I got there, I saw the policeman keeping the crowds back and decided it was best to leave it alone, he already looked annoyed.'

'But you didn't leave it alone did you Stanley?' Inspector Kelly's words were enough to throw the bait and encourage Stanley to continue nattering.

'No. I mean I went around the other side and saw there was a second hole, there wasn't anyone guarding it so I thought I would chance a look. I wasn't doing any harm and nobody was there to stop me so I had a look.'

Stanley continued retelling his account of what had happened. The Inspector fought not to laugh as Stanley's nervousness as he got faster and faster in his recount of events. By the time Stanley had made it into the open door of the underground room, he had heard enough.

'I'll stop you there.' Inspector Kelly interrupted with a raised hand and Stanley fell silent. 'I can tell you've never been in this position before.'

'What? Arrested, you mean? Well no, never.'

'I can tell,' he chuckled and flipped open the notepad. 'Most people sit quietly on that side of my desk and yet you haven't shut up and I haven't even asked you a question yet.'

Stanley blushed as he realised how silly he must have looked to the seasoned detective. Any career criminal would have kept quiet, refused to say anything, yet Stanley had sat down and started talking the moment the silence in the room became too uncomfortable. Had the situation not been as serious as it was he may have laughed himself.

'Before we go any further,' the policeman interrupted Stanley's train of thought, 'I just want to clarify something. You say the door was already open?'

'Yes.'

'Interesting.'

'When I fell down the hole I didn't expect to find anything, maybe some old pipes but nothing like that. All I had with me was my granddad's old lighter and I used that to look around.'

'So, you went into the room?'

'Well yes, of course I did.'

The Inspector's furrowed brow and disapproving gaze melted any flippancy Stanley was feeling.

'What did you see in there?'

Stanley felt uncomfortable with the Inspector's sudden shift in temperament. A moment ago the policeman had almost been joking about Stanley's inexperience, and yet now the air was once again serious. As he sat on the other side of the desk Stanley felt uncomfortable in talking about what he had seen in the curious room.

'Stanley,' the Inspector warned as he removed the glasses from his face and rubbed the bridge of his nose. 'It won't pay you well now to sit there. If I were to tell you the church have lodged a formal complaint that someone stole a priceless and rare antiquity from that room perhaps you'd reconsider holding back whatever it is you think you don't want to tell me.'

Stanley let the comment sink in. Having explored what little he had of the underground room, he could tell the items were old and had some value. In all truth, it had never crossed his mind to take anything; it wasn't in his nature to do that. Judging by the look on Inspector Kelly's face the other man was having a hard time believing that. 'I had a look around but none of it made any sense to me.' Stanley continued. 'There was some weird skull in a glass box and lots of boxes on shelves.'

'What was in them?'

'I have no idea, I didn't look.'

Inspector Kelly raised an eyebrow.

'The curator said that at least half a dozen of the boxes had been opened and searched.'

'Not by me.'

'So you say.' He thumbed through the pages. 'Curious as it was there was only a single item taken. All those boxes and yet whoever was responsible was searching for something very particular.'

Stanley had no answer. In the brief time he had been in the room he had looked at the boxed skull and nothing else. He hadn't had time to look any further before his nerves had gotten the better of him.

The Inspector took Stanley's silence as defiance and refusal. In a swift move the Inspector stood from the chair and rounded the desk in two lengthy strides. Towering over Stanley, he pressed his finger into his chest as he spoke.

'You and your girlfriend had better come up with something better than the stories you are giving me at the moment.' Inspector Kelly hissed. 'You want me to believe a priceless item was stolen and the only two people found near the site had nothing to do with it?'

'I didn't take anything.' Stanley stammered, but the policeman was not listening.

'I have three officers searching every inch of your house as we speak. They will leave nothing unturned until they find what you have stolen,' there was controlled menace in his words. 'Your mother was already upset when we took you, imagine how she will feel with my officers taking apart her home. Imagine what the neighbours would think.'

'There's nothing there for you to find.' He pleaded.

'So you've already sold it?'

'I never had it!' Stanley bit back, raising his voice louder than he had wanted. 'All you will end up doing is upsetting the wrong people. I have nothing to do with this, my family have nothing to do with this and you're accusing the wrong person.'

'Really?' Inspector Kelly hissed as he took a step back from Stanley. 'Perhaps a little more time in the cell while I speak to your girlfriend and see what she has to say.'

'I don't have a,' it dawned on Stanley he was referring to the woman who had helped him from the hole. 'Hazel? The woman who got me out? I never met her before today, if it wasn't for her I'd still be stuck down there.'

'Likely story.' Inspector Kelly barked and ripped open the door to his office. 'Constable, take this young man back to the cells.'

In an instant a uniformed constable marched into the office and guided Stanley from the seat. As he approached the door, Stanley gasped as two other officers escorted Hazel Johnson towards him.

'You!' She growled, her face screwed up with anger. 'That's the last time I help some fool out of a hole.'

Stanley moved aside as they guided her into the Inspector's office. As the constable was about to lead him

away Inspector Kelly offered him one last parting fit.
'I'm guessing right about now you were wishing you were
back with your friends in France?'

The fact Inspector Kelly knew he had served on the
front line stunned him. It dawned on him that the
Inspector knew far more about him than he realised.
'I wish I was still there every day.' Stanley sighed.

Stanley's answer seemed to catch the Inspector by
surprise. Even more so the exchange had been heard by
Hazel, who now looked at the deflated Stanley as they
marched him back down to the cells. The last thing Stanley
heard was the Inspector as he descended the staircase into
the old station's cellblock.
'Right Miss Johnson, let us see if we can't get to the truth.'

Stanley found the confines of the cell even more dreary
once he had returned from the Inspector's office. The final
slap in the face had come when Inspector Kelly had
revealed how much they knew about him. The look in the
policeman's eyes told Stanley he believed he was guilty.
There was nothing he could say, or do, to convince him
otherwise and the fact he was telling the truth made it all
the more frustrating.

With his mind racing he tried to make some sense of
what was happening and how he could, for the second
time that day, get himself out of the sudden hole he found
himself in. Looking through the small window in the top
of the cell wall, he saw the sun had set, and it shrouded
the world outside in night. He had already been here for
hours and wanted to be home.

The sudden thought of home filled him with a sense of
guilt as he pictured his parents waiting for the police to
finish searching the house. What must they think of their
son as he sat in the cell? He was their only child and in the
last six months he had disappeared to war, returned

injured and now sat in a police cell accused of a crime he hadn't committed.

He understood how it must look and accepted that, without evidence, everyone would believe he was guilty. What other explanation could there be from an outside perspective. An injured soldier with no job, supporting his family in wartime London stumbles across a room filled with valuable items and one goes missing. Why wouldn't they suspect him?

Resting his head against the icy stone wall, Stanley admitted to himself that even he, in their circumstance, would believe he was guilty. That simple realisation filled him with fear as he tried to work out how he could get out of this mess.

Closing his eyes, he thought back to the tunnel, the door and the curious array of boxes and items in the shadowy room.

Who had opened the door?

Why was it open?

What could he do to find anything out to help him?

As he replayed the memory in his head, he thought back to what he had seen. The crumbled roof opening up to the sky, the dusty floor and footprints.

Footprints! In the dust, on the floor and leading into the room. They had seemed so inconsequential before, but now, facing accusations, it was suddenly something very important. Clamping his eyes shut he pictured the footprints in the dust and tried to make sense of them if for nothing more than to give him hope there was a way out of this mess.

CHAPTER SIX

THE night rolled by far slower than Stanley would have liked. He was left in the cell, alone, having been served a very basic meal before the night shift arrived. Being secured in the police station's cellar station it was deemed a safe enough place when another night of bombing began.

The crescendo of explosions carried in the air and Stanley could not dismiss the feeling of fear he felt for his parents. Aside from being deployed to the front, he had not spent a night away from his parents since the war had begun. For all he knew, as another explosion echoed through the night air, that could have been his home engulfed in flame.

It made him feel sick as he sat alone in the cell.
'I can't believe I'm in this mess.' A familiar voice groaned from the cell next to his. 'I should be out there making sure people are safe.'

They had interrogated Hazel for hours and returned her to the next cell as Stanley had finished his lukewarm meal. He had fleetingly glimpsed her as they paraded her past his cell door, but she said nothing. Having relived the events in his memory, he felt a fresh feeling of guilt as he saw her trudge past the cell flanked by the uniformed officers.

'I'm sorry.' Stanley offered, unsure if she could hear him. 'So you bloody should be.' She snapped, she had heard him. 'Can't you just tell them where this thing is so I can get back to my life?'

'If I knew what they were talking about then yes, I would tell them.' Stanley snapped at the blank wall. 'I touched nothing down there, I wish I had never even gone into the churchyard but I promise I took nothing.'

'You expect me to believe that?'

'Not really, no.' He sighed in defeat. 'I'd feel the same if I was in your position. You have no reason to believe me.'

His sincerity seemed to catch her by surprise as when she spoke again her tone was softer. From the sound of her voice she was sat in a similar position to Stanley, head resting against the wall perched on the bed looking up towards the moonlight in the small window.

'Can I ask you something?'

'Go for it,' Stanley sighed. 'There's nothing else to do at the moment.'

'I heard what the Inspector said to you, about wishing you were in France, have you been to the front line?'

Stanley rubbed the wound on his shoulder as he once again had a flashback of the crack and whip of the rifleman's shot. Sensing his pause, Hazel was about to offer an apology when Stanley answered.

'I was there for six months and eighteen days.' His voice was much quieter now, the memories forming a lump in his throat. 'I still have nightmares about the day I had to come back.'

'What happened?'

Stanley had not even spoken to his parents about the details, he had wanted to save them from the fear if he could ever return to the front line. His friends were still there, and he had nobody he could confide in so relived the memories alone. Perhaps it was the shared sanctuary of the sealed cell, but for the next hours, between the bombardment of the city outside, he explained the course of events of what had brought him home.

He spared no detail, not out of some macabre reason just more the fact he could tell Hazel was listening and wanted to know. By the time he had finished his account of initial training and deployment she had not muttered a word. For a second he thought she had fallen asleep.

'What did it feel like?' Hazel asked after a brief pause. 'Knowing you were heading into battle, that you could die?'

'I don't think I considered it,' Stanley confessed. 'It's hard to believe, but we all wanted to be there. There's that collective belief we are invulnerable, immortal and we are fighting for the right cause. Even when we disembarked and you could hear the gunfire in the distance, I still felt I would somehow be safe, somehow make it back without a problem.'

Hazel allowed him to continue as he explained what had happened as they progressed through the French countryside with only minor skirmishes against the unseen enemy. Furloughs at camps gave them respite, and the camaraderie between them grew until the fateful day arrived.

By the time Stanley had reached the moment, the patrol in search of the platoon of hiding German soldiers, he didn't know how hooked Hazel was on his every word. In her own cell, she was sat cross-legged on her bed facing the wall listening.

As he reached the moment, the gunshot from the church tower and the searing pain as the bullet ripped through his shoulder, he hadn't realised he was crying. Grateful to be alone in the shadows of the cell, he wiped the tears from his face and looked up at the waxing moon.
'What did you think when it happened?'
'Do you want to know the stupid thing, the first thought I had?'
'Yes.'
'I was angry I would have to come home, it embarrassed me I was a coward and would be leaving my friends behind.' It was the first time he had articulated that thought. 'I was also scared I would die.'
'That's natural, and it's nothing to be ashamed of.'

Stanley struggled to carry on and fought to hide the sound of his crying from passing through the cell wall. Staring up at the moon, he tried to control his breathing and sound calmer than he was.
'I'm sorry I was rude to you in the street.'
'What do you mean?'
'When I said you should have been fighting on the front, I didn't realise you had been there.'
'It's fine.' Stanley choked. 'You had no reason to know anything, and you were right in what you were saying. I should be back there fighting and not messing around in graveyards.'
'Now I feel bad saying it though,' she confessed. 'I shouldn't have jumped to conclusions.'
'You had no reason not to.'

The conversation had taken an uncomfortable turn and Stanley could not blame Hazel for what she had said. It was a reasonable thing in his eyes considering all the circumstances.

'So,' she broke the silence. 'If you didn't take what they're saying then how do we get ourselves out of this?'

Stanley was glad for the change of conversation. The memories had brought with them a fresh feeling of upset and guilt that he longed to bury. Wiping the tears from his face he held the bridge of his nose and took a deep breath in before answering.

'To be honest, I can't see them letting us go until they find it.'

'Do you even know what went missing?' Hazel pressed.

'Not a clue.' Stanley confessed. 'The only thing the Inspector said was something about a priceless antique.'

'What was down there?'

'A room full of weird stuff but I didn't have time to look around much before I heard you and thought I would get in trouble.'

'Looks like we both did.'

'Who took it then?' Hazel pushed as she sat back against the wall. 'Somebody had to have left that rope there, somebody else went down there before you did.'

'I didn't see anyone.' Stanley groaned. 'I wouldn't have even gone for a look if there had been anyone else around.'

'There's got to be something that can help the police, something that can help us prove I, sorry we, had nothing to do with it.'

'It's fine, you've still got no reason to believe me.'

'Strange thing is though, I do.'

Her answer took Stanley by surprise as he turned to look at the wall. Separated by the bricks, it was curious that he had just shared his memories so easily. There was something about her that made him feel at ease, or at least enough to share things he had kept to himself since coming home. Maybe it had been that sincerity, that willingness to share with her that had somehow softened her distrust for him.

'There was one thing I remember.' Stanley trailed off for a second. 'I was thinking about what was down there while you were in with the Inspector and I remembered something I hadn't thought about before.'

'What was it?'

'Footprints. There were other footprints in the dust on the floor.'

'That's not surprising.'

'Let me finish.' Stanley joked, his tone light enough to break the tension. 'They were small, a lot smaller than mine. I think they belonged to a child.'

'Why would a kid be down there?' No sooner had she asked did she realise how ridiculous it was. 'You should tell the Inspector.'

'Somehow I don't think he will believe anything I tell him. I've met people like him in the army, people who believe they are right and won't accept anything other than that.' Stanley huffed. 'No, if I am going to prove it wasn't me I will prove it myself, on my own.'

'Hey!' Hazel snapped from the other cell. 'You've already dragged me into this little mess, you can think again if you're dumping me now to prove your own innocence.'

'I didn't mean it like that.' He defended with haste. 'Like you say, I've already got you in enough bother.'

'Besides,' she interrupted. 'If the Inspector keeps you here, then I might be your only chance if they let me out.'

'Fill me with confidence why don't you?' Stanley chided but knew she was right.

The tables had turned and now, sat in the confines of the small cell, it was hard to see any other way out than to

trust the strange woman he had only just met. Everything about his situation felt absurd, beyond any realm of possibility but the truth was inescapable. Sat in the dungeon-esque cell, he wasn't in any position to argue.
'It's more about the fact I'm a realist.'
'Brilliant.' He groaned in response. 'You sound like my bloody mother.'
'Ok then,' she played. 'If they do let you go for whatever reason, then what, what will you do?'
'I'll try to find who the footprints belong to.'
'One child in London, a big task for one injured soldier on his own.'

She delivered her response tactfully enough that Stanley didn't take offence. Far from it in fact, as a smile appeared on his tired face.
'And I suppose you have a better suggestion?'

Hazel let the question go unanswered for a moment as a sound outside the cells in the corridor stole her attention. When nobody meandered past the cells, she leaned closer to the wall to whisper through the stone and mortar.
'There are some advantages of being an Air Warden, you know,' she teased. 'You get to see a lot of things, many people, that don't want to be found.'
'How does that help?'
'Because there are some children who didn't want to catch the train out of the city. They hide in the hope they can stay here. I might not have an idea who it is but I know someone we can ask.'
'If we ever get out of here.'

It was a glimmer of hope in the darkness but it was enough. Tiredness had taken hold of Stanley as he felt his eyelids closing as he rested on the uncomfortable bed.
'What say we get some sleep and see what happens in the morning.'

'Listen,' Hazel answered, sensing Stanley's tiredness. 'I am sorry I said what I said, you may not feel it but I think you're a hero for wanting to go back.'

Her words played on his mind as he once again drifted into the familiar disturbed sleep that had plagued him since returning home. As he closed his eyes, he wanted to reply but felt too tired to muster a comprehensible sentence.

Unbeknownst to the two of them, Inspector Kelly had been sat silently in the corridor listening to every word they had shared. With the familiar notebook in his hand he had remained the silent assassin, concealed in the shadows, until his pencil had dropped to the floor as his own tiredness crept over him.

Making sure he remained unseen, the Inspector rose from the floor and tiptoed back up into the station. The air raid was drawing to a close and the all-clear would soon sound and he could, as was becoming routine practice, get some sleep in his office until morning.

CHAPTER SEVEN

ALL the while Stanley and Hazel were being interrogated and questioned in the police station, the truth was moving further away from them. Shortly after Stanley had returned to his cell, Colin arrived at the salubrious meeting place they had given him directions to.

Colin had not questioned the address that had been scribbled on the piece of paper. In all honesty, he would have been happy to meet anywhere for the money he was to be paid for the exchange. Fifteen pounds was nothing to be sniffed at and considering Owen had been the one taking all the chances, it was easy money.

Walking through the pillared gates of Highgate Cemetery, he felt an odd chill as he passed through. Looking around, he had been careful to make sure he wasn't being followed. For the last fifteen minutes he had retraced his steps and circled back through the alleys more than once to make sure he was alone.

Satisfied he was safe, having seen only a handful of people, he had made his way to the cemetery entrance. Checking the scribbled instructions on the paper, Colin cast one last glance around and followed the path through the graveyard.

He had never been to Highgate before, never needed to meander through the thousands of tombstones and crypts, but the mystery of the place was undeniable. As he ventured deeper into the eerie graveyard, he could not shake the feeling that he was not alone. Less the people he expected to meet, but more as if there were eyes watching him from the gravestones.

Casting aside the ridiculous notion, he moved past the impressive church building near the entrance and followed the scribbled map in his hand. Passing beneath the crooked trees more than once, he checked the shadows in the doorways of the crypts and mausoleums he passed. With the sun setting behind him, the shadows seemed deeper, longer and more capable of disguising things within them.

Wanting to be done with the meeting, he hastened his pace and navigated towards his destination. Reaching a fork in the paths Colin checked the paperwork one last time and decided. Taking the left path, he followed it for a scant distance before he found what he was looking for.

The crypt he saw in front of him sent an icy shiver tracing down his spine. A set of iron gates were secured in front of a dark archway that led deep beneath the ground. Flanking either side of the metal gates were two pairs of carved columns into the smooth face of the crypt. The design had the feel of something Greek or Roman, yet the growing ivy disguised the intricate details etched and carved into the stone.

The adjoining building to the left was almost covered

in shrubbery, but Colin could just make out a round window facing back down the path he had come along. Pausing a distance from the dark entrance, he looked around for any sign of his mysterious employer.

Checking the time on his cracked watch, it relieved him to find he had arrived a little earlier than he had planned. As he was about to look around again the sound of creaking metal caused him to jump as he turned to look back at the sealed entrance.

Much to his surprise a ghostly figure, a man dressed in a light-grey hooded coat pulled open the gates and stepped out into the dying sunlight. Colin's eyes went wide as he watched the man take a handful of steps towards him then pause as if to take him in. After a few tense seconds the man reached up to the hood and pulled it back off his head, revealing the face beneath.
'Christ!' Colin exclaimed as he recognised the white-haired man. 'You almost had me running for the hills, I thought you were a bloody ghost.'

The white-haired man looked a little older than him, maybe in his mid-thirties, but his white hair made him look older. The man had introduced himself as Mr Masters, but Colin was sure it wasn't his actual name. There was something sinister about Masters, and the way he had emerged from the derelict crypt only heightened Colin's nervousness in dealing with the man.

Chastising himself, remembering the deal they had struck and the fifteen pounds that they had promised him, Colin waited for Masters to answer. Without muttering a word, Masters stepped across the path, his footsteps crunching on the pebbled footpath until he moved to stand in front of Colin.
'I trust you have acquired what I asked for?'

Masters' voice was distinct and well-spoken. His

demeanour and the way he carried himself told Colin he was a man of money, background and status. Quite how Masters had happened across him he would never know but the deal was too good an opportunity to miss.
'You think I'd come here if I hadn't?' Colin was careful not to sound too flippant as he sensed Masters' patience were not to be tested. 'Why did you choose here, anyway?'
'I conduct my business in places where idle eyes don't pay me attention.' Masters replied, his tone flat and emotionless. 'May I see it?'
'May I see the money' Colin feigned an attempt at matching Masters' pronunciation but failed.

Masters cast him a disapproving glare but raised a hand as if to summon his butler. True to form, a second figure appeared from the now insecure gates of the crypt and moved to Masters' side in silence. Passing him an envelope, he offered Colin no greeting as he turned and returned to stand at the crypt's entrance.
'You're all mysterious.' Colin scoffed as Masters handed him the envelope.

Although it was rude to check, the insatiable thirst to see the money took over as Colin unfolded the flap and looked inside. Thumbing through them, he counted fifteen pound notes stuffed into the envelope and fought to contain his jubilant smile.
'And the box Mr Farley?'
'Wait,' Colin looked up from the money. 'How d'you know my full name?'
'You don't think I would trust such a task to any street urchin do you?' Masters retorted, his hand outstretched awaiting his prize. 'For something this valuable I needed to ensure I was using the right person to get the job done.'

There was no denying the fact this mysterious member of the gentry's level of knowledge about him was disturbing. Having the money in his hand, Colin wanted nothing more than to be rid of the box and on his way to the King's Head and his Hidden Boys. The prospect of meeting Masters had lost its appeal.

Reaching into his jacket, he took hold of the ornate wooden box and handed it to Masters. For a moment the white-haired man stared at the ornate triple-skulls etched onto the lid of the box. He seemed almost transfixed as he traced his long fingers across each of the skulls.

'What is it anyway?' Colin asked, his curiosity getting the better of him for a moment.

'Have you not looked inside Mr Farley?'

'No need to,' Colin answered. 'I was just curious to know who would pay fifteen pounds for a little box.'

'This is the key to my life's work Mr Farley.' Masters' demeanour changed as he returned his attention to Colin. 'Would you like to see?'

Colin wished he hadn't asked, all he wanted to do was get as far away from the creepy man as he could and yet he felt he couldn't refuse. The look on Masters' face told him it would be unwise to refuse the offer. With great reluctance Colin offered a nonchalant shrug, and Masters moved to the side.

'Away from prying eyes Mr Farley, come.'

Colin's heart sank as Masters pointed towards the open gates of the eerie crypt entrance. More than anything he wanted to run, but he suspected he would not get very far. Stuffing the envelope into the inside pocket of his jacket, Colin accepted the invitation and walked alongside Masters back through the gates of the crypt.

As they passed by the silent guard that had handed over the envelope, Colin watched as he too stepped through the gates and pulled them shut behind them.

'Wait a minute,' Colin declared and stopped in the mouth

of the enormous archway. 'I don't think I need to see anything more, I should get on my way.'

'Oh come now Mr Farley, you've come this far.'

'No, I need to get back.' His voice was almost shrill with nerves. 'I've got people who need me, they'll be worried where I am. I should get going.'

He turned and managed two steps before Masters' reply stopped him dead in his tracks.

'You mean your Hidden Boys at the King's Head?'

Just how much did this creepy man know? Turning around he looked at Masters wide-eyed who was now shrouded in the ominous shadows of the crypt.

'This box,' Masters began as Colin drank in the sinister threat in his simple declaration. 'Will take me on a journey to a place I have dreamt of all my life. There is just one thing that stands in my way.'

Colin swallowed as a lump formed in his throat. The damp air of the crypt chilled him. The dangerous look in Masters' eyes filled him with dread yet he daren't turn his back on the man. Instead he felt rooted to the spot as Masters closed the gap between them so he was once again stood in front of him.

'Do you want to know what stops me?'

Colin couldn't answer, his mind raced to find a way out of his situation.

'I will take your silence as a yes.' Masters sneered. 'This box is centuries old and is protected by ancient magic.'

'Magic?' Colin scoffed. 'You had me going for a moment then.'

Colin sighed with relief as he realised Masters was nothing more than a crazy fool who played on theatrics. Colin felt a wave of relief and could not suppress the laugh that bubbled up at how well masters had made him fear for his life.

'Listen mate,' Colin laughed as he placed his hand on Masters' shoulder. 'You can keep your little magic box and I'll be on my way with my fifteen pounds. Fairs fair and all.'

Turning around, Colin didn't make it a single step before something passed in front of his face. Having been swallowed by the shadows, the other man now stepped out in front of him and passed so close that Colin felt his skin brush against his face. Almost as fast as he had appeared, the man disappeared back into the shadows. 'What stops me Mr Farley is my bloodline,' Masters hissed as Colin attempted to take a step.

His leg buckled beneath him, and he tumbled to the floor. It was only then, as he dropped his hand to the mossy floor, did he see his hand was covered in blood. Landing in the light cast by the setting sun he saw, to his horror, that his hand was soaked in blood.

As he tried to understand what was happening, he felt the warmth of something trickling down his neck. Reaching his quivering hands, he was overcome with fear as he felt warm blood oozing from a gash across his throat. 'You see Mr Farley, as I say there is a curse on my bloodline that would stop me opening the box. Yet yours,' Masters towered over him and grabbed his hair tight in his fist. 'Unlike me, you are innocent in the eyes of the magic that protects this box. You have no idea what it pertains to.'

As the life flowed through the neat cut across Colin's throat, Masters tilted his head upward and allowed the blood to spray out onto the ground in front of him. Holding the box beneath the arterial spray of crimson blood, he soaked the lid until the spray had become nothing more than a trickle.

Satisfied enough of Colin's blood had soaked the

carved wooden box, Masters released his grip and allowed Colin's body to fall lifeless to the floor.

'Excellent work.' Masters commended the man who once again appeared from the shadows. 'Your precision and craft are a rarity my friend.'

Masters watched as the man cleaned the blood off a razor-thin piece of glass. Laying in wait he had been the silent assassin, ready to strike at Masters' command and when the time was right he had traced the curious blade across the unsuspecting street thief's throat.

In the confines of the damp crypt, Masters could not suppress his smile as he pulled the tethered rope from the lock and felt his heart race as he lifted the lid of the ornate box to reveal the contents within.

CHAPTER EIGHT

WITH dawn came freedom. Much to Stanley's surprise, they provided him another basic meal and escorted from the cells into the police station's drab entrance.

'Constable,' Inspector Kelly's voice interrupted as Stanley was signing the paperwork to retrieve his belongings. 'I'll finish up here. I need a word with Mr Grand before he goes.'

'All yours, sir.' The constable replied and disappeared away from the reception desk.

Stanley looked tired. Another night of uneasy sleep stressed the black rings around his eyes and he was in no mood for the Inspector's questioning. Doing his best to remain quiet, he counted the coins in his hand and slid them into his pocket.

'What is it Inspector?' Stanley asked as he slid his coat over his arms. 'I'm tired and I want to go home.'

'We found nothing in your house.'

'Like I told you, you wouldn't.' Stanley bit.

'That doesn't mean you're in the clear. If it weren't for the fact they hit another station during the raid last night and they are transferring their prisoners here, I'd be keeping you as long as I could until I find what I'm looking for.'

'I can only tell you so many times I had nothing to do with it.'

The Inspector rounded on him and stared at Stanley for a moment.

'I've seen enough people in my career to know when I'm looking at the right ones.' Inspector Kelly declared with confidence. 'Our paths will cross again, sooner than you'd like I expect.'

With their exchange over the Inspector turned on his heels and stalked back into the police station leaving Stanley alone in the reception. Glad to be free, he checked outside and saw it was raining. Pulling his collar up, he pushed open the door and stepped out into the chilly morning air.

'Still want to buy me that tea?'

Hazel's voice caught him by surprise as he reached the bottom step of the station. Taking shelter beneath the alcove of the custody entrance, he had missed her as he had stormed out of the door. Feeling the rain soaking his hair and face he turned to look up at her.

'Sure, why not?' He feigned a smile. 'Beats walking in the rain and I don't think I'm ready to face my folks yet.'

'Good!' hazel seemed in friendly spirits. 'I know just the place, your treat.'

They left Inspector Kelly and police station behind them as Hazel guided them through the London streets. The spring rain had done little to discourage people from their daily lives, and it surprised Stanley to see how many people were still braving the torrential downpour going about their daily business.

Hazel's confidence still surprised him. She carried herself different from what he would have expected but realised the war had changed people. They were both almost soaked to the skin by the time they arrived at a small café.

The windows had been reinforced with tape and the exterior had seen better days, but Stanley would not argue. Places like these were gems, all things considered, and he was grateful to be out of the rain as he pulled the door open to let Hazel go in.

'Hazel my dear.' A warm voice declared with glee. 'I haven't seen you all week, how have you been?'

An old woman in her sixties shuffled around the makeshift counter and disappeared into a compact back room to boil the water.

'I see you have a gentleman friend,' the old woman's voice brimmed with curiosity. 'Will he be joining you?'

'He'll be paying!' Hazel declared and guided Stanley to a seat by the cracked window.

'Lucky girl.'

'She's innocent enough,' Hazel soothed as she picked up on Stanley's discomfort. 'She's been a friend of my mum's since I was a little girl. It's nice she always looks after me and I expect will be dying to tell my mother I've been here with a man.'

Stanley felt out of place and was glad they were the only patrons in the café that morning. As the old woman busied herself in the back, Hazel shouted their orders to keep her busy so they could talk. Not giving Stanley a choice in the matter she ordered him tea and a slice of Victoria Sponge.

'So, Stanley,' Hazel started as she ran her fingers through

her sodden hair. 'Where do we go from here?'

'I'm not sure,' he confessed. 'You were the one who said you'd have an idea where to start.'

'Excellent!' She beamed. 'So you will not do this on your own?'

There was a mischievous glee in her voice and Stanley sensed she had prepared a lengthy argument had he seen fit to tell her he would prove their innocence alone. Looking at her across the table, Stanley couldn't help but smile at her tenacity. She was nothing like his mother; she would never have been so confident and forthright when she had been Hazel's age.

'What are you thinking then? Where are we going to start?'

'I know a few places around the town where some of the evacuee boys hide out. We would do well to start there, I suppose.'

The old woman emerged from the back room carrying two generous slices of Victoria sponge. Shuffling over to their table, she placed the plates down and beamed down at Stanley.

'Best you'll find with the rations we have, dear.' The old woman chuckled as Stanley sized up the enormous slice of iced cake. 'Almost tastes as good as I used to make it before the war.'

'Thank you.' He smiled as the old woman offered Hazel a cheeky wink and she moved to get their drinks from the counter by the back room.

With their drinks served the old woman loitered for a moment but took then hint and returned to a well-thumbed paperback at a table on the far side of the café. Welcoming the warmth of the tea and the powdery taste of the sponge cake, Stanley enjoyed the quiet while it lasted.

'Can I ask you something?' Hazel asked as she laid her fork on the empty plate.

'I feel you'll ask, anyway.'

'You're probably right,' she chuckled. 'Are you an only child?'

'What makes you think that?'

'I have two brothers and they wouldn't ever let me tell them what to do. You seem happy enough to listen to me, which I'm not used to.'

'I am an only child, yes,' Stanley sipped the last of his tea. 'That's the main reason I'm not looking forward to going home. The Inspector turned up and arrested me in front of my parents. My mother was in pieces when they handcuffed me.'

The memory of his arrest made him feel uncomfortable. Although he had been keen to get out of the cells, he was not looking forwards to returning home. He recalled the look on his father's face as they drove him away in the police car and knew he would not hear the end of it. Even the thought of their disappointment was enough motivation to prove the Inspector was wrong.

'Lucky for me they collared me when I was heading in for my shift. My folks probably think I've slept at the shelter again.'

'Where are your brothers?'

The question caused a sudden change in Hazel's face. Sensing he had pushed into the realms of something she would rather not discuss, Stanley corrected himself and changed the subject.

'Sorry, I didn't mean to push like that.' He offered. 'Why don't we talk about the places, we can look for this kid.'

'Excellent idea.' Hazel welcomed the change of conversation.

Stanley found her hard to read. One moment Hazel

was jovial and almost playful with him, but the question about her brothers had added an icy chill to her façade. As they both finished the last of the tea, Stanley moved to pay the old woman as Hazel took a moment to compose herself. By the time he returned she had somehow pushed aside the coldness and seemed once again relaxed and focussed on helping him.

'Do you want to go back and see your parents before we go traipsing through the backstreets?'

'I'd rather not.' Stanley confessed but saw the disapproving look on Hazel's face.

'I think it's better that you do.' She declared as they stepped back out into the rain. 'If there's one thing I've learned during this bloody war, it's the fact you shouldn't leave things for another day.'

'I don't want to sit and listen to my dad preaching to me. If you think the Inspector was relentless, my dad can give him a run for his money.'

What she did next caught Stanley by surprise. Taking his hand in hers she looked him in the eyes, the tenderness to her touch caught him off guard for a moment and he stood in the rain entranced by her. There was a look in her eye that told him she was speaking from experience and with sincerity.

'Regardless if it is today or tomorrow, you will have to face them. Trust me when I say there's too much to lose by putting things off for another day.' She locked her gaze with his as she spoke. 'Go home. Accept what they have to say even if you know it's wrong.'

'Something tells me there's no point in arguing, is there?'

'No!' She laughed and gave him a peck on the cheek.

Stanley didn't know if it was a friendly peck or something more, but he felt his cheeks burn red. Conscious she was still smiling at him, he took a step back and smiled sheepishly.

'I'd rather get on with looking for the kid.'

'How about this then?' She sighed with mock frustration. 'Speak to your parents and meet me at four o'clock on Tothill Street near Westminster. We can start from there, deal?'

'Fair enough!'

Having separated, Stanley wasn't sure how to part ways, having accepted the peck on his cheek. Conscious there was a strange tension building between them, he offered her a smile and made his way back towards home. As he reached the junction, he cast one last glance back, but there was no sign of Hazel as she had disappeared into the flow of pedestrians along the pavement.

'What is going on?' Stanley mumbled to himself as he lowered his head and set off for home.

By the time he arrived at the end of his street, he had played through the conversation he was soon to be having with his dad. As he reached the front door he had built himself up for every plausible argument and accusation they would throw at him.

Taking a deep breath, he pulled down the handle and opened the front door. No sooner had the door opened an inch than they welcomed him back how he had expected.

'About bloody time Stanley Grand, get your arse in here and explain yourself.'

Fighting the urge to turn and run, Stanley steeled himself for what was about to happen and shuffled into the living room.

CHAPTER NINE

STANLEY endured the onslaught from his father. Never in his life had he seen his old man as enraged as he had been when he had returned home. Although the embarrassment of having Stanley carted away by the police played a big part, Stanley sensed there was more to it. He knew deep down his father's frustration was born from disappointment.

Try as he might Stanley could not get a word in edgeways. At every opportunity his father had interrupted him or silenced him with a raised hand and steely glare. Resigning himself to the barrage of anger, Stanley sat himself down and fought back the urge to argue.

When his dad had finished and there was enough room to speak he had offered them his account of events. His mother remained silent, a handkerchief held to her face as she fought back tears. Seeing her like that fuelled his determination to prove he was innocent but it was his father's look that surprised him the most.

The pure look of disappointment burned Stanley as he sat in the chair. He knew, as he watched his father brooding in silence, he didn't believe him.

'I've explained everything and you can believe me or not.' Stanley declared as he launched up from the seat.

'I don't believe you.' His dad grumbled.

'Well in that case there's no point in staying.'

Against the protesting of his mother, Stanley snatched his coat from the hook and ripped open the front door.

'I didn't raise you to be a thief.' His father bellowed as he stepped out onto the pavement.

'You didn't,' Stanley fought the urge to yell at the top of his voice. 'That's why I'm not.'

Closing the door behind him he didn't hear his father's reply and cared not to hear anything more from his parents as he stalked off back up the road. Checking his watch it was early for his meeting with Hazel but he couldn't take any more from his mum or dad.

Leaving them behind Stanley was glad for the respite as he walked the streets towards Westminster. His whole world had been flipped upside down in the last twenty-four hours and he had hardly any chance to process anything that was happening. As he reached Tothill Street he found a wooden bench and sat down to watch the world go by.

It was perhaps, aside from being in the cells, the only time he had taken a moment to stop and think since the banks of the Thames. Everything felt like it had been revolving around him at a hundred miles an hour. Resting himself back against the damp bench he looked at the people that meandered around him.

The rain had stopped but the lumbering grey clouds

threatened to release a fresh downpour at any moment. Looking from the sky he caught sight of a man loitering in the entrance to an alley between two buildings. Dressed in a brown trench coat the man seemed out of place and as he caught sight of Stanley paying him attention he dipped into the alley and out of sight.

The man seemed too well-dressed and much too interested in watching Stanley as he sat on the bench. 'He's not the only one.' Hazel interrupted as Stanley craned to see where the man had gone.

Jumping a little in his seat, Stanley was relieved to see Hazel as she dropped onto the bench next to him. 'What was that?'

'The man in the coat, he's been following me all day.' Hazel was very calm and matter-of-fact as she spoke. 'I suspect Inspector Kelly wanted us watched in case we led him to anything interesting.'

'Maybe.' Stanley answered, his mind still distracted. 'How did it go with your folks?'

'As you'd expected,' Stanley sighed in reply. 'Dad wouldn't listen and mum was in bits.'

'It's ok,' she soothed and put an arm around his shoulder. 'Come the end of all this you'll be able to prove you were right.'

Feeling the same confusion he had with the peck on the cheek he shrugged his shoulders and offered her no reply. Allowing the moment to pass Hazel withdrew her arm and rose from the bench. Looking down at Stanley she was not about to let him wallow in self-pity and quickly changed her tact.

'Right, enough melancholy! What do you say we crack on with it and get looking for the owner of those footprints?'

Grateful for the sudden steer and direction, Stanley offered her a smile and stood up. Following her lead he had no idea where she was taking him but the fact she remained as focussed as she had in the café filled him with hope.

The pair walked away from Westminster and along Tothill Street before Hazel guided them off the main streets. A lifetime resident of London it soon dawned on Stanley how little of the vast capital he had actually seen. Circling around the streets they soon came to a cold, desolate and empty row of terraced houses.

The street felt lonely and as Stanley looked around he realised that almost every house showed signs of damage from the air raids. Every window, as far as Stanley could see, had been blown in and glass littered the pavement and road.

'What happened here?' Stanley asked as they walked down the centre of the road.

Although the houses were mere shells of their former selves, Stanley could not shake the feeling they were being watched. From the dark shadows cast by the crumbling walls and roofs he suspected their presence was being watched by those who chose not to leave the derelict street.

'One of the earlier raids the Germans hit a gas main,' Hazel's tone was filled with an air of sadness. 'I was on the night it went up.'

'I can't imagine what it was like.'

They followed the line of the road and Stanley stopped short as the sight of destruction stole his breath. Two houses in the row had been completely annihilated in the blast and now only a deep crater remained. The houses on either side looked on the verge of collapse, their walls leaning precariously over the hole.

The bricks that were left exposed had been charred black from the flames and the sight was terrifying to behold.

'Fifteen people died.' Hazel added as she moved to stand beside Stanley. 'This is the side of things Churchill doesn't want everyone to know. They want us to think we're winning but every night I see another set of dead eyes staring up from the wreckage of another family home.'

Stanley remained quiet as he allowed Hazel her moment of grace in the presence of the destroyed street. Feeling more than a little uncomfortable he found himself relating to the feelings he knew Hazel was having. Perhaps, he thought to himself, that had been why it had been so easy to speak of France through the walls of the cells.

'Come on, we should get moving.' Hazel declared. 'No time to dwell on things like this.'

Suspecting it was more a matter of speaking to herself, Stanley traced the back of his hand along her arm to offer silent comfort. Grateful for the gesture she offered him a smile and continued along the street leaving the destruction behind them.

'Who still lives here?' Stanley pressed as they rounded onto the next street.

'A few families refused to leave but for the most part everyone evacuated.'

'Is this where you think they may be hiding out?'

'Not quite,' hazel answered as she looked along the next street. 'There are a few houses where children congregate under the protection of older ruffians, think of them like Fagin from Oliver Twist.'

'That's a comforting thought.'

'Most areas have their own. This one is run by a scruffy little urchin by the name of Thomas and he normally hides around here.'

'What do they do?' Stanley asked as Hazel led them up the

street.

'They survive,' hazel sighed as she moved towards a wooden door that had once been nailed shut. 'Any way they can but it normally sees them resorting to petty crime for food. The handlers take payment for giving them a roof over their heads.'

Hazel pushed on the front door but it would not budge. Moving to help, Stanley pressed his good shoulder against the door and between them they forced it open. 'This is the one,' Hazel announced as a foul odour wafted through the open door.

'Smells delightful.' Stanley complained as he followed her into the derelict house.

'They aren't the best condition.'

Venturing into the house it was obvious to see it had been lived in since it had been abandoned. Wrappings and cartons littered the floor and the remaining furniture had been turned into beds. The smell, Stanley realised, came from the fact the plumbing had long since stopped working and the house was more a den than a home.

Stepping carefully over the littered belongings he noticed a small teddy tucked beneath a crumpled sheet on the overturned sofa. Still tied around the bear's neck was the familiar hand-written nametag children had been given when being evacuated from London. A sudden sense of sadness washed over him as he read the label and saw the owner's age was only nine.

'Why didn't they go with the other evacuees?'

'Most are just scared,' Hazel answered as she looked around the empty house. 'Imagine leaving your parents to go to a place you don't know. For someone that small it must be terrifying.'

After searching through the house it was obvious it had been empty for some time. Maggots wriggled in the half-eaten cans of rationed food but there was no sign of life.

'They move around a lot,' Hazel ground as they emerged back out into the street and the fresh air. 'This was the last place I knew Thomas was hiding with his little gang.'

'What now?' Stanley asked, the fleeting sense of hope he had had now waned a little.

'Quit your fretting,' Hazel chuckled as she took her bearings. 'This isn't the only place I know about you know.'

'So where are we going next?'

'Colin Farley's place, the King's Head.'

'A pub?' Stanley scoffed.

'It's empty, well it was until Colin got his hands on it. It's only a short walk and maybe he'll be able to point us in the right direction.'

'Bit of a long shot though isn't it?'

'Not really,' Hazel laughed. 'You really aren't a boy of the streets are you?'

'Meaning what?'

'If someone took something valuable they'll need to shift it, anything like that would pass on the grapevine like fireweed. If Colin or his lot don't know where it is, they might be able to tell us who does.'

'Better than nothing.'

'Exactly!' She offered with a cheeky smile.

CHAPTER TEN

MORE battered houses surrounded them as they made their way towards the King's Head. Taking another turn the sky was growing darker as more rain clouds formed in the sky.

'What are the chances that we will-' Stanley stopped speaking and stood mouth open almost dumbstruck.

As they had rounded the corner, the boarded up pub dominated the street. Flaking white paint, pockmarked from shrapnel, added to the abandonment of the pub but it wasn't that which had caused him to trail off. To the side of the pub, beneath the creaking sign that had the silhouette of the King on it, stood a boy Stanley recognised.

The chance encounter, a fleeting moment of passing in the street had slipped his mind but seeing the young boy stood outside the pub brought it all back. Owen had been the boy that had bumped into Stanley as he walked towards the smouldering Abbey. In such a hurry, hands holding something inside his jacket, it had seemed like nothing. So insignificant an event, his brain had seen fit to store it in some forgotten part of his memory until that moment.

Owen, bedraggled and somewhat forlorn, had not seen them as they emerged onto the street and Stanley ground to a halt. His back was turned while Hazel made her enquiry as to what had silenced him. It was only as Stanley offered his disbelieving reply that Owen turned and noticed them.

'Him,' Stanley pointed at Owen.

'What about him? He's one of Colin's boys.'

'He was there.'

'Where?'

'It's him!'

'You're not making any sense.'

Having seen the strange man point in his direction, Owen was not taking any chances. As soon as Stanley raised his hand and pointed he was on his toes.

As Owen disappeared around the back of the derelict pub Stanley gave chase. Hazel was hot on his heels but still did not understand what was going on. As Stanley burst into the empty beer garden he scanned for any sign of the boy, but he had all but vanished into the unkempt garden and yard.

The overgrown lawn and remnants of furniture offered the small boy many places to hide, Stanley was about to search when a flurry of movement caught his eye. From a clump of grass, Owen exploded and sprinted past Stanley. Too fast to take hold, Stanley turned and watched as Owen skidded across the floor and dived through the open wood that secured the back door. Before Stanley could reach him, Owen pulled the wood behind him and heaved enough items to barricade the door from opening. 'Get around the front!' Stanley barked at Hazel. 'He will get out that way.'

Ferreting along the rear of the pub, Stanley was desperate to speak to Owen and find out why he was running.

'Come on kid, I'm not going to hurt you.' He bellowed at the boarded windows.

He could hear the sound of Owen scrambling through the pub's interior but couldn't see what he was doing. Desperate not to lose his only chance of a lead, he waited to see if the boy would answer.

'I only want to talk.' Stanley pleaded, doing his best to sound calm.

Looking up towards the second level of the pub, a piece of brick flew past his head and smashed onto the cracked patio paving by his feet. Turning around, Stanley saw Owen hanging out of a window above him.

'Hey, kid. Just hear me out will you?'

Owen responded with a second piece of masonry that smashed close to Stanley.

'Go away!' Owen yelled as he searched for another missile.

'Where's Colin?' Hazel asked as she hurried around to the back of the pub.

Having heard the commotion and checked the ground floor was secure, she had returned to the sound of raised voices. Looking up she saw Owen, wide eyed and glaring down at the two of them from a room on the second level.

'What's it to you?'

'We need to speak to him, I want to know what you took from underneath Westminster Abbey.'

Owen turned his attention to Stanley. The look of frustration was now replaced with one of pure fear.

'Go away, Colin has gone and I need to find somewhere to live.'

'Where's Colin gone?' Hazel pressed as she moved to Stanley's side.

'You know!'

'No we don't.' She argued. 'That's why we came here.'

'I don't believe you.' Owen tossed another piece of debris but his aim was wide this time and neither of them flinched. 'He went to meet you people, to take them that box, and he hasn't been back since.'

'It's not like Colin to stay out at night.' Hazel hushed so only Stanley could hear her. 'Being a handler puts you on the nasty side of a good many people you'd rather not cross. This place was like his kingdom, if he's been out all night I doubt that's a good sign.'

'What people did he go to meet?'

'Your people.'

It was obvious Owen was terrified, and the desperation was clear in his behaviour. There was something he wasn't telling them.

'Whoever it was,' Hazel tried to soothe, 'they weren't anything to do with us.'

'LIARS!' Owen shrieked and threw a plank of wood at them. 'You're here for the same thing.'

'What?' Stanley's patience was wearing thin as he kicked aside the plank.

'You said yourself, the thing from the weird room.'

Stanley wanted to blurt a hundred questions at the boy, but before he could speak Hazel placed her hand on his arm to silence him.

'We aren't with anyone, the police have accused us of stealing whatever it was and I think Colin might know who has it.' Her words were calm and kind, her voice level to keep from escalating Owen again.

'I don't believe you, you're here to finish the job. I know you are.'

'Finish what job?'

Stanley didn't like what the boy was saying. The look of terror on his face told him there was a genuine fear in the immature boy that wasn't explained by the two of them turning up at the pub.

'They killed him.' Owen declared and climbed out of the window onto the flat roof of the outside toilet.

'Who?' Hazel pressed as Owen sat himself on the edge of the flat roof and buried his head in his hands.

'He told me to get something to eat, but I thought he would leave us. I knew the box was worth a lot of money and I thought he might run off with it.'

'What happened?' Hazel asked as she moved closer.

Hazel's demeanour was much softer than Stanley had expected. He could see a motherly quality as she kept her tone soft and caring.

'I followed him,' Owen sighed. 'I wanted to make sure he wouldn't leave us.'

'Where did he go?' Hazel pressed with caution, keeping her distance but inching closer to the crying boy.

'Highgate graveyard, I followed him in there and saw him meet with someone.' Stanley was about to interrupt, but Hazel silenced him with a raised hand. 'Who did he meet?'

'I don't know but I watched them and…' Owen trailed off, his cries louder in his hands.

'It's ok, take your time.' Hazel murmured as she moved to stand beneath Owen now. 'I'm not here to hurt you, neither of us are.'

Owen peeped through his fingers and looked like a startled rabbit as he realised how close she was. Stanley feared the boy would run as he realised Hazel had closed him down, but her raised hand and warm expression seemed to defuse his flight response.

'I've never seen a dead body before,' Owen sniffled. 'I mean I've been into houses after the bombings but Colin always kept the bodies away from us.'

'Come on down from there, what's your name?'

'Owen.' He replied as he considered the offer of her outstretched hand.

'Well Owen, I'm Hazel and that silly oaf is Stanley.'

Stanley huffed in the background but remained quiet, offering Owen a curt nod at the less than flattering introduction Hazel had made.

'Why did the police think you took it?'

'Because that silly bugger fell down the hole and got stuck.' She leaned closer and lowered her voice as if shielding Stanley from embarrassment. 'I had to help him get out, and that's when the police found us. When they realised something had been stolen they came looking for us but I mean, come on, do you think he could be a thief?'

Owen cast a curious glance at Stanley and laughed. The sudden change in the boy's expression caught him by surprise as he could not hear what Hazel was saying. Hiding the frustration, he watched as Hazel worked her magic on the boy.

'He wouldn't last five minutes on the streets with the Hidden Boys.' Owen wiped the tears from his dirty face and smiled a crooked-tooth smile.

'Is that what you call yourselves, the Hidden Boys?'

'It's what Colin called us.'

'If he got you to get whatever it was from that hole I expect you were his best?'

'Of course!' Owen brimmed with pride. 'He said he only trusted me to fetch it.'

Hazel wanted to press but knew it best to let the boy

tell her in his own time. Teetering on the edge of running. Hazel was ever cautious not to push too much as the boy sat perched on the flat roof. She could have reached up and taken hold of him, but that would not have helped their cause. She knew Owen would have a mistrust for anyone outside of Colin and his Hidden Boys. The fact he was even speaking told her he was afraid.

Not wanting to push, she continued to offer her hand up at him in the hope he would make his own decision to take it.

'Did Colin take it with him to the graveyard?' Hazel longed to know what *it* was.

'Yes, when I got back, he was keen to get to the meeting.' Owen looked towards the upturned milk churn in the centre of the grass. 'He was sat on that when I got back.'

Hazel and Stanley looked at the upturned churn and waited for Owen to continue.

'I've never seen anything like it.'

'If it was kept in that room, buried underground I imagine it was very special.' Hazel offered just enough encouragement to tease more out of the boy.

'I thought it would be more impressive to be honest,' Owen scoffed as he remembered the box. 'It was just a wooden box but the way they decorated it was interesting.'

'What made it interesting?'

'The skulls, the ones Colin told me about, three of them carved into the lid.'

'Sounds amazing.'

'I never looked inside it, I didn't care, I just brought it back and gave it to Colin.'

'Who did he meet in the graveyard, Owen?'

'I don't know,' the sadness returned to his face again. 'I was too far away, hidden among the graves but I saw them take him into the crypt and then only they came back out.'

'What did they do to Colin?'

The tears formed in his young eyes again. Looking up, Hazel felt a pang of sorrow at what Owen had seen and experienced in his junior years. No child should endure what he had gone through and she felt a strong sympathy for the once innocent boy.

'You promise you're not with them?'

'I promise.'

Hazel watched in dumbstruck horror as Owen mimicked drawing his finger across his throat.

'The sliced him from ear to ear and left him to die.'

'That's horrible.'

'Do you want me to show you?'

The sudden offer was a macabre gesture, but one that neither Hazel nor Stanley would refuse. As Owen took Hazel's outstretched arm he had somehow composed himself from the sobbing boy perched on the roof only seconds earlier. At ground level he seemed a boy ten years older than he was as he offered to take them to Colin's body.

CHAPTER ELEVEN

WALKING to Highgate Cemetery was sombre and as they walked through the gates, the rain had started again. Owen seemed nervous as he led them along the paths and past the mausoleums and crypts.

'Do you want to just tell us where to go?' Stanley offered as he sensed Owen's trepidation.

'No.' The boy replied with determination. 'I feel bad I didn't go to the police, but I didn't want to be sent away.'

Stanley had wondered why Owen hadn't alerted the police when he had found Colin's body. Self-preservation had been the reason and Stanley couldn't fault him. If he had gone to the police, then he would have been re-labelled and sent as an evacuee to the countryside and away from everything he knew. Seeing how much Owen had been forced to protect himself in lieu of the war was a humbling feeling for Stanley.

'You did what was right for you,' Stanley attempted to

comfort Owen as they neared the gated crypt where Colin's body was hidden. 'It can't be easy hiding all the time.'

'No, it isn't' Owen replied very matter-of-fact. 'He's in there.'

Owen pointed to the wrought-iron gates that sealed the crypt. Standing on the path, Owen was reluctant to go any further and remained in place as Hazel and Stanley moved towards the gates.

'You'll have to climb over,' Owen told them as they reached the gates. 'They locked them when they left.'

Stanley looked at the gates and was impressed Owen had made it over them. Standing almost twice his height, the gates were topped with jagged spikes. Looking at Hazel, she offered him a shrug and tested the gate's security.

Much to their frustration, the gates had been secured with a thick chain and padlock. Rattling the gates, Hazel looked at Stanley and frowned.

'Leg up?' Stanley smirked and pressed himself against the gates, offering Hazel his knee.

'Why am I going first?'

'They do say lady's first!'

'Oh come off it,' she laughed and put her foot on his bent knee. 'Admit it; you're just scared to go first.'

The jovial banter seemed inappropriate considering they were searching for a dead body, but that didn't stop them. As Hazel hoisted herself up onto the gate and over to the other side she was careful not to catch herself on the jagged spikes. Once she was up, Stanley turned and offered her support as she lowered herself down the opposite side of the gate with care.

'So how do you plan on getting over?' Hazel quizzed as they stood face-to-face either side of the gate.

It was a fair question and one Stanley had been thinking about as they had walked up to the gates. As a teenager Stanley had spent many hours climbing and getting into places he shouldn't have been. Ever an explorer and curious soul, he had taught himself the skills he needed to venture into the more dangerous places he discovered. The only difference now, aside from being older and heavier, was the injury to his shoulder.

Casting aside the worry about his shoulder, Stanley removed his jacket and took a handful of strides backwards away from the gate.
'Step back.'

Stanley waited as Hazel moved away from the gate and he eyed up his route up the metal fencing. Feeling Hazel's curiosity growing, he propelled himself forward and sprinted at the gate. Making the jump, he slipped his foot between the bars and onto the sagging chain and lifted himself until his hands reached the horizontal bar between the spikes. Feeding from the momentum, Stanley hoisted himself up and over the row of spikes.

The tips grazed against the backside of his trousers as he launched up and over the top of the gates. Much to Hazel's surprise, Stanley flew over the gate and landed on the dusty floor a few feet in front of her. Although he had moved with surprising grace for someone his size his landing had been unsteady and heavier than he had planned.

Catching his breath and hiding the fact his shoulder screamed with pain, he rose to his feet and tried to dust himself off as casual as he could.
'Well I wasn't expecting that!' Hazel exclaimed as she stepped up to him. 'Full of surprises, aren't you?'
'I like to keep people guessing.' Stanley smirked. 'Pass me that will you please?'

Stanley pointed across at a spare piece of metal railing leant against the rough wall. Using the pole for leverage, Stanley made quick work of ripping open the padlock and removing the chain from the gate.

It may have been a figment of their imagination, considering Colin's body had only been there a few hours, but there was a smell of death in the air. With the gates open Stanley dropped the piece of metal to the ground and turned to look into the black mouth of the crypt.
'It's not ladies first this time.' Hazel chortled and pushed Stanley in the small of his back.

The light from outside struggled to breach into the crypt and once again Stanley withdrew the lighter from his pocket. As his eyes adjusted, he ventured into the shadowy recess of the underground burial tomb and he could make out the silhouette of a body on the floor ahead of him.

Allowing his eyes to adjust to the flickering flame, Stanley reached the body and dropped to his knees.
'Come and hold this for me.' Stanley asked as he held out the lighter.

Hazel was nervous but tried her best to hide it as she moved to Stanley's side. In the light of the flickering flame Colin's body lay face down in the dirt, a pool of blood having soaked the ground around his head.

Stanley inspected the body and peered at the jagged gash across Colin's throat. His lifeless eyes stared up towards the sealed gates as if his last thought had been of escape and freedom from the shadows of the crypt.
'Not a pleasant way to go.' Stanley muttered as he moved to check Colin's pockets.
'Police!' Owen's shrill voice bellowed from outside in the graveyard.

As Stanley rose, he saw Owen sprint off through the

gravestones as two uniformed constables appeared on the path.

'Go!' Stanley barked as he ripped the lighter from Hazel's hand. 'I'll explain this, you get yourself out of here.'

Although she wanted to protest, she knew Stanley was right. As she ran towards the open gates, another figure stepped from the side of the crypt's mouth and blocked her escape. Skidding to a halt, she gasped as the familiar face of Detective Inspector Kelly stepped into view.

'Why am I not surprised?' The Inspector groaned as the two constables moved to his side.

'It's not how it looks.' Hazel protested as she stepped back to Stanley's side. 'We've only just got here.'

Inspector Kelly left the constables at the entrance and moved past Stanley and Hazel to inspect the body. Dropping, he pressed his fingers into the dead man's neck and smiled to himself.

'Do you take me for a complete fool?' Inspector Kelly snapped as he turned to face the two of them.

'No.'

'Lucky for you I've seen enough bodies to know that this poor chap has been here longer than you have.'

'What do you mean longer than we have?'

'We had a tip in the office about the body this morning,' Kelly explained as he wiped the cold blood from his fingertips and stood up. 'I had the scene under observations in case the killer came back.'

'We didn't kill him.'

'No?' Kelly let his question linger a moment as he made sure all the blood was gone from his hand. 'Lucky for you I'm aware of that fact.'

'How?' Hazel snapped but already knew the answer.

'Because my officers have been watching you since you left the station.'

'I knew it!'

'Lucky for you they were or else it would look bad for you right now stood over a corpse wouldn't it?'

Stanley was about to answer when a movement behind the two guarding constables caught his attention. At first he thought Owen had returned for another look but as he watched, a smartly dressed man appeared from between two headstones and moved towards them.

There was something about the man, the way he seemed oblivious to the two uniformed men and the events in the dark crypt. Stanley was about to speak when he saw the stranger pull open his jacket and draw a revolver from inside.

Acting on instinct, Stanley shoulder-barged into Inspector Kelly while pushing Hazel away from him. Before the Inspector could protest a single gunshot echoed in the air and one constable fell to the floor.

As Inspector Kelly crashed to the floor, he fumbled inside his own jacket for the issue revolver they had given him. A second shot echoed along the tunnel as the assassin fired at the second constable. The distraction was enough for Kelly to find the firearm and unleash his own rounds in the attacker's direction.

Stanley turned to watch as the Inspector and the unknown assassin exchanged a volley of fire before the assassin turned and fled. Having fired all of his rounds the Inspector made a quick reload but by the time he was back on aim the man had gone.

'What are you pair involved with?' He growled in anger as he moved to the open gates in search of the other man.

As the Inspector scanned the graveyard, there was no sign of anyone else amongst the gravestones. Owen had disappeared and their would be assassin had faded back into the undergrowth.

'We should get moving,' Kelly barked as he moved to check the two dead constables. 'I don't want to be here if he comes back, I've only got six more bullets.'
'I'm not going to the police station!' Stanley protested as Kelly scanned around wide-eyed.

Inspector Kelly squared up to Stanley and pressed his face into his. Whereas the policeman had been calm and collected, his composure was different now. For the first time Stanley felt intimidated by the older man as he glared at him.

'Someone that's willing to murder two police officers in broad daylight isn't likely to be put off by a handful of reservists in a police station.' Kelly snarled.
'So where are we going to go?' Hazel asked, trying to break the tension between the two men.
'Do you trust me?' Kelly asked but kept his gaze locked with Stanley.
'Not in the slightest.' Stanley bit back.
'Good!' Kelly slammed a hand on Stanley's shoulder. 'But for the moment I'm your best chance of getting out of the mess you find yourself in. Now follow me, I know somewhere we can hide.'

Stanley was not happy with the sudden deadly change of events but with little else in the way of choice he shrugged at Hazel and they both followed Kelly out of the crypt.
'Where are you taking us?'
'Somewhere safe! Now save your breath and get ready to run.'

The three of them exploded from the crypt's opening and disappeared amongst the footpaths out of Highgate Cemetery. Unbeknownst to them, Owen was watching as they ran but he didn't follow. He would have if he had been able, but the tight hand wrapped around his mouth and the muzzle of the revolver pressed into his temple kept him silent.

'I know someone who would very much like to speak to you.' The assassin hissed as he dragged Owen through the cemetery in the opposite direction of the fleeing policeman and his newfound companions.

CHAPTER TWELVE

BEHIND a small and indistinguishable wooden door facing out onto Piccadilly was Eric Masters' second home when in London. The Whisper Club was one of London's best-kept secrets and membership was beyond select. Less than a hundred names counted themselves amongst the members and the only way to attain membership was through family lines and elite recommendation.

Sitting beside the roaring fire, a crystal glass of whiskey in his hand it was hard to think there was a war raging in the world outside. Everything about the room brimmed with luxury and expense and the air was thick with cigar smoke.

'Mister Masters,' a well-dressed attendant interrupted. 'You have a call.'

Taking his time to sip the fiery whiskey, Eric placed the glass down on the table and pointed to it as he waltzed past the waiter. Offering him a nod at his silent order, the waiter scooped the glass from the table as Eric made his way to a small booth at the back of the room.

'What is it?' Eric groaned into the mouthpiece as he held the receiver to his ear.

'They found the body,' the voice replied on the other end of the call. 'The boy led them back.'

'I suppose you dealt with them?'

There was an uncomfortable silence on the other end of the call, and Eric felt his temper rising.

'The police arrived before I could intervene,' there was hesitation in his words. 'I tried to eliminate them all, but the Inspector intervened.'

'Where are they now?' Eric snapped into the telephone.

'I don't know.'

'Why didn't you follow them?'

'Someone saw me.'

Eric's anger boiled over as he slammed his fist into the wooden table in front of him. Although the man on the end of the line was his most trusted associate in London, his displeasure at the news was hard to disguise.

'Please tell me you dealt with that?'

'It was the boy, I have him with me now.'

Eric had been made aware from a contact that one of Colin Farley's boys had witnessed his actions in Highgate. The boy had been hard to find and although he had sent men to watch the King's Head, the boy had not made an appearance.

'Who did he take to the body?' Eric pressed, the aggravation in his voice subsiding.

'The two the police arrested.'

'It would appear your recommendation of Colin Farley and his crew of miscreants was an ill-informed suggestion. It seems that man has brought me nothing but complications and problems.' Eric tapped on the glass of the booth as the waiter moved past with his drink on a tray. 'I hold you responsible for everything that has happened in London.'

Eric opened the door and snatched the whiskey from the tray without a word. Shutting the door again, he took a long drink from the crystal glass and contemplated his options.

'I take full responsibility.' The voice declared on the crackled call.

'Good! Now bring the boy here, I'll arrange a private room and we will find out how much of a mess we find ourselves in.'

Without waiting for an answer, Eric slammed the earpiece into the cradle and ended the call. Pressing the glass against his forehead, he took a moment to compose himself before he planned for a private room within the Whisper Club.

In hindsight, he should have made the arrangements himself for the recovery of the artefact. Even though he had been away from London for several years, Eric believed his contacts would have found him better sources of help than the services provided by Colin Farley. Leaving the booth, he seethed with frustration how such a simple task had become a complicated mess that threatened to bring his exploits into the limelight.

His one stipulation, the one thing he had been insistent upon when he had struck the deal with Farley, was discretion. Nobody was supposed to know of the removal of the box, nobody should have known for decades, or until it was too late, and yet in a matter of hours news of the theft had been fed back to him.

'Jonathan,' Eric barked as he swallowed the remains of the new glass. 'I require a private room for the afternoon and entry for two guests.'

'Certainly Mister Masters, will they be using the club entrance?'

'No, I will send them to the back. They are not the clientele we would want our reputable members worrying about.'

'As you wish.'

The Maitre D' was a respectful man and knew of the discretion his club afforded to its members. Such a request of a private room and subterfuge for non-guests was commonplace and nothing out of the ordinary. They had built the original building with such accesses embedded within the design for just that purpose.

'You may have the Diamond Lounge if that will be to your liking?' The Maitre D' checked through a large leather-bound register behind the desk. 'I will ensure it is ready for you within the hour sir.'

'Excellent,' Eric Masters loved the power his status brought with it.

Leaving the empty glass on the reception desk, he moved back to his chair and removed a cigar from a box on the side table. Rolling it between his fingers, he waited until the young waiter returned to offer him a light. As the end of the cigar burned, Eric inhaled the smoke and cast the plume out towards the roaring fire.

'Another drink Mister Masters?' The waiter enquired as he finished lighting the cigar.

'Yes please,' Eric conceded as he tasted the rich flavour of the cigar. 'In fact, make it a double.'

Left alone in the empty lounge, Eric watched the smoke billow up towards the vaulted high ceiling. Leaning back in the chair, he watched the smoke wallow and dance each time he exhaled as he tried to work out how the recent turn of events had altered his plans.

With the murder of Colin Farley it had granted him

access to the cursed box, but it had come at a price. Not only were the police investigating the theft, they had connected the murder and the theft. There was no other explanation why the two people they had arrested had turned up at the scene.

Eric had been reluctant to return to London, the shadows of his past were always lingering and yet the discovery of Ad Firmamentum's location had been too much of an opportunity to ignore. For ten years Eric had searched for the fabled Vault, the home of hundreds of historical artefacts seized by the church and protected by the Secret Order of the Benedictine Brotherhood.

When he had first learned of Ad Firmamentum's location it had filled him with suspicion. A place of such treasures, to be buried beneath London's largest Abbey, seemed ludicrous. Having spent more money than many could quantify on confirming the information, he had confidence this was The Vault's location.

He had paid a generous sum to a mercenary to expose the subterranean vault in a simulated explosion during the nightly raids of the capital city. With such theatrics, Eric had secured access to the vault. As the waiter placed another fresh glass on the table, he paid him no attention as he recalled the events of two nights earlier as he had watched the ground rip open with the simple press of a button.

The mercenary had been a skilled man, his professionalism had been the only reason Eric had honoured their agreement and spared him the same fate as Colin Farley. Shrouded by the shadows of the parliament building, he watched the man with eagerness as he set about planting charges in the ground between Westminster Abbey and St Margaret's Church.

They had planned the rigged explosion for a night

earlier but the German's had failed to launch a significant foray and it had forced them to delay their plans. The following night however, the German's true to form had rallied an onslaught of bombs that had offered them the perfect cover.

With the streets empty, everyone housed in the safety of their Anderson shelters or the community shelters, they were left alone to execute Eric's plan. When he had been handed the innocuous device to detonate the buried explosives, Eric's hand had trembled. For years he had dreamed of finding Ad Firmamentum and retrieving the key to his life's obsession, and now its exposure rested in his hands.

'Wait until the bombing starts,' the mercenary had warned.

As the bombing runs began, it was like a concerto of instruments. Distant at first, the whistle and blast of the bombing raid grew into a crescendo until, feeling like a composer, the moment was right and he depressed the small plunger. At his command, the ground was torn open in a violent explosion that rocked the ground and sent dirt and debris flying in every direction.

The explosion ripped through the wide trunk of a tree that crashed to the ground and yet, despite the explosion's violence, nobody cared. To everyone else it was just another bomb dropped by the passing Luftwaffe, but for Eric it was the first steps on the last part of his journey.

As the smouldering ground billowed smoke and dust into the sky, they ventured to see what they had exposed. With his heart racing in his chest, knowing he was so close, he felt elation as the secret tunnel had been exposed by the mercenary's controlled explosion. Fighting the urge to clamber into the subterranean room, he paid the man and had disappeared into the night.

Replaying the night's events in his mind brought a twisted smile to his face as he rested in the Whisper Club lounge. He had achieved so much in his search, much more than anyone before him, and he could almost taste his victory.

By the time his guests arrived at the Whisper Club, Eric had planned everything about the boy's interrogation. As the Maitre D' informed him his guests were waiting in the Diamond Lounge, it filled Eric with resolve. Passing by the reception desk, he admired his reflection in the vast mirror by the main entrance.

His head of white hair was parted perfectly. Adjusting the tie around his neck, he brushed down the collar and made sure he oozed wealth and decorum. Smiling at his reflection, he felt a sense of power as he disappeared up a flight of narrow stairs to the Diamond Lounge where his two guests were waiting.

Reaching the door, he wrapped his long fingers around the handle and pushed the door open. By the window sat his most trusted friend, while Owen had been bound to a chair in the middle of the room.

Hands bound and a piece of cloth tied around his mouth, Owen's eyes went wide as he recognised the vile man that walked through the door.
'Judging by that look young man, you recognise who I am?'

Eric's words were bitter and sent a shiver down Owen's spine as he closed the door behind him, leaving the two men and the boy alone in the Diamond Lounge. Regardless of any sound that came from the room, Eric knew they would not be disturbed.

He could, and would, do anything he wanted to the boy to find out what he had seen and who he had told.

CHAPTER THIRTEEN

THEIR journey from Highgate Cemetery was uneventful. Much to Stanley's surprise Inspector Kelly didn't lead to them to an awaiting police car but dragged them at a pace towards the bus stop. As a familiar double-decker bus rumbled up the street, the Inspector had scanned around for the assassin and any sign he had followed them from the graveyard.

Thrusting his hand out to stop the bus there had been an air of tension as the lumbering vehicle made its way at a snail's pace towards them. Stanley expected to hear another *crack-thump* from another round but nothing came. As the bus pulled up next to the pavement Inspector Kelly ushered them on and all but threw his change at the flummoxed conductor.

'Keep the tickets,' he snapped at the surprised woman and flashed him his warrant card.

'Rides are free officer.' The conductor protested but Kelly

was too busy thrusting Hazel and Stanley to the upper deck of the bus.

The trio had sat on the back two rows of the top deck and stared down at the world outside. As they rumbled along the route Stanley allowed himself the chance to relax as the events of the last few hours replayed in his head. 'So,' Hazel interrupted as Inspector Kelly was checking the remaining rounds in his revolver. 'Where are we going and why are we using a bus?'

Counting only four remaining rounds, Kelly frowned as he reloaded the gun and rotated the cylinder into position. Sliding the weapon back into its holster he looked at Hazel and thought of the best way to answer her questions.

'Who did you tell about the body?'

'Nobody, it was Owen who told us.'

'The boy?' Kelly pressed and Hazel answered with a nod. 'I don't suppose you know who he told do you?'

'No idea,' Stanley answered, dragging himself back from trying to make sense of the day's events. 'We found him while we were trying to find out what had happened to the box that he stole.'

Inspector Kelly's ears pricked up at the mention of the box, Stanley noted the sudden shift in attention. 'How do you know it was a box?' The inherent suspicion rising in him, a consequence of being a very effective investigator. 'I made sure I didn't tell you what they took from The Vault. So tell me innocent Stanley Grand, how do you know it was a box?'

'Easy there,' Hazel interrupted. 'Until we found Owen we had no idea what any of this was about. We still only know some wooden box was stolen and not a lot else.'

Raising an eyebrow with suspicion Kelly looked at his two young companions.

'It was hard enough getting what we did out of him.' Stanley confessed, remembering the standoff outside the King's Head pub. 'If it hadn't been for Hazel, I think I'd have got nowhere with the stubborn git.'

'I see,' the Inspector pondered as he looked out of the almost panoramic view as the bus trundled up the road. 'When we get to where we're going I think it's time I gave you an explanation.'

'That's the most sense you've made since we met you.' Stanley quipped.

'I take it by that, you're not taking us to the police station?' Hazel watched as Kelly answered with a distracted shake of his head. 'So, where are we going?'

'It'll be easier once we get there to explain everything.'

'Any reason you're not taking us to the station?' Stanley pressed.

'Because, young man, there are only a handful of people who knew about the body in the graveyard. Three of them are here, two of my constables who are now dead and it would seem the boy and whoever wanted you dead. I told three other people in my office and something tells me the tip was a stage to flush out those who knew about the murder.'

Kelly left his words to linger as he tried to pull together the events of the last hour. Slipping into silence the rest of the journey was uneventful, and it wasn't until Kelly pressed the bell to stop the bus that Stanley tried to work out where he was taking them.

Disembarking the bus, Inspector Kelly offered the flustered conductor an apology for his gruffness. Smoothing over his actions he offered the woman a smile and wave as the bus pulled away from the pavement and continued along its journey.

Ignoring the exchange, Stanley looked around trying to

work out where in London he was. The streets were familiar but only by the design of the houses. To his recollection he had never been to this part of the city. Where they stood, close to the mouth of a wide junction, the biggest feature was an ornate church-building sat on the junction.

'We're heading there.' Kelly declared and pointed in the church's direction.

Throwing a confused look at Hazel, she responded with a shrug and followed Kelly as he crossed the road towards the paved path leading to the impressive church building. A trio of imposing doors sat beneath an enormous ornate arched window. A pair of battlement-styled spires flanked either side of the church front and as they walked towards the handful of steps leading to the doors Stanley read the simple sign planted in the grass to the side of the path.

In what appeared to be hand-painted lettering read:

EALING ABBEY
CATHOLIC CHURCH
OF
ST BENEDICT

As Stanley was about to ask why the Inspector had brought them to a church, the rightmost door opened and a man in his early sixties sauntered to the top of the steps. Dressed in the familiar black habit of a monk, the man looked at the recent arrivals and offered Kelly a knowing nod of greeting.

'Greetings brother,' the monk offered as Kelly led them up the steps of the church.

'I thought monks were silent?' Stanley hissed at Hazel but blushed as Kelly rounded on him and answered.

'There's a lot of misinformation, silly beliefs about things people do not understand.' There was an obvious frustration in Kelly's voice. 'Perhaps we can save the explanation for when we are safe and out of the street?'

Accepting the sudden berating from the Inspector, Stanley followed in silence as the monk shared a hushed greeting with Kelly and led them into the church. Passing through the door, a second monk secured the door behind them as he guided them through the narthex of the church and into the wide nave beyond.

Taken aback by the vast size of the nave, Stanley took a moment to admire the beauty of the room. Turning around, his attention fell to the impressive stained-glass window that sat above the doors. From the outside, with the lights inside dimmed as expected, the light from outside was enough to illuminate the intricate artwork.

Although not in any sense religious, Stanley had always found churches to be fascinating places. Now, as he looked up at the rich reds, blues and gold within the glass, he could not help but admire its majesty. Not understanding the images in the glass, he tried to makes sense of the three gathered figures and praying children that dominated the centre of the red circle.

The window showed signs of damage, shrapnel and bomb damage from the air raids and as he looked towards the back of the church, Stanley realised the magnificent building had suffered.

Pulling his attention from the stained-glass, it surprised Stanley to see the walls and archways were bland and almost featureless. The magnificent vaulted ceiling sat high above them, held in place by arched columns with little or no decoration to them. Although an enormous section of roof had been damaged and the rear wall was missing, the church still looked resilient in its refusal to be levelled by the bombs.

'It still stands despite the damage from the bombs.' The monk that had welcomed them declared as he saw Stanley taking in the damage. 'We have lost the organ chamber and the east end but we remain hopeful the worst is done.'

The monks had done an impressive job of cleaning through the debris and damage. From the outside, or at least the way Kelly had brought them to the building, there was little to show the extent of the damage caused to the church. Where piles of debris had been sorted, there was a path through the centre of the nave to where the altar, or what remained, stood.

'There are but a few of us that remain to protect the church.' The monk explained as he guided them through the path in the debris. 'Many have been called to fight and others have sought to spread the word of God hoping peace will one day return. I, along with my other Brothers, are all that remain to protect the church.'

'I seek your hospitality.' Kelly announced as they reached the nave's centre and the monk stopped in his tracks.

'A Brother of the Benedictine Order is bound to offer hospitality.'

'I come in search of hospitality in a time when stability is required against the rising darkness, through my obedience I stand a light to others.'

'A candle must burn in the darkest of times, even in darkness there must be light for conversatio.'

'I am the light in the dark, the guide into the depths.'

The curious exchange sounded like a strange riddle to Stanley as he watched the two men speak. Sensing Hazel's curiosity, they watched as the two men recited words like some old pre-prepared script until the monk looked from Kelly to them.

'And these?' The monk pressed.

'In need of light, in need of guidance through dark times.'
'You are of the Order?'

Casting a glance at them Kelly returned his attention to the monk and nodded.
'I wear the medal of Saint Benedict.'

Stanley watched as Kelly removed his jacket and unbuttoned the top of his shirt. Moving the fabric aside, he exposed the left-side of his chest to the monk as Stanley craned to see. Moving around, it surprised Stanley to find an intricate tattoo of black ink etched above where Kelly's heart would be. Letters arranged in a circle around a black cross with more letters made no sense to him, but the monk recognised it.

Looking up at Kelly, the monk's demeanour changed to one of awe as he admired the tattoo. Reaching out a finger, the monk touched Kelly's flesh and traced around the circular lettering and cross.

'I have never been presented with a Brother of the Secret Order. We are humbled you seek hospitality in my home.'
'I am no different from you Brother.' Kelly offered as he moved to cover the tattoo.
'You are welcome to stay.' The monk offered Kelly a curt bow and scurried off towards the ruins of the altar.

'What was that about?' Hazel asked as Kelly retrieved his jacket from the rubble pile and put it under his arm.
'There is a lot I need to explain, perhaps we should find somewhere to sit?'

Looking around, Stanley realised they had stacked the benches on the far sides of the nave. As they weaved through the piles of debris and rubble Stanley sensed the same curiosity in Hazel that was now bubbling inside him.

CHAPTER FOURTEEN

ALONE in the nave of Ealing Abbey Church, Stanley watched as Kelly fidgeted on the seat opposite. Not wanting to press the Inspector, feeling this would be an enlightening conversation, he waited with patience as did Hazel by his side.

'I should begin with introductions,' Kelly fiddled with the cuff of his shirt, appearing nervous. 'Right now I'm talking to you as myself, not as a police officer.'

'What do you mean?' Hazel enquired, trying to make sense of Kelly's words.

'My name is Damien Kelly and while I work as an officer of the law I am also part of a much bigger secret.' There was a heaviness in his voice, a sense that he was revealing things to them that made him feel more than a little uncomfortable. 'What you saw with the monk, the tattoo and the things we said are all part of something much bigger than you would believe.'

Stanley could not deny the curiosity that bubbled inside him. The sudden change in Kelly's demeanour was curious to observe, and Stanley wanted to push.

'Before I joined the police, I sat alongside men like the Brother who welcomed us here.'

'You were a man of the cloth?' Hazel's expression mimicked Stanley's surprise.

'I took my vows as a much younger man but lived my life in the world, respecting the vows but serving God outside where I felt I could have more influence and impact.' Kelly traced his hand across the tattoo beneath his shirt for a moment. 'Beyond my vows, however, I came across a part of the brotherhood that piqued my interest.'

Stanley sensed Kelly was holding things back but respected what was happening enough to let him speak. As they sat in the empty nave, Kelly explained his life as if it had been leading to that moment.

During his early years in servitude a curious Friar, a learned man of few words but worldly knowledge had mentored him. The stories he had shared with Kelly had fed on his curiosity and, when the time had been right, the Friar had offered Kelly the chance to walk amongst the ranks of a secret order within the church.

'Within every element of life be it the church, the police or the military there are layers of secrecy. I was part of the Benedictine Monks and yet the Friar told me of the Secret Order, an order charged with…'

Kelly trailed off and looked at each of them. Hanging on the unfinished sentence, Stanley perched on the edge of his seat as he waited to hear what Kelly had to say.

'Charged with what?' Stanley pressed, his urge to know taking over.

'I've never told a soul of this outside of the church,' Kelly mused. 'I've never had a need to and yet, here I am feeling nervous.'

'Why?'

'Because saying it aloud to people who don't understand the workings of the brotherhood, the vows and the things I've seen it sounds ridiculous.'

'What does?' It was Hazel's turn to press.

'I am a member of the Secret Order of the Benedictine Brotherhood and they charge us with protecting humanity from the darkness, the things we know and are yet to discover.'

Stanley sat back in his seat and looked at the Inspector. The confident policeman looked like a different man as he sat opposite him. There was something, albeit ridiculous sounding, but the look on Kelly's face told Stanley there was truth in the older man's words. Even though Stanley suspected it was nothing more than religious fairytales, he could see enough in Kelly's expression that he believed what he was saying.

'Ok,' Stanley started, choosing his words so as not to offend Kelly. 'I'm not saying I don't believe you but what does any of this have to do with us?'

'Until two days ago it had nothing to do with you. Our paths were not destined to cross until you stumbled across Ad Firmamentum.'

'Ad what?'

'The Vault, the place buried beneath Westminster, is a secret vault overseen by my Brothers. Your inquisitive nature caused our paths to converge and now we find ourselves entwined in a dark web.'

'I didn't take anything.' Stanley bit, the frustration still fresh that Kelly was still pressing his suspicions towards the theft.

'I know you didn't!' His reply stunned Stanley. 'The looks on your faces tell me you've never heard of The

Brotherhood or Ad Firmamentum, had it been different none of this would be new to you.'

'So what was in there?'

'Many things,' Stanley raised any eyebrow at the obvious attempt to avoid the question. 'The important thing remains what was taken, what no longer sits under our protection.'

'This box thing?'

'Yes.' Kelly sighed. 'The box pertains to an ancient evil, a cursed soul that has been buried for thousands of years. Until two days ago it was forgotten to history, and we intended to keep it that way. We had heard of people searching for the legend, but nobody had come close.'

'Until two days ago?'

'Someone learned of The Vault's location. The war has forced us to keep it in situ longer than we would have liked and gave them an opportunity.'

'You said it's something to do with an ancient evil?' Hazel pressed, her curiosity was beyond piqued as she hung on Kelly's every word.

'There are things you are better off not knowing,' Kelly replied. 'For your own protection I expect the less you know, the safer you will be.'

'Bugger that!' Stanley snapped, catching his companions by surprise with his outburst. 'In the last few days you have arrested me, I've pretty much been kicked out of my house, found dead bodies, been shot at and now you're saying we might be in danger.'

'My Brothers can protect you until this is over.'

'What do you expect us to do, sit by while you recover whatever this box is?' Hazel interjected. 'I'm sorry but that isn't going to happen. We will not sit back and wait.'

Her tenacity once again surprise Stanley and he had to smile as she glared at Kelly. The Inspector sighed as he rested his head in his hands as if wrestling with his own thoughts on the matter. For a few tense moments the nave fell silent as both Stanley and Hazel waited for Kelly to speak again.

'I don't enjoy exposing you to harm,' Kelly started, but Stanley interrupted.

'Isn't that our choice?'

'If you let me finish,' Kelly snapped with irritation. 'Protecting The Vault is mine and my Brother's responsibility and we cannot ask or expect anyone else to take that charge in our stead.'

'You're not asking us,' Hazel soothed. 'What Stanley is trying to say is, we want to help.'

'That decision is far above anything I can make.' Kelly sighed. 'I would need to speak with the Friar and my Brothers before we could accept your offer.'

'Then ask them so we can get on with it.' Stanley huffed.

Kelly rose from his seat and stepped to the centre of the empty church. Scanning his surroundings, he caught sight of a robed monk stood by a pile of rubble and shattered glass on the far side of the nave. As Stanley turned to see what had taken Kelly's attention he realised the new monk's face. The labour of the monk's movements made Stanley believe it was an old man beneath the robes. With a waft of a wrinkled hand, he beckoned Kelly over to him. The two shared a hushed conversation, their quiet voices impossible to hear as Stanley and Hazel waited.

'What do you think is going on here?' Stanley asked as he watched Kelly and the mysterious monk.

'I have no idea but looking at Inspector Kelly, he believes everything he's telling us.'

'And he seemed so normal!' Stanley scoffed but felt Hazel cast him a disapproving glare.

'We may not know him very well but he doesn't strike me

as a fool, far from it.' Hazel's words were true and Stanley couldn't disagree. 'All we can do is listen to what he has to say. I don't think we are any safer out there, especially if that man was trying to kill us.'

'He could have been after the Inspector.' Stanley mused. 'We could have just been caught in the middle.'

'Do you believe that?'

'Not really,' he confessed.

'Quiet, he's coming back.'

Everything felt so dramatic and theatrical as Stanley sat on the bench and watched the proceedings. There were so many questions he wanted to ask but knew, judging by Kelly's behaviour, it was not the best time to push. Kelly offered the older monk a respectful bow before the robed monk turned and walked away.

A sudden flurry of wings stole everyone's attention as a flock of pigeons flew from their perch on the exposed beams of the damaged church roof. As the trio watched the birds lift up and out of the jagged hole in the roof, Kelly took advantage of the distraction and returned to his seat. Taking advantage of the brief pause, he took a deep breath and prepared to explain to his two young companions the truth about the world they had stumbled into.

'The box leads to an ancient tomb.' Kelly announced once the birds had disappeared.

Stanley turned on the spot and looked down at Kelly. The simple declaration had dragged him from the distraction of the birds and back into the conversation. 'Tomb?'

'What lies in the tomb is an evil the likes of which the world has not seen before.' Kelly explained as they sat back down. 'It is a creature with no name, history has seen fit to destroy his legacy but we know him only as The

Iceman, a creature that has slumbered for five-thousand-years.'

'What do you mean by creature?' Hazel was struggling to understand what Kelly was trying to say. 'You mean some beast or animal?'

'If only it were an animal or beast,' Kelly sighed. 'To understand the threat, we now face, I need to take you back almost five-thousand-years to a time when the world differed greatly from how it is now.'

As Kelly settled himself back in his seat he was not surprised to see both of his young companions staring at him, hooked on his every word. Kelly recalled the time he had first heard the legend of The Iceman. He suspected his face reflected the same expectant look he saw on Stanley and Hazel's face right then.

Outside of the Brotherhood, and the ones who sought to release the creature, there were but a handful of people that knew of its existence. He was sure that neither Stanley nor Hazel understood the magnitude of what he was about to tell them. Unbeknownst to them it had been the Friar who had been observing them from the ruined altar had been the mentor Kelly had spoken of.

Kelly had known his mentor was at the Abbey, he had received a summons to attend when news had travelled that Ad Firmamentum had been breached. Allowing the Friar to observe the conversation, concealed in the shadows, it had been a simple nod of approval to share The Iceman's legacy with Stanley and Hazel.

By doing so Kelly knew, with a heavy heart, that by sharing this with them they were forced upon a path of darkness and danger. Once he had shared with them the secrets, there would be no turning back for them.

'I will explain something to you that happened five-thousand-years ago. Some of it you won't believe, but trust me when I say every word is true.'

For the rest of the day and into the night, Kelly explained what he knew of the origins of the creature he had warned Stanley and Hazel of. As they sat in silence and absorbed what he was saying they could almost see it in their mind's eye.

CHAPTER FIFTEEN

5,000 YEARS AGO

THE Ötztal Alpine mountain range dominated the landscape with its zig-zag of peaks clambering skywards. The rich blue sky was crystal clear and not a solitary cloud moved. A snow storm that had raged through the night had long since dissipated and the village people had emerged from their conical-roofed huts to be welcomed by the crisp morning sun.

A Chalcolithic settlement was an impressive sight. Nestled in a large clearing there were three distinct levels within the modest village. Most activity was taking place amongst the houses in the lower section as children scrambled around while adults prepared for a day of hunting.

The settlement sat close to the divide of modern Italy and Austria and was home to almost two-hundred people. Constructed of a mix of mud, stone and straw the houses had been built in a neat pattern, all feeding towards a larger central conical-roofed dwelling that stood on a natural rise in the land.

Twine fencing surrounded the central building and two straw cones sat either side of the principal building. In front of the trio of buildings a fire raged in a pit and two men appeared in heated conversation in front of the dancing flames.

In a language long since forgotten, the older of the two men was almost shouting at the other.

'What do you mean you can't find her?' He bellowed in their native tongue, his voice echoing in the wide opening of his home.

'We have searched the village and there is no sign.' The second man professed and lowered his gaze to the floor.

The Village Chief was enraged, his tanned skin flushed as he kicked out at a log protruding from the roaring fire. As a shower of sparks erupted into the air, he turned his back on the quivering man and stormed across to the neighbouring dwelling.

Lifting open the door, he descended a set of steps into the sunken interior. This roof was set at ground level but most of the habitation was below ground level and belonged to the Chief's Shaman, a man he had known since childhood.

'Where is he?' The Chief bellowed as he looked around the empty dwelling.

Much to the Chief's surprise, the interior was in a state of disarray. The Shaman had always been a careful man and kept his habitat neat and ordered. What he saw now was chaos and disorder with items strewn over with a mix of plants, herbs and tools.

'The guardsmen at the gates say he left at sunrise.' The timid man seemed fearful of the Chief. 'He is the only one to leave the village today.'

The Chief turned and stalked back out into the dry air. Although snow-capped mountains loomed behind his attention was focussed on the stone wall that surrounded his village and the gates leading out into the open land. 'Bring me my guards,' he barked in anger as he stormed back towards his own hut. 'If you are certain she is not within the village, then he must have taken her.'

In recent months the Shaman's behaviour had become unpredictable and concerning. The Chief had spent many hours listening to the Shaman's beliefs and how they had shifted from the Mother Goddess to that of the Forest Goddess. More often the Shaman had disappeared beyond the safety of the village and explored the nearby glades in search of a voice he claimed to have heard.

Once an open man he had retreated more into his own company and denied anyone, including the Chief, access to his workshop and home. Retrieving the copper-tipped spear and axe from the walls of his hut, the Chief emerged into the bright sun as two leather-clad guards sprinted up the hill towards him.

'My wife is missing, as is the Shaman.' The Chief barked as he tested each of the weapons in his hands. 'Your brother's say he is the only person to have left this morning, he cannot have travelled far.'

'Is it wise for you to travel beyond the walls?' The taller of the two guards interjected.

The Chief was on him in an instant. Covering the gap between them he pressed the cold copper blade of the axe against the guard's throat until the metal pinched at his skin.

'My wife is with child, it is my responsibility to protect her.'

'But beyond the walls, if the other Chiefs learn of your

departure the village will be at risk.'

It surprised the Chief that the guardsman continued his protest despite his precarious position at the edge of his axe. Although passion flowed through him, the Chief could not deny the guard's logic and what he was saying. Their settlement had sat in the centre of a bloody feud between their neighbouring villages since the Chief's youth and his enemies would exploit any chance of weakness.

Faced with the tough choice, he kept the sharpened blade against the guard's flesh a little longer as he considered what to do.

'Might I suggest a hunting party?' It was, to the Chief's surprise, the timid man who interrupted the tense silence.

'How long since he left the gates?' The Chief growled through gritted teeth.

'The sun had barely crested the mountains.'

'Take horses, take whatever you need.' The Chief declared as he removed the blade from the guard's neck and took a step back. 'Return my wife and child to me or else you and your family will have no home within my walls.'

The Chief turned and disappeared back into the Shaman's hut.

'Take another with you,' the timid man began as he watched the Chief descend the steps into the hut. 'Do not let him down, we are vulnerable to attack at any time and the Chief needs to be clear of mind should that happen.'

'We understand.' The guard agreed as he massaged the tender flesh where the Chief had pressed the axe blade into his neck.

'Go.' The timid man instructed and watched as the two guards disappeared in search of a third companion and the horses to carry them in pursuit of the absent Shaman.

Oblivious to the turmoil in the Chieftain's

encampment, the village was alive with daily activity. Animals meandered the serpentine paths between the huts on all three levels of the village as families went about their business. Although the day had not gained momentum, already plumes of black smoke billowed towards the sky as the smiths set about smelting the ore and forging weapons and tools.

The Chief, alone in the Shaman's hut, collapsed into a heap against the far wall and stared at the open doorway. Resting his weapons on the ground, he felt fear course through him at the thought of what was happening to his wife.

Although the Shaman had been different in himself it was not uncommon. Across the generations it was know that they knew those who danced the lines between the Mother Goddess and the land were seen as more eccentric. When the Shaman had spoken of the Forest Goddess it had been unusual, but the Chief had brushed it aside as a flight of fancy of his curious mind.

Sitting alone inside the hut, he remained with his head buried in his hands for some time before he could pull himself to take in his surroundings. All that raced through his mind were the infinite possibilities of what had happened to his wife and why the Shaman would have taken her. He had shown no malcontent towards her before, their interactions had been few as his wife had never warmed to the Shaman or his presence in their lives. Sitting alone, the morning crept by until a sudden cry of laughter from an unseen child outside dragged him back from his melancholy.

Returning from his musing, he looked around at the interior of the Shaman's hut. Sat on the floor of the hut, the Chief looked around and saw the intricate carvings and images the Shaman had scribbled and scratched on every space within the hut. The stone walls were etched with images of trees, men and animals, and in their native language he had inscribed words and phrases that made no sense to the Chief.

Dropping his gaze to the floor, he was amazed to find the Shaman had even inscribed passages and symbols into the compressed earth that made up the floor of the building. Although disguised by a layer of dust the Chief brushed his hand against the surface and exposed a series of symbols between his legs.

Although they were like their language, they were not symbols he recognised. Clearing out a larger piece of ground, the Chief uncovered a spiral-pattern of words interlaced with the unfamiliar symbols.

Before long the Chief had followed the spiral out until he had uncovered almost a quarter of the dusty floor. Pushing the makeshift table out of the way, he sent the contents of herbs and tools clattering to the floor.

As if guided by the hands of fate, a small dagger fell from the table and buried itself almost to the hilt in the softer earth where the table had stood. As he moved, the Chief's attention was drawn to the dagger as the sun caught on the glistening copper blade.

Bending to inspect the weapon, he ripped the dagger from the floor and admired the weapon's craftsmanship. It was not something crafted within the village, he knew that from the etched decoration on the handle. The dagger had been crafted in another settlement far from his village. How the Shaman had come by such a prize was another unanswered question, but more so was the blood that stained the blade and the handle.

Raising the dagger into the sunlight, the Chief inspected the blood and, to his horror, found it still wet. Feeling a rising sense of fear for his wife, he looked down to where the dagger had embedded in the floor. The lettering and symbols were familiar to him and he read the words aloud as he toyed with the bloodstained dagger. 'The Goddess spoke to me, her voice sang like the birds in an opening in the depths of the trees. I saw her there, in the middle of the glade, a woman of beauty. She promised me life eternal for blood.' The chief's mouth went dry as he continued to read. 'A sacrifice of my own was not enough. She accepted but demanded more. To her I am not innocent, she wanted a sacrifice of life that was pure and untouched by the Mother Goddess and her blinding thoughts.'

Brushing the floor, the Chief searched for more but there was nothing else etched into the compressed earth. Fuelled by desperation he scurried on all fours to find something, any clue where the Shaman had gone, all the while knowing what innocence the Shaman intended to offer his newfound deity.

As he brushed aside a clump of dried heather and lavender the Chief recoiled from the bloodied mess, his fingers pressed against. There, on the floor, lay the mutilated corpse of an unborn sheep. The foetus was partly developed and still encased inside the amniotic sac. Only the foetus' head had been drawn from the now crusty sack.

The skin had been peeled back across one side of the animal's head and someone had pressed a thin copper needle through an eye socket and out through the open mouth. Whatever the Shaman had done to the poor creature had left it looking like some cruel and twisted experiment.

The sight of it sent an icy chill down the Chief's spine as he fought the rising taste of sick from his stomach. Taking the dagger with him, he made his way out of the hut and allowed the warm sun to bathe him as he stepped back outside.

He prayed to the Mother Goddess for the safety of his wife and unborn child. With no power over her fate, he relied on the guards he had despatched to seek and find the absconded Shaman and bring his wife back to him.

For the first time since childhood, the Chief felt powerless and alone.

CHAPTER SIXTEEN

5,000 YEARS AGO

NOTHING disturbed the Shaman as he moved around the open glade in the forest. Entirely focussed, he moved around the writhing bound woman on the floor without a care for her comfort. The Chief's wife was bound and gagged on the snow-covered floor of the forest. Although her voice was muted with a tether of leather her eyes were wide with terror as she watched the Shaman prepare for his rituals.

A short man, standing just over five-feet tall he sported an unkempt beard and a look in his eyes of a man with purpose. The glade was deep within the forest and offered him cover from the more trodden tracks used by the villagers.

'Not long now,' he murmured as he removed a bag from the horse that had carried them from the settlement. 'I promise it will not be painful.'

Dropping the bag to the ground beside the woman's head, he reached down and pulled the taut leather from between her lips. Gasping for air she pleaded with the Shaman but instead of listening he silenced her by placing his thin finger against her lips.

Leaning close he whispered into her ear.
'You should feel honoured the Goddess of the forest has chosen you.'
'My husband will not allow this,' although her voice quivered she spat the words with venom. '
'The Chief will be powerless to deny me when I return to the village, my Goddess will see to that.'

The Shaman had always been a man to be wary of. In the eyes of the Chief's wife there had always been something unnerving about the Shaman. Reclusive in his studies, emerging less and less in recent months, he looked even more frenzied as he busied himself laying out a trail of blood on the surrounding snow.

The Shaman squeezed the thick blood from an old leather bladder until there was nothing left inside. Discarding the bladder on the ground, he traced his finger through the blood and set about etching bloodied symbols in a circle around the struggling woman.
'Keep still; there are animals in these woods that would see you as food.'

As if on cue, the howl of a wolf echoed through the forest and the Chieftain's wife froze. Smiling to himself, the Shaman continued to decorate the incantations on the ground until he had completed the circle.
'You don't have to do this.' The woman sobbed as she watched the Shaman. 'Please, my child has done nothing to you.'

The Shaman was indifferent to her pleading as he prepared for the sacrifice. Returning to the horse tethered to a nearby tree, he removed his outer coat and shivered as the icy chill of the air touched his skin. Clad in his leather vest and furred headwear, he hung the thick fur coat over the horse and dipped his hand into another bag.

Rifling through the contents he found what he was looking for and removed a small leather pouch and a matching dagger to the one he had left in his hut. Admiring the blade in the sunlight, a snowflake tumbled from the sky as the heavy clouds dulled the sunlight, adding an ominous air to the glade.

Feeling the wind pick up and whistle through the alpine forest, the Shaman turned and stalked through the snow back to the bound woman. Laying the pouch on the floor by her head, he untied the cord securing the top. Opening it, the inside was filled with an array of various sized copper needles and curious instruments. Fingering through them the Shaman found the one he was looking for and lifted it from the leather pouch. Holding it in front of his face he inspected the delicate instrument and nodded with satisfaction.

'I will make this as painless as I can.'

'Why are you doing this?'

'Your sacrifice will ascend me to a place above mortality,' the Shaman hushed as the snow started fall between the evergreen trees. 'I have been promised a life beyond death for your blood, the blood of an innocent.'

The Chief's wife went rigid as she watched the Shaman's gaze drop from her face to her bulging stomach. Almost ready for birth she had carried her unborn child through a harsh winter and now this twisted man wanted to take it from her.

Powerless and bound with her hands behind her back, all she could do was thrash as the Shaman opened her leather outer garment, exposing the woven frock underneath. Without a word he lifted the dagger and pressed the tip against the tight fabric and sliced from her chest down the length of the frock.

'Please,' she wept, too terrified to move for fear of it slicing through the stretched skin that protected her unborn child.

Ignoring her sobs, the Shaman pulled aside the fabric and exposed the swollen stomach. Placing his hand against her warm skin, he leaned close and pressed his ear against her stomach to feel the baby moving beneath her skin.

To the Chief's wife it was sickening to see the bearded man listening to her baby's heartbeat in her stomach. He looked almost serene as he closed his eyes and pressed his ear to her warm flesh. Still holding the dagger, he tapped his finger on her swollen breast in time with the heartbeat he heard from her womb.

'There is nothing more innocent than the blood of a child.'

The weather had changed since they had travelled from the village. Where the sun had shone down, the snowstorm from the night before had returned with a vengeance. Although protected by the enormous trees the wind whipped between the trunks and flurries of snowflakes broke through the canopy as the Shaman prepared himself for what needed to be done.

Feeling the chill against his exposed cheek, he opened his eyes and saw the look of terror on the woman's face. Ignoring the silent pleas in her eyes, he lifted from her stomach and placed his hand against her skin. At his touch the baby moved, perhaps sensing the evil that he was about to perform.

'The Forest Goddess demands only the blood of an innocent but I would see you relieved of the pain,' the Shaman pressed the dagger against the woman's neck as he knelt above her. 'You do not need to see what I will do.'

'I would rather you see my hate as you do it.' The woman growled in defiance, catching the Shaman by surprise. 'As you wish,' he scoffed and focussed his attention back to her stomach. 'Then I will let you see.'

Pressing the dagger against his own palm, he sliced the metal blade across the length of his hand. Feeling the blade bite into his skin, he winced at the pain but knew it was necessary for the ritual. Feeling the warmth of his own blood, he clenched his fist and allowed the blood to stain his entire hand. He placed his bloodied palm against her stomach, smearing her skin with his blood.

Tears streaming down her face she watched as the Shaman held the thin copper needle above her navel. Feeling the razor-sharp tip press against her stretched skin, she winced and prepared herself to feel the searing pain as he pushed the needle through her flesh.

To her surprise it was not pain that followed but a sense of relief as a voice bellowed from the tree line at the edge of the glade.

Both the Shaman and Chief's wife turned to look towards the edge of the glade. The flurries of snow had increased but not enough to obscure the view of three village guardsman emerging from the trees.
'How?' The Shaman snarled as he moved around the woman's body and pressed the knife once again to her throat. 'One step closer and I will kill her.'

His voice carried in the wind and the three armed guardsman stopped dead in their tracks. Looking at them, the Shaman weighed up his options as the storm increased around them. Two of the men were armed with nothing more than axes and spears while the third had knocked an arrow and aimed the bow in his direction.

The Shaman knew they would not release the arrow. He was too close to the woman, but he could not stay there forever. As his mind raced through his options, the woman shouted to the guardsmen.

'He's mad, kill him! He wants my baby.'

Hearing her voice snatched him from his contemplations and the Shaman acted on instinct. 'Perhaps your blood will be innocent enough.' He hissed into her ear and drew the dagger across her throat in one swift move. 'My Goddess see the blood I spill for you in honour of your power, in honour of my promise.'

The copper blade sliced through her flesh with ease and pierced her windpipe, silencing the scream she tried to release. Seeing her eyes grow wide the blood oozed from the rough gash in her neck but the Shaman had no time to complete the ritual and draw his hand through the warm blood as the bowman released the arrow.

More by luck than anything else, the arrow flew but missed its mark. Hearing the whistle and thump of the arrow, the Shaman dropped to the snowy ground and scurried away from the dying woman, taking flight away from the three men.

He had no chance or time to reclaim the tethered horse, he had no other choice than to make his escape on foot. Casting a quick glance behind him, he saw the first of the three men drop to the dying woman's side and fight to stem the flow of blood from her neck.

Knowing there was no chance to save the woman, he looked to his hand and saw his fingers speckled with the woman's blood. As he turned and ran, he took a moment to lick the lukewarm blood from his fingers and savoured the metallic taste on his tongue.

'You will pay for this.' One guard shrieked as a second arrow flew wide through the air. 'Get him.'

The Shaman wasted no time and knew the enraged guards were a force to be reckoned with. No stranger to protecting himself in his travels beyond the walls of his settlement, he knew when he was out skilled and the three men now chasing him were superior warriors than him. Heart racing, he dodged through the trees, making it difficult for more arrows to be fired at his back.

As his heart raced, he felt the blood oozing from the jagged cut on his palm and tore a strip of material from his clothes as he ran. Doing his best to stem the flow of blood as he zigzagged through the forest he did not know where he was heading but knew what lay ahead of him as the forest led to the jagged cliffs and the deep valleys that marked the edge of the Ötztal mountains.

With no other choice, he raced towards the vertical cliffs and almost certain promise of death.

CHAPTER
SEVENTEEN

KELLY smiled as he saw the attentive looks on Stanley and Hazel's faces. His recollection of the events that had unfolded in the Ötztal mountains some five-thousand years earlier had swallowed their attention. As he drifted away from the story he allowed them to come back from their imagined versions of what he had been saying.

'What happened?' Hazel gasped as she realised Kelly had stopped talking. 'The Shaman, the man in the woods. Did they catch him?'

Before Kelly could answer, the robed monk announced his arrival with a cough that startled Stanley and made him jump in his seat. Turning their attention to the monk the pair watched as he moved between the trio and handed a leather-bound book to Kelly. Without as much as a word the monk stole a glance at both of them before retiring silently back into the shadowed ruins of the altar.

'What's that?' Stanley enquired as Kelly admired the cover of the oversized book.

'Follow me,' Kelly announced as he rose from his seat and led the pair to a door on the opposite side of the church. 'I'd rather be out of sight when I discuss this part.'

Kelly set off across the width of the church as Stanley looked across at Hazel. Offering him a shrug she too rose from her seat and followed in Kelly's wake.

'I don't know about you but I'm curious what any of that weirdness has to do with us.'

Not waiting for an answer she disappeared through the door. Stanley groaned and followed them into the church annex.

The annex to Ealing Abbey was a stark contrast to the grandeur of the church building. Consisting mostly of residence and rooms of prayer Stanley fell into step by Kelly's side as they navigated towards a small private room on the far end of the annex.

'Wasn't it safe in there?' Stanley quizzed as Kelly led them into a small room and closed the door behind them.

'We have already attracted the attention of dangerous people. The Brotherhood have protected this, and other secrets, it would be unwise to let our guard down now.'

Clearing a table in the room's centre he dropped the leather-bound book and lit a candle on the sideboard. Hazel, acting on instinct, was about to tell the Inspector off for his light discipline but realised the room had no windows. Smiling to herself she dropped her attention to the cover of the leather book.

The book was obviously old, the spine was covered in a thin layer of dust and pages appeared yellowed from what they could see. The bound leather cover was intricately decorated with the pattern of a tree that encased a crucifix in the centre. Beams of light spread in all directions from the tree and beneath it the tree the lettering seemed to grow from the roots of the tree.

'What does that say?' Stanley asked as he struggled to read the Latin words on the cover.

'The archives of the Brotherhood are divided into volumes, each one focuses on a particular element of our history that requires our attention.'

'How many are there?' Stanley pressed.

'Enough,' Kelly replied with a dismissive wave of his hand. 'This is the only one that we are concerned with.'

Magnitudo
CDXII

Homo Glacies

'Homo Glacies?' Hazel mused as she interrupted her companions. 'If I can remember the Latin from school doesn't that say Ice Man?'

'Very good,' Kelly replied with a look of surprise. 'This volume covers the legend of the Iceman, the Shaman I was telling you about back there.'

Kelly opened the cover and leafed through the pages. As he did, Stanley looked closer at the handwritten calligraphy that covered each individual page. The

artwork and lettering was like nothing he had ever seen
before and reminded him of the old bibles he had once
seen in a museum. The ink looked so rich, as if it had only
just been written but, judging by the age of the book, he
expected they were a lot older than that.

'They hunted the Shaman through the forests until they
trapped him by the cliffs of the mountain,' Kelly continued
as he found the page he was looking for. 'He put up a
valiant fight, defying the guardsmen's demands for him to
return to face justice for the murder he had committed.'

'Wait a minute,' Hazel interrupted. 'How do you know
any of this? I mean, this is a lot to have been written on the
walls of some cave somewhere.'

'You're right,' Kelly smirked. 'Every Volume within the
archives represents the life's work of many of my Brothers.
Lifetimes dedicated to uncovering the forgotten secrets of
our history, following delicate slivers of information to
their conclusion along paths long since forgotten.'

'So, these could be nothing more than stories?' Stanley
huffed. 'A nice collection of bedtime stories.'

The change in Kelly's mood caught Stanley by surprise
as the older man slammed his hands down on the table
either side of the book.

'Story or not, the people that are trying to kill you believe
it.' Kelly fought to keep his voice calm. 'This Volume
represents the work of my Brothers and if they saw fit to
commit them to these pages then I believe they are of
worth.'

Stanley was silenced by the stern reply from Kelly and
lowered his gaze back to the table. Defusing the tension
Hazel encouraged Kelly to continue his account of the
Shaman and his flight through the forest.

'The Shaman was cornered, the guards were the pride of
the village and skilled huntsmen. In those times survival

relied on tracking and even though the snowstorm raged they were able to locate him. Outnumbered and in no way their equal the Shaman killed one of the troop but was felled by an arrow.'

Once again Kelly allowed the two of them the time to picture what he was telling them as he continued.
'The Shaman was not killed in the snow that day,' Kelly continued. 'His injuries should have killed him, an arrow buried beneath his arm and bludgeoned with weapons he remained defiant.'
'How is that possible?'
'The Shaman believed he was securing his immortality with the sacrifice of the unborn child, the truest form of innocence.' Kelly turned the book to face Stanley and Hazel as a series of sketches filled the pages.

The pictures looked like medical sketches, something similar to those drawn during the Renaissance with the human body and lines of dissection. One of the pictures showed a long-haired man and a series of lines identifying places of injuries and beside them the weapons that had inflicted them.
'This is the Iceman. As you can see the arrow landed here and with all these other injuries you must see that death should have been a certainty.'

Stanley inspected the image of the Iceman and the array of injuries that the sketch showed. Arrows, swords and other weapons littered the space around the figure and, although it was an artists' impression, the lifeless face staring up at him somehow unnerved Stanley.
'They returned the injured Shaman to the village along with the body of his murdered wife.' Kelly turned the page and read from the passage. 'The Chief presented the Shaman for the entire village to see in the village square. Mourning the murder of his wife and child the Chief saw

fit to execute the Shaman as a lesson for anyone who would dare to challenge him. History tells that the Chief plunged a dagger into the Shaman's chest and him proclaiming his immortality at the grace of his newfound Forest Goddess.'

'How can that even be possible?' Stanley exclaimed.

'There are many things, many dangerous parts of history that are best forgotten.' Kelly explained as he thumbed through the remaining pages. 'If mankind knew of every creature in the shadows, every legend that echoed through history you would never sleep for fear of what may come for you.'

'It sounds like ghost stories my dad made up for me when I was a boy.' Stanley scoffed but felt a nervousness how serious Kelly appeared as he regaled the account from the book.

'What has any of this got to do with your vault and us?' Hazel pressed as Kelly found the page he was looking for.

'These pages,' Kelly announced as he pointed to a gap where two pages had been torn from the book. 'These are what were secured in The Vault and under the protection of the Brotherhood since they were written and the Volume completed.'

'What was on them?'

'The final resting place of the Iceman, the tomb he was buried in after his execution in the village square, a cursed tomb in the depths of the Ötztal Alps long buried and forgotten.'

'A dead man's tomb, why would that be of interest to anyone unless you're telling me they want to repeat the weird sacrifice for immortality.' Stanley was about to laugh but felt Kelly's stern gaze and stopped himself.

'There are those, aside from my Brotherhood, who have devoted their lives to rediscovering the Iceman and realising his potential. Those same people have heard the whispers that the Shaman did not die at the hands of the Chief, the dagger that plunged into his heart did not end his life but demonstrate the fearful villagers that the Shaman had ascended above them and was, as he declared, immortal.'

Kelly let the words hang in the air as Stanley tried to make sense of what he was hearing. He knew the disbelief the two of them felt, he had experienced the same thing when he had first been trusted with the fable. The sense of whimsical storytelling made the story feel beyond the realms of possibility but he had been shown something to solidify the truth in the story.

Closing the book Kelly opened the rear cover and opened a flap on the underside. Trapped against the hardcover was a stretched piece of leathery flesh with a series of simplistic tattooed lines inked into the skin. 'What is that?' Hazel asked, a strange look of disgust on her face as she lent closer.

'Proof,' Kelly mumbled as he removed a fountain pen from his pocket. 'I understand your disbelief, I had that same feeling when I heard this story for the first time.'

'What changed your mind?' Stanley pressed as he watched the Inspector.

Holding the pen in his hand Kelly did not need to speak, he offered his answer in the form of a practical demonstration. The tethered flesh, pulled tight between four screws attached to the inside of the book's cover, was the focus of his attention. Removing the lid from his pen he pressed the pointed nib against the flesh and heard the intake of breath from both his companions at what happened.

Despite being nothing more than a dried square of flesh, as the metal touched the surface the flesh twitched.

Beyond the realms of possibility the piece of tether skin was somehow still alive.

'How?' Hazel stammered as she watched the flesh twitch and move.

'This was taken by the Chief as a warning against anyone searching for the buried tomb. It was passed from generation to generation along with the story and warning that the Shaman was no longer of the earth but a twisted creature of death and darkness.' He let his warning linger for a moment. 'Cutting a piece of the man's flesh he was buried in a deep tomb in the heart of the mountain and sealed inside to spend his days in darkness.'

'Surely he's dead.' Stanley gasped in disbelief.

'The fact this flesh still lives would say different.'

Against his better judgement Stanley reached out and touched the taught dry skin with his fingertips. As he felt the odd warmth from the leathery skin he recoiled his hand and looked on in shock and horror.

Kelly's retelling of the macabre sacrifice some five-thousand-years ago no longer felt like a strange work of fiction. As Stanley stared at the impossibly living tattered piece of flesh he realised the truth in the words and with it he felt an icy chill trickle down his spine.

'What have we got ourselves into?' Stanley hushed as he tried to make sense of everything.

'You are part of something more dangerous than you could have ever believed.' Kelly answered solemnly. 'You are on a path that will lead you to places you will wish had remained hidden from you.'

CHAPTER EIGHTEEN

SLEEP was evasive as Stanley tried to settle himself on the cot in the room he had been guided to. Through the thick walls he could hear the *thump* of another air raid, but it wasn't the German bombardment that was keeping him awake.

Stanley could not shake the image of the piece of skin moving on the inside of the book's rear cover. Each time Kelly had pressed the metal nib of the fountain pen against the skin, it had twitched and moved, as if the skin was still attached to a human body. It was impossible and no matter how hard he tried, Stanley could not explain it.

In the windowless room, he stared up at the ceiling and watched the shadows dancing in the candlelight. A quiet knock on the door startled him as he laid on the sheets. Questioning himself if what he had heard was knocking, the silence was disturbed again with the tap of knuckles on the wooden door.

Rising from the bed, he moved to the heavy door and lifted the oversized latch. Inching the door open it surprised him to find hazel stood in the corridor outside. 'I take it you couldn't sleep either,' she said with a warm smile.

'Guess not.' Stanley peered either direction along the corridor and invited Hazel in. 'No point in standing out there, come in.'

Opening the door, Stanley moved back to the bed and sat down with his back against the wall. Making her own check of the corridor, suspecting a woman in a man's room would be frowned up by the remaining monks, she crossed the threshold and closed the door.

'What's bothering you?' She asked as she pulled the chair from beneath the desk on the opposite side of the room.

'I'm struggling to make sense of the last twenty-four hours, if I'm honest.'

'You're not the only one.' She quipped as she dropped onto the seat and tipped it back on the rear legs. 'I can't quite believe what I saw.'

'I know, the skin in the back of the book was the weirdest thing I've ever seen.'

'Do you think it was real?'

Hazel's question was something he had been considering himself. Maybe deep down he *hoped* it was some elaborate joke but he doubted it. Everything pointed to the fact the taut piece of anchored flesh was real.

'I'd love for it to be a joke, I would,' Stanley confessed as he toyed with a broken pencil between his fingers. 'Everything that's happened points to all of this being real.'

'I know,' Hazel sighed as she tried to balance on the back two legs of the chair. 'I don't know what scares me most, the fact it's real or the fact I believe it.'

They discussed what they had been told of the Iceman through the night. Each of them tried to reason with the other, to convince themselves that it wasn't real but, as the all-clear siren wailed outside, neither had changed their mind.

The pair sat and discussed everything they had learned and realised how little they understood of their current situation. As both of them felt their eyes growing heavy, they fell asleep side-by-side sat on the bed, Hazel's head resting on Stanley's shoulder. That was the position Kelly found them in the morning when he crept into the room to wake Stanley.

'I don't think this would go down too well,' Kelly declared in his Irish twang, a smile painted across his face.

Stanley woke first and felt Hazel's weight on his shoulder. Panicking he gave Hazel a quick jolt to wake it relieved her as she lifted her head from its resting place. 'It's not like that,' he stammered in defence. 'We were just talking, trying to make sense of everything, I promise.'

Kelly could not help but laugh as Stanley blurted out in defence of them being found in the room together. For a moment it reminded Kelly how young his two companions were and how much the world was changing the youth.

'I understand Stanley,' Kelly chuckled. 'You'd do well to get yourself ready in your own room, I'll wait for you and we can see the Friar together.'

Holding the door for Hazel, he waited as she hurried from the room, her cheeks flushed from the same realisation Stanley had about how it must have looked.

'If I may Stanley?' Kelly interrupted as Stanley rose from the bed.

'What is it?'

'You'd do well to take note of her,' Kelly offered a nod in

Hazel's direction as she walked off along the corridor. 'She quite likes you.'

It was Stanley's turn to blush and once again Kelly could not help but smile.

'I don't think so, I'm not her type.' Stanley muttered with nerves.

'You'd be surprised.' Kelly sensed Stanley's discomfort, again realising his interrupted youth with the war, and changed the subject. 'The friar wishes to speak to you.'

'What does he want?'

'I'll let him explain, it is not my place and the last thing I want to do is upset our host.'

Dropping a set of fresh clothes on the bed, Kelly excused himself and left Stanley to wash and change. From their escapades in the graveyard and their hasty retreat to Ealing Abbey it had taken a toll on his clothes and, sniffing the collar of his shirt, Stanley wrinkled his nose at the odour.

Grateful for the solitude and new clothes he made quick work of cleaning the grime from his face and donning the new clothes Kelly had left him. As he unfolded the clothes it relieved Stanley to find the clothes were the type he would normally wear and he hadn't been handed a robe or something similar to wear. A little oversized, he tucked the cream shirt into his trousers and tightened the belt before meeting Kelly back in the corridor.

'Glad you could join us!' Hazel smirked as she stood in the corridor talking with Kelly.

It took Stanley a moment to take her in as she stood in fresh clothes with her hair now tied in a ponytail and a light layer of make-up hiding the tiredness he had seen only a short while ago. She looked a different woman, somehow more mature and, if it was even possible, more confident.

'Let's not keep the Friar waiting,' Kelly interrupted as he sensed the mood between them near a level of awkwardness.

Stanley made his apology and joined his companions as they meandered back through the annex of the abbey and into the main church building. Sunlight streamed through the broken roof and particles of dust danced in the beams of light as if they had a life of their own.

The sun glinted on the remains of jagged stained glass from a windowless arch, and Stanley felt a wave of sorrow wash over him as he looked at the almost ruined church. The war, he realised, was eroding away the city around him and yet it was something that had been accepted. As they walked through the church, he realised it was a side-effect of survival. If buildings had to tumble, homes had to be destroyed and monuments be evaporated by the bombs, it was acceptable if people survived. Stanley mused to himself how different the world was becoming around him and, for the first time in a long time, he longed for his youth before the war.

'Good morning.' An unfamiliar voice greeted and jolted him back from his melancholy.

Looking down from the dancing dust and beams of morning sunlight, Stanley saw the robed and hooded Friar waiting for them where they had sat the day before. The Friar's hood concealed his face and standing in the shadows it gave him an air of mystery that Stanley sensed was done on purpose.

Following Kelly's lead, they made their way back to the pews and Kelly made their introductions. It was strange to see Kelly seem nervous in the hooded Friar's presence, but Stanley kept his observations and amusement to himself as he waited to be introduced.

'Once again,' Kelly started. 'Thank you for your hospitality for myself and my companions. May I introduce you to Stanley Grand and Hazel Johnson, both have been unfortunately thrust onto our path.'

For a moment the Friar said nothing. He tilted his head enough to see them but not enough to reveal the face within the shadows. As Stanley stood rooted to the spot, he could feel the frosty gaze of the Friar from beneath the hood.

'There will always be sanctuary beneath his roof,' the Friar announced as he reached his trembling hands to his hood. 'Brother Kelly has told me of your troubles and the unfortunate series of events that brought you to my door.'

Both Stanley and Hazel watched with almost bated breath as the old man pulled back the hood. Stanley didn't know what he had expected, perhaps the theatricality had built up an expectation, but the face that looked back at him was normal. Well into old age, the Friar's brilliant white hair was ruffled and stood in many directions. Wrinkles surrounded his slight squinting eyes yet his face was soft and warm, his narrow lips turned into a warm smile which Stanley was not expecting.

Having expected some stern and discerning figure, the warmth from the Friar took him by surprise. As the old man looked at each of them Stanley watched with curiosity. At last, after what felt like an age, the Friar reached out a trembling hand and offered Stanley a welcoming handshake.

'I have heard much about you, both of you,' the Friar smiled as he moved to shake Hazel's hand. 'Your bravery and tenacity is a credit to you both. My name is Brother Jacob.'

'Nice to meet you,' Hazel offered as she waited for what would happen next.

'Having spoken with Brother Kelly at length last night, I believe it faces us with something of a conundrum.' The Friar moved to sit on the nearest of the pews and reached to his side. 'Tea anyone?'

Much to their amusement, Jacob poured a cup of tea from a still steaming kettle. As they settled on the surrounding seats there was no denying there was a strong air of friendly eccentricity about the old man. Stanley nodded at the offer of tea. He sympathised in the knowledge Jacob would not have seen the horrors of London and beyond for some time. Taking the cup, the uncontrollable tremble in Jacob's hand had the cup clattering on the saucer.

'Brother Kelly tells me you would rather not sit back and allow the trusted Brotherhood protect the treasures of Ad Firmamentum?'

Stanley paused with the cup pressed to his lips and sensed the same discomfort in Hazel at the old Friar's accusation. Hearing it phrased in such a way Stanley realised how, with such a perspective, their desire to help could be read as an insult.

'We didn't mean it like that,' Stanley defended as he lowered the cup back to the saucer. 'We only want to help, we weren't saying that you weren't capable.'

'Not at all,' Hazel interrupted, feeling the same defensiveness as Stanley. 'What we were trying to say is…'

Jacob chuckled aloud as he watched the two of them stammer and stumble to apologise. Even having observed them from a distance, the old Friar had seen enough to know they were humble if not naïve. Raising his hand he silenced the two of them and yet the warmth of his smile softened the move.

'We take no offence at what you've said and, in your

defence, Brother Kelly agrees that you should not be idle in the Brotherhood's endeavours to retrieve that which was stolen.'

'The pages pertain to the Iceman's last resting place and we know whoever has them now will search to decipher the contents and make their way there to unleash the creature.'

'Is there no way to get them back, to stop them deciphering them?' Hazel pressed between sipping her tea.

'I will task Brother Kelly with seeking those who hold the pages, that is why we granted him grace to live in the outside. It well suits his skills to his position of protection and investigation.'

'What about us, are we going to help him?' Stanley pressed, sensing the Friar was delaying.

'You will help me in another way.' Kelly answered and watched as Stanley deflated in his seat. 'I fear we are already far behind those who have the pages and I would seek an alternative avenue if I cannot locate them.'

'We want you to retrieve the only tools we know that, should they release the creature, can slay him.'

The sudden weight of Jacob's words hit them both like a tonne of bricks. Gob smacked they both sat in silence as they listened to the old Friar's explanation of what he would have them do.

CHAPTER NINETEEN

SEATED in the rear of the Rolls Royce
Phantom II, Eric Masters stared at the wooden box on the
seat beside him. Having watched the suburbs of London
fade away, he had allowed his attention to turn to the box.

The blood had stained the wood in a strange pattern
and as the car rumbled along the road, he traced his
fingers across the bloodstained skulls. He had waited so
long to take possession of the box and what it held inside.
Countless fortunes had been spent and lives redirected,
much like the boy in the Whisper Club, and yet it now sat
on the seat by his side.

'My entire life I've yearned to find this,' he murmured to
himself as he lifted the box onto his knee. 'Something so
small and delicate.'

Gingerly he lifted the lid and looked down at the two
folded sheets of aged yellowing paper. His heart raced,
although he knew what they signified it was the

culmination of a life's obsession to set his eyes on them.

Removing a pair of white cotton gloves from his pocket, he pulled them on before daring to touch the delicate paper. Against the vibrations of the car, Eric removed the pages and unfolded them.

Eric had inherited his obsession from his parents, and a sudden sense of sadness consumed him as he looked at the calligraphy on the page. Both his mother and father had never even come close to seeing the contents of the box from the legendary Brotherhood's Vault, and yet now he was holding them in his hands.

For a moment he considered how they would feel if they were sat beside him, how he would feel if they were with him. It was a moot point. Their death had provided him the resources to succeed where they had failed. If they were with him now, then he would not have received the pages. Casting aside the momentary stir of emotion and sentiment, he set about translating the scripture inked onto the pages.

The world passed by as the Rolls rumbled along the quiet roads. The car was a statement, one that Eric wore proudly, and he had long since learned to ignore the glances and shrieks of excited children as he was driven along the streets. Having left the suburbs of London behind, they were now surrounded by rolling countryside as they snaked their way south towards the coast.

His driver was a quiet man. He paid no attention to Eric as he examined the paper but kept his attention on the roads. Wearing a nondescript black suit, the chauffer was all that could be expected and blended in with the exuberant exterior of the expensive car.

Eric Masters' estate sat near the Dorset coast on the outskirts of the quaint village of Sandford. Far away from the bustle and destruction of the capital, Eric had longed to return to his sanctuary once he had taken possession of the pages. Now, knowing London was far behind him, he could revel in the victory as he worked through the elegant calligraphy.

The pages regaled the account of a Benedictine Monk who had spent his life in search of the Iceman's legacy. In the fifteenth century the first rumblings of the Iceman had reached the ears of the Brotherhood, and they had despatched a monk to seek proof of the fable's validity.

Allowing his mind to wander, Eric placed the folded sheets onto his knee as he reminisced and looked out of the car window.

Eric had been home for the summer when he had first learned of his family's obsession with the Iceman. It had been a typical English summer, rain hammering down outside and he had been a teenage boy bored with little to do. The immense size of his family home offered him many rooms to amuse his inquisitive nature, but he had never ventured into the cellar.

His parents had kept the cellar as their own and refused to let him venture beneath the house. As a child it had been a source of curiosity, but having been sent to Boarding School he had all but forgotten about the imposing oak door and mysteries that lay behind it. That day he had explored almost every corner of the house before his adolescent mind had wondered towards the cellar door.

Checking he was alone, both his mother and father out in the vast gardens entertaining friends, he had dared to search out a way to bypass the solid wood door. All afternoon he had searched through his father's study, but it was in the depths of his mother's bedside table that he had found the curious looking key that fit the door. Shaking with excitement and nerves, Eric had unlocked the door and descended the stone steps into the vast cellar beneath the house.

What he had found in the darkness had been a turning point in his life. It had been the moment he had taken the first steps on the path he had devoted his life to. Lit only by a flickering candle he had stolen from the shelf on the other side of the door, he moved past the racks of fine wines until the cellar opened into a wide stone-walled room.

The air had somehow felt colder as he stepped into the open space. The racks of bottles had made the cellar feel claustrophobic, yet the room beyond felt much wider as the flickering candlelight failed to find the surrounding walls. Moving with nervousness, Eric pressed deeper into the room until the candle caught something on the far wall.

At first he had stopped in his tracks, curious as he tried to make out what adorned the far wall of the cellar. Moving closer, he illuminated a wall filled with pieces of paper. Pages of books, scribbled notes and an enormous hand-drawn map of the globe dominated the wall and as he moved closer Eric tried to make sense of what he was looking at.

Moving with care he read the pages, scoured through the scribbled notes, but nothing made sense to him. Tethers of twine had been attached to various points on the map and connected to the collection of notes, but there was one piece of twine that caught his attention. Unlike the others, it did not connect a place on the map to any of the notepaper but stretched beyond the pieces of paper.

Holding the sting between his fingers, he moved along the wall and followed it to its destination. Engrossed by the fine thread between his fingers, he had reached the adjoining wall before he raised his gaze and took a sharp intake of breath in shock at what he saw.

Someone had covered the stone wall in a layer of plaster, while the edges were uneven the surface had been rubbed smooth like paper. Almost like a framed picture, someone had painted a mural that dominated the wall from floor to ceiling. Standing proud in the centre of the pale plaster patch was a strange and primitive image of a cave man. The detail was astounding and its appearance stole Eric's attention.

The painting was like nothing he had seen before, it was simplistic and yet seemed very much alive. The paint was a hue of crimson that appeared almost black in the flickering light. Looking back now he knew it was not paint that had been paint but blood that had been used to recreate a solitary image that had survived five-thousand years. It was, as he now knew, the only image of the Iceman.

Eric had been mesmerised by the painting. There was something about it that captured his attention. In the flickering candlelight he stood in front of the image, absorbed by its simplicity. It had been in that position, as the candle wax pooled in the tray in his hand, that his mother had found him.

'How did you get in here?' She had barked, snatching him back from his silent admiration.

'I didn't mean to,' he had stammered but felt the sting of her hand on his face.

'Get out and to your room.' He had never seen her so angry. Her eyes burned like fire.

Not wanting to push her, Eric turned and ran back up out of the cellar, leaving his mother alone in the eerie room. Falling over his own feet as he ran, Eric made it to his bedroom and slammed the door shut behind him. Jumping onto the bed, he had sobbed into the pillow until his mother had knocked on the door.

'Go away.'

'Eric, my love, we need to talk.' Her voice was calmer and more familiar to him as she whispered through the door.

He had been cautious, recalling the terrifying look on his mother's face but he knew better than to keep her waiting. Inching to the door, he opened it just enough to peek through the gap and was relieved to see his mother calmer, her expression no longer tainted with anger.

'I'm sorry about that Eric, I just don't want you down there.'

'Why?' Eric asked as he opened the door wider.

'Because that world is something for your father and I. You are too young to understand.'

'What was it, the painting on the wall.'

Even though she remained calm, Eric could see the bubbling frustration in his mother's expression. Keeping calm, she dropped to her knees in front of Eric and took hold of his shoulders.

'When the time is right Eric, you will know everything about what you saw but please, please be patient.'

Eye-to-eye with his mother, Eric was awash with guilt and fought to hold back the tears that welled in his eyes. Holding his gaze for a moment, his mother finally pulled him close and in that moment all worry was gone.

Coming back from his memory, Eric saw the world outside the Rolls and smiled. It had been another six years before Eric had returned into the cellar. His parents had secured the solid door with a padlock, the same padlock he now wore around his neck as a reminder to the task in hand. Pulling it from beneath his shirt, he toyed with the lock as he remembered the promises he had made to both his parents before their death.

A chance discovery by a curious young boy had been

his first steps onto the path to discover the Iceman. Now, as his youth had passed through adolescence and adulthood, he now stood closer than anyone before him in discovering his final resting place. That thought alone excited him as a crooked smile appeared on his face.

With the pages from Ad Firmamentum now in his possession, it would only be a matter of time until he would see the source of his family's obsession. What had been merely a bloodied painting on the cellar wall was close to becoming a physical thing before him. Once back at his home he would take the time to decipher the text on the pages and, in doing so, learn of the Iceman's resting place.

There was much yet to be done, but with London behind him, Eric knew he was on a new path never trodden by anyone in history. Closing his eyes, he listened to the rumble of the car's engine. Deep down Eric was glad to be free of London, to escape the looming depression and fear that hung in the air like a fog. Away from the capital he would be free to move with ease and the connections his family had around the world, he hoped, would transcend beyond the idiotic squabbles of nations at war.

But for now, he took a moment to rest as his driver carried him home.

CHAPTER
TWENTY

THEIR conversation with Jacob lasted most of the day and as the afternoon rolled on both Stanley and Hazel felt overwhelmed. Kelly noticed their interest waning and interrupted the flow of Jacob's explanations.

'You will be provided an archived copy of the Magnitudo, transcribed by the Brotherhood as best we can into English. There will be parts that have been removed.'

'Censored?' Hazel scoffed.

'In short, yes!' Kelly threw her a warning glance with his reply. 'A lot of the Magnitudo has been secret and held amongst only the Brotherhood for centuries.'

'While we accept your help in the matter of Homo Glacies, see no offence in us keeping some elements secret.'

'We understood.' Stanley added, doing his best to diffuse the sudden increased tension.

'The pages you will have, relate to the journey of Alessandro Ramos, a member of the Brotherhood who sought the tools we may need to slay the creature should he be resurrected from his resting place.'

'I shall seek to stop the man who now holds the stolen pages but we would see you find the tools should I not succeed.'

'Sounds like you're expecting to fail?' Hazel pressed as Jacob handed her a leather-bound book.

'I already have,' Kelly sighed, his shoulders and gaze dropping. 'The fact the pages have already left The Vault highlights how ill-prepared I was.'

'How ill prepared *we* were.' Jacob corrected, his voice soft and calming. 'The world is changing, people are no longer docile and ignorant to the darker world. We have, and will continue, to do all we can to protect humanity.'

Jacob's declaration was humbling. All eyes turned to him as he spoke. Kelly, Stanley and Hazel waited for him to continue, much like a revered teacher stood in front of an eager class of students. Rising from his seat, Jacob took a moment to look at each of them.

'This path will not be easy, you will all be tested and pushed more than ever before.' Jacob moved to stand in front of Kelly. 'Damien, your efforts to protect The Vault have been admirable, your faith has never faltered, do not let it now.'

'I won't.' A lump formed in his throat as he answered the Friar.

'As for you two, you are yet to discover your faith.'

'I'm not a religious person.' Stanley corrected as Jacob moved to stand in front of him and Hazel.

'Faith does not rely on God, it relies on the person.' Jacob reached down and tapped Stanley's chest above his heart. 'The faith you are yet to discover is the faith in yourselves. I promise, by the end of this, you will see your own strength and worth. Both of you.'

Leaving the three of them humbled by his words, Jacob took his leave and left them alone within the Abbey building.

Stanley and Hazel excused themselves and returned to Stanley's room in the annexe of the Abbey. Eager to scan the pages of the abridged Magnitudo, Hazel dropped onto the bed and opened the leather cover with care. Unlike the original text whose cover was emblazoned with the tree, roots and cross, the leather cover on the book she held was far more subtle. The leather had been embossed with only the Roman numerals and a smaller tree and roots in the bottom corner.

'Makes you wonder what they took out.' Stanley mused as he sat beside Hazel.

Their abridged version was only a third as thick as the original they had seen, and yet they both knew whatever pages had been included would be enough for their journey. More tentative than she had expected, Hazel opened the first pages to find a sketched image of a man on the first page.

'Guess that's the Alessandro bloke they were talking about.'

The image was a sketch of an aged man, weathered face and dark eyes, dressed in similar garb to Jacob. Around his neck the man wore an ornate cross and across the right side of his head, arching above his right ear and down his neck, was a jagged scar.

For the next few hours, the pair scanned through the translated pages. Where elements had been translated, notes had been added to the pages making the book feel more of a journal than a direct copy of the original Magnitudo. Maps had been copied from the original texts with amazing detail and soon they could see where they were headed.

The original maps had been crude and simplistic, place names written in Latin and translated into English underneath, but they meant little to them. Reaching the final pages they had seen sketches of machines, rooms and pages filled with curious numerical combinations and explanations of machinery and mechanisms that made no sense to them.

'Alessandro's Test,' Hazel read aloud as she turned the page. 'That doesn't sound good.'

A light knock on the door silenced them as Stanley moved to open it. Standing in the corridor, now dressed in more traditional clothes of the Abbey, Kelly waited in the corridor outside.

'You're lucky Brother Jacob accepts your help, I somehow doubt a female in a male's room would be accepted by him otherwise.'

'It's not like that,' Stanley defended with haste. 'We were just looking through the book.'

'I know, don't worry.' Kelly's laugh disarmed Stanley. 'May I?'

'Yes, come in.'

Kelly's appearance in religious clothes took Hazel by surprise, but she was curious about what they had discovered on the pages.

'What's Alessandro's Test?' She quizzed before Stanley had closed the door behind Kelly.

'You need to read the pages on your way. Everything you need is contained within the texts of the Magnitudo. It is all in there.'

'But it doesn't say where it is or how we get there.'

'You're right!' Kelly smiled and pulled a folded sheet from his pocket. 'Sometimes it is safer to keep parts separate from one another.'

'You don't make this easy, do you?' Stanley groaned as he

took the paper from Kelly. 'Why can't it just be a simple book of *here you go and this is how you do it*?'

'That's the nature of our ways, doing what we can to protect the secrets we keep.'

Stanley unfolded the paper as Hazel moved to join him. The sheet was a large map of a series of towns far from London. On the map two parts had been circled in ink, both labelled "Alessandro?"

'Where's this place, I've never heard of Grassley?'

'Greasley,' Kelly corrected with a grin. 'You two are set on a journey to the heart of England in the East Midlands, a fair way from here. Greasley is a small parish on the outskirts of Nottingham and, we believe, the location of Alessandro's Test.'

'Why there?'

'Alessandro's reasons are his own. Every member of the Brotherhood does what they think is best to protect the secrets they discover. For whatever reason, Alessandro chose this location for his test.'

'How are we supposed to get there?'

'We have purchased you tickets on the train, you will leave in the morning.' Kelly removed another envelope from his pocket. 'This will see you through your journey.'

Hazel took the envelope and peered inside. Her face dropped as she hurried to hand it back.

'No, we can't do that, I mean we can't take that.'

'What is it?'

'This is the least the Brotherhood can do to help. Money is not a thing that should hamper your journey and I suspect neither of you would survive on the money you have with you now.'

It was Hazel's turn to blush as Kelly wrapped her hand around the envelope and pushed it back towards her.

'It feels wrong.' She sighed as Stanley peeked in the

envelope to the handful of crumpled notes contained within.

'Consider it an investment; you will be busy enough on your journey that the distraction of funds would be an unnecessary hindrance.'

'What are we looking for, what are these tools you've been talking about? Even scanning through the pages there's no mention of what they are.' It was Hazel who pressed.

Kelly looked uncomfortable for a moment and moved to perch on the desk leant against the far wall. Tracing his hand over the place with the Benedictine Medal was tattooed on his chest, he remained quiet for a moment. 'The truth is Alessandro never shared that in the Magnitudo.'

'Great!' Stanley scoffed. 'So we could be searching for anything.'

'Every Brother creates their volume for the archives and The Vault. As with the map to the Iceman's final resting place, some parts of kept separate, a sum of all the parts reveals everything.'

'But alone they just leave unanswered questions and incomplete clues?'

'Yes.' Kelly sighed as he looked at them. 'Truth be told, I don't know what waits you in the test, I don't know what the tools are that the text speaks of.'

'Weapons?' Stanley pressed.

'Perhaps, consider the fact this creature comes from a time long forgotten to history. The ways of his people, of civilisation that long ago are a mystery. It could be anything.'

'I'm dreading this the more I learn,' Stanley groaned as he laid himself back on the bed. 'I mean I know less now than I did when we started.'

'No journey is ever easy Stanley, no test is ever

understood from the outset or else what would be the point in doing it?' Kelly moved towards the door. 'Alessandro was a devious Brother, he learned all there can be known about the Iceman, if there is a way to counter his curse then Alessandro will have secured it for such a time as what we are facing now.'

'What about the missing pages, do you think you can get to them before they reach the burial site?'

Kelly paused at the door before offering his answer. Hazel could, from the look on the tired Inspector's face, already see what the answer would be. Opening the door, Kelly offered his reply as he stepped back out into the corridor.

'Truth is I am already far behind whoever has the pages now. It will be a hard task to intercept them before they reach their destination.'

'Do you know where they are heading?'

'Yes. As you've seen, the Magnitudo are archived and copied, as a protector of Ad Firmamentum it is my task to know of its secrets, the location of the Iceman's tomb is one of those secrets.'

'If you can't find them before they leave, will you meet them there?'

'As a last resort and if I do, I will need whatever it is that Alessandro buried.'

'How will we find you?'

'If my attempts to retrieve the pages are unsuccessful, then I will ensure we meet, the eyes and ears of the Brotherhood stretch further than you can imagine. You will not be far from our protection, no matter how isolated you feel.'

Leaving them with the ominous promise, Kelly left the two of them alone in the room. With the door closed, they shared the time trying to make sense of the translated pages and hand-written notes on every page. By the time night settled the two of them had fallen asleep rested against one another on the small bed.

Unbeknownst to them Jacob chanced a check on them as he retired for the night and smiled at them rested against each other. Choosing not to disturb them he left two plates of food on the small desk and scurried back out of the room. As he closed the door, he extinguished the lights and left them to sleep.

In the morning they would be set upon a journey, and Jacob knew the trials and tests that followed would be nothing like they expected. It was only right to leave them to rest and calm themselves before the storm.

CHAPTER TWENTY-ONE

KELLY hurried them from Ealing Abbey under the cover of darkness. Dawn had not even broken and Stanley had been sure the all clear had not even sounded. Still, without protest, they packed and made for Paddington Station before the capital awoke from the latest onslaught of nightly bombing.

Reaching the station Stanley watched as Kelly approached a constable outside the station and spoke with him in secret. After a few tense moments of conversation, Kelly beckoned them over to join him.

'You'll be safe here until first light, I've secured you passage on the right train.'

'Where do we need to go?' Hazel pressed as she held a satchel tight around her body, conscious the Magnitudo was hidden inside.

'That's for you to choose, you've got the maps I gave you?'

'Yes.'

'Use them as you travel and decide on the best place to get off. Knowing what I do about the likely locations you'll be hard pressed to get close, you must do some walking I suspect.'

'Thank you.'

'No Stanley, thank *you*. What you're doing will help in case I fail.'

Kelly had shaken both their hands before leaving them under the watchful eye of the tired constable. As dawn broke, the train pulled into the station and before long the impressive locomotive had pulled out from Paddington and transported them away from London.

'This is the first time I've left London alone.' Hazel had mused as the scenery changed from urban to rural outside the train.

'I've seen a fair few places,' Stanley comforted, lost in a memory of his trip to Portsmouth when he had been deployed to France. 'Last time was a little different though.'

'Do you want to talk about it?'

'Not really.'

Feeling she had pushed too far, Hazel checked the half-empty carriage and placed the satchel on the table. Admiring the curious stitching and ornate patterns on the bag's cover, she reached inside and pulled out the bound items. The Magnitudo book along with a handful of folded sheets of paper had been tied together before being placed in the bag and handed over to Hazel.

'I suppose we should start making plans.' Hazel offered, determined to break the sudden tension that had arisen with her questioning once again.

Unfolding the map, she pinned the corners down on the table and they both inspected the contours and roads. 'Listen,' Stanley began as he looked at Hazel across the table. 'I don't mean to be abrupt, I'm just not used to sharing.'

'It's fine, you need not explain to me.'

'My folks are not ones for sharing, especially my old man. Since coming back he often tells me I've changed but has never once sat down and asked why. As for my mother, well she just pretends the war isn't happening and is doing everything to keep me from going back to the front line.'

'I suppose it's the same with my brothers, my parents just leave me be but every time I come home I know they hope it's one of my brothers and not me.'

Hazel held Stanley's hand as they talked. For a moment Stanley felt, and looked, vulnerable. Looking across the map at her, he realised how comfortable he felt sharing the feelings he had continued to keep to himself since returning home. Following Hazel's lead, he wrapped his hand over hers. Their silent gaze met above the map as the carriage around them faded away.

'What a pair we are,' his voice barely above a nervous whisper. 'Two days ago I was just a street urchin that you thought was hiding from the war.'

Hazel blushed at the thought. Although Stanley treated her remarks with a light-hearted feeling, she could not hide the guilt she felt at having been so rash to judge him. 'I never meant it that way.'

'It doesn't matter, you were right at the time. Now look at us.'

Leaning closer Stanley could not deny the fact he had taken quite a shine to Hazel. Her abrupt nature was weakened by the softer side he had seen more than once now. Having been thrown together into such an impossible journey as the one they were on, he had, since boarding the train, decided it was time to take advantage of the situation. Awash with nerves, Stanley leaned closer and, much to his relief, Hazel returned the gesture.

With the rocking motion of the train, Stanley could feel the heat from her face as they moved closer.
'Sorry for the interruption, tickets?'

The sudden voice snatched them both back from the tender moment and Hazel recoiled back, folding over the map so it was no longer on show. The conductor, a man no older than Stanley, looked uncomfortable as he held his hand out for the tickets Kelly had given them. Punching the tickets, he handed them back and shuffled off along the carriage leaving them alone.

'Look, I'm sorry.' Stanley apologised, but the moment had passed and Hazel's attention was back on the task at hand.

Not wanting to push, Stanley accepted that the interruption had cut short their connection and focussed on the map on the table.

'The train stations are here and here,' Hazel offered as she traced the train line across the map to two outlying towns south of the circles that had been marked.

'What do you think these places are?'

'I was looking through the book and I think one of them is a ruined Priory in a place called Beauvale.'

'And the other?' Stanley leaned closer to see if he could make out the details, but the ink circle had scored out the name beneath.

'There's mention of a castle, but I can't see anything like a castle.'

'Then I guess we start at the priory and hope for the best.'

'This place is the best then, we'll find somewhere to stay the night.'

Hazel pointed to a small town on the outskirts of Nottingham, a few miles from the priory marked on the map. Having decided on their destination, Hazel spent the rest of the journey trying to make sense of the abridged pages in the Magnitudo while Stanley scoured the miscellaneous sheets that had been piled atop the leather book.

The rest of the journey saw the pair make a single stop and before long the locomotive drew them across the Bennerley Viaduct before pulling into Kimberley station. Having been engrossed in the literature, they had almost missed the spectacular views of the rolling countryside from their vantage point atop the viaduct. As the train passed high above the flood plains, the conductor made his announcement from the far end of the carriage.
'Next stop, Kimberley.'
'That's us.' Hazel smiled and made quick work of returning all the paperwork into the bag.

In a matter of minutes the train rolled into the station and the pair of them disembarked. Standing outside the double-building station they watched as the smoke billowed from the train and it pulled the trio of carriages off on the rest of its journey. Coughing against the smoke that billowed around the platform, Stanley waited for the train to be clear before taking in his surroundings.
'Any idea where we will stay? I don't like the idea of wandering to find this priory and it ends up getting dark on us.'

The small town was all you would expect from a rural settlement. Rows of houses lined the streets and an enormous factory dominated the skyline. Neither of them knew the town, and soon they wandered the narrow streets in search of somewhere for food and a place to rest.

The afternoon passed by in a heartbeat as they explored the town. Having made their enquiries Stanley and Hazel soon found themselves in the hospitality of a local pub. Having made their brief introductions, they were shown to a pair of rooms and invited back into the main pub for food before dark.

'Feels strange not worrying for the air raids.' Hazel confessed as the sun started its descent towards the horizon. 'It doesn't feel right, everyone is a lot calmer than back home, there isn't the constant fear in the air like I'm used to.'

Climbing a steep hill, they walked into a large graveyard and towards an isolated chapel standing proud above the town. The small chapel seemed out of place atop the desolate hill, surrounded by gravestones. A solitary statue of an angel looked to be standing watch over the doors of the chapel as they walked around and took in the picturesque view from their vantage point.

'Now that isn't something you get in London.'

Finding a bench, they shared the sunset in silence, two companions locked on an unknown path. Seeing the dying rays of light disappear, giving way to the clear starry sky, the temperature soon dropped. Hearing Hazel's teeth chatter, Stanley removed his thin jacket and handed it to her.

'Quite the gentleman.' Hazel chuckled as she slipped the jacket over her shoulders.

'We should head back and eat.'

'Sounds like a plan.'

'What about tomorrow?'

'We can ask about the priory with the landlord if you like?'

They walked down the steep winding path between the gravestones and towards the enormous gates leading back to the main road.

'I think two strangers asking about ruins may be a little suspicious. Knowing what has happened so far, I think it best we keep our business to ourselves.'

The sudden memory of the ambush at the site of Colin's murder set them both on edge. As they walked towards the gate, they both scanned the graveyard around them for any sign they were being followed. As they reached the gates Hazel slipped her hand in Stanley's and he returned the gesture with a gentle squeeze.

'Thank you.' She hushed as they walked back to the pub.

'It's the least I can do, after all I'm the reason we are both in this mess.'

'I can't argue with you there!'

'Alright, give me a little bit of credit, will you? I am trying to make it right.'

'I know.' A sudden sound from an alley near the graveyard's entrance stopped them in their tracks.

Edging closer to a large bush, they waited as the sound of footsteps grew closer to them. At last a figure emerged from the alley and, much to their combined relief; it was an elderly man with a small dog marching by his side.

'Bit late for you young ones to be out. Better get in before the local Bobby finds you!' The man chortled as he crossed over the road.

'Come on, he's right.' Hazel agreed and tugged at Stanley's hand. 'We should get back and get some rest, we have no idea what tomorrow will bring.'

Stanley did not answer, but in his head he agreed with her. The uncertainty of what they would find unnerved him, but he was determined not to show it. Since boarding the train he had scanned every face they had passed, hoping to identify anyone trying to follow them. There was nothing to say anyone lay in wait for them but the memory of gunshots from Highgate Cemetery were still too fresh in his mind to let him lower his guard.

In a matter of minutes they were back within the warmth of the pub and they soon forgot the uncertainty of the world outside against the jovial banter of the local patrons scattered around the surrounding tables. In fact as they ate and relaxed, the worries of the last few days faded away enough for them to enjoy the quaint public house and quirky landlord's hospitality.

CHAPTER
TWENTY-TWO

UNDISTURBED sleep without the
disruption of raids or the echo of distant fire-fights was a
welcome change. Stanley had spent the night tossing and
turning in his bed, dreams haunted by his time in France,
but still he awoke refreshed. Having wolfed down a
curious ensemble of breakfast served by the friendly
landlord, they had soon set on their way in search of the
priory ruins.

The small town was already alive with people. The
factory was a hive of activity while farm machinery
trundled along the wide streets servicing the surrounding
countryside. Albeit they accepted the glances of curiosity
at "outsiders" but neither Stanley nor Hazel felt
threatened or unwanted. On the contrary, the townspeople
seemed friendly enough and offered their morning
greetings as they passed the visiting pair.

Following their route on the folded map, Hazel led the

way and soon they had left Kimberley behind. Venturing
north of the town, they happened across a curious sight as
they followed a freight line. As they had ventured along
the train line, their path had been blocked by a less than
welcoming military man stationed in a pillbox outside a
submerged bunker. Having offered their apologies and
retraced their steps, they had soon set back on the proper
path and navigated through fresh ploughed fields.

It was not long before both of them were covered in
mud and found their feet dragging heavily beneath them.
'I need a break.' Stanley groaned as they reached a narrow
country lane that cut through the fields and towards a
large copse of trees in the distance. 'Have we got much
further to go?'

Pulling a drink from her bag and finding a fallen tree to
sit on, Hazel inspected the map and did her best to find
where they were. Following the rough line of the
horseshoe shaped lane, she pinpointed where they were.
'I thought you'd be the map reader,' Hazel mocked as she
rotated the map to face Stanley. 'What with your military
training and all.'

'It was more tactics and shooting for me.' Stanley retorted
as he looked along the length of the road and towards the
marked ruins.

'Probably better suited to this then.' Hazel realised she had
once again bitten with more sarcasm than she had
intended. 'I mean, well, you should be…'

'Stop worrying when you say things like that. I promise if
I'm upset by something I'll tell you.'

'All right then, just as long as you will.'

'Just because you've got older brothers, doesn't mean I'm
afraid of you.' The chuckle and light-hearted tone broke
through the sudden concern of Hazel's words, and they
shared a more relaxed moment.

Before midday they crested the horseshoe track and found themselves at a vantage point over a narrow valley. A short distance away, nestled behind fences and trees, stood the impressive ruins of Beauvale Priory. Even from a distance, the ruins held an air of mystery and grandeur. What remained of the monastery walls clambered skyward and hollows where impressive stained-glass windows would have once stood framed the view beyond like a painting.

Taking a moment to admire the ruins and the nearby farm building, they found a space in the hedgerow and climbed into the field. Stepping from the main path brought with it a sense of nervousness as they both checked for any sign someone had spotted them, or followed, as they ventured down the steep grass towards the priory building.

Reaching the towering walls of the old monastery and pressing towards the Prior's House ruin, they made one last check they were alone. Satisfied they were, Stanley found an opening and crawled through into the Prior's house and out of sight from anyone passing.

The air was cold in the ruin's shelter, and something about their surroundings added a chill to the air. Although they had not seen another person since crossing the path of the guardsman at the bunker hours before, there was an unshakable feeling they were being watched.
'What now?' Hazel pressed as she looked around the crumbled interior of the house.

Vines and trees had long been tangled amongst the weathered stonework, and beams of sunlight passed through small holes where pieces of masonry had fallen from position. Taking a moment to admire their concealed surroundings, Stanley reached into the bag on Hazel's side and removed the Magnitudo.

'Remember there are two potential places,' Stanley mused as he skimmed through the pages looking for one in particular. 'There was this and something else.'
'There's got to be some clue.'
'Maybe this?' Stanley announced as he found the page he was looking for.

Handing the Magnitudo to Hazel, he pointed to a rough sketch of the priory ruins and a singular brick that had been drawn on the page. The brick, unlike the others, was etched with the Roman numerals **CDXII** the same numbers relating the volume of text itself.
'Seriously? You expect to find that in here?'

Hazel looked at the surrounding building to emphasise her disbelief.
'It's all we've got to go on.'
'It's a needle in a hay stack.' She scoffed, kicking aside a bramble in the room's corner.

Stanley knew she wasn't wrong. If they searched the entire Priory house there was still the remaining walls of the church and monastery outside. Frustrated, Stanley slammed the book shut and tossed it at Hazel.
'I don't disagree,' he snapped. 'But we have nothing else to go on. It's not like Jacob or Kelly gave us any idea what to do.'

Pushing past Hazel, he began in the far corner of the room and started searching the tangled vines and branches for any sign of the brick etched with the lettering. It was not long before the thorns had cut his hands and he felt the sting of nettles as he searched each individual stone and brick.

They worked in silence, Hazel knowing all too well from her brothers it was best to leave Stanley be. Moving along the opposing wall she found nothing amongst the bricks and was surprised to find Stanley squirreling his way up to where the upper level of the Prior's house had once been.

All that remained of the floor above were the rotten wooden beams long since snapped and weathered. Balancing himself above, he shuffled around the second level of the ruin using what parts of the stonewall he could to keep his grip. Dripping with sweat, Stanley inched his way around the upper levels until something caught his eye.

'I think I've got something.' He declared as he adjusted his position, balanced on the broken beam.

'What is it?'

'It's not all the letters, just the one.'

Brushing off a layer of moss, Stanley was right as the numeral I had been chiselled into the surface of the brick, discreetly etched in the bottom corner. Convinced it was no coincidence, he brushed the surrounding bricks until he found a second and third with other numerals etched into the surface.

'What have you got?' Hazel pressed as she craned her neck to see what he was doing.

'I've got a C, D, I and I but no X.'

'So X marks the spot then?' Hazel chuckled as she watched Stanley perched above her.

The bricks were spaced apart in no particular pattern. As he brushed them off the only difference was the surrounding mortar that seemed more brittle than that between the others. Reaching to his ankle, Stanley removed a short knife from a sheath at his ankle and dug the blade around the edge of the nearest brick.

Much to his surprise, the mortar all but crumbled with little effort. Scraping it free Stanley wedged his fingers into the narrow gap and wriggled the brick free from its position. At first the brick remained secure, but after a few attempts it slid free with relative ease.

As the end of the brick slipped out of the wall, it surprised Stanley to find the back face of the brick was not flat. Someone had attached a metal plate to the rear of the brick that moved at his touch to reveal a secret compartment within the brick itself.

'Grab this.' Stanley huffed as he lowered the brick and dropped it down to Hazel's waiting hands. 'There's a compartment inside with something in it.'

Not waiting for her to open it, Stanley set to work extracting the remaining bricks until he had passed all four down to Hazel. Working his way back down the wall to ground level, he was happy to reach terra firma.

'What's inside?' He pressed as he wiped his sleeve across his sweat-coated brow.

'Keys.' Hazel announced as she unwrapped the last key.

Each brick had contained a single metal key wrapped in discoloured linen. The head of each key looked similar and had been created into the familiar shape of the embossed tree that had been pressed into the cover of the original Magnitudo Jacob had shown them.

'What are they for?' Stanley asked as he inspected the key in the beam of sunlight from outside.

'I have no idea, I haven't found the X, it was the only one that's missing.'

Looking around them the only thing they had not searched as the cobbled floor buried beneath a thin layer of moss and earth. Holding the key in his hand Stanley kicked at the earth at his feet but found nothing resembling the etched bricks.

'Could have been part of the floor before it rotted away and somehow it's now gone?' Hazel asked as she looked up to where Stanley had been balancing moments before.

'I hope not,' he sighed. 'I mean look at this place, I'd like to think this Alessandro would have chosen parts that were likely to survive the decay.'

Scraping back the moss, Hazel found a smooth stone where a fireplace had once stood when the building had been occupied. The damp earth had discoloured the smooth hearth and as she followed it into the old chimney her gaze settled on the fireback through the face of the fireplace.

'Stanley, look.'

At first, the centuries of soot and scorch marks of flames disguised the indentation in the stone's surface fireback. Inspecting the stone closer, Hazel brushed her hand against the pitted stone and felt the undeniable diagonal lines scratched into the surface.

With rising excitement she traced the lines until her hand found the horizontal line at the top of the line. Despite the scorched stone her finger slipped into a narrow hole at the apex of the line and inside she felt the metal of a lock.

'Here, give me the keys.' She barked and held out her hands.

Handing her the four keys, Stanley stood back and watched. In the dark shadows of the fireplace he could just make out the Roman numeral X on the dark fireback. Trying the keys in turn Hazel made quick work of finding the corresponding locks until all four sat proudly from the face of the stone.

'What does it unlock?' Hazel hushed as she rotated each key.

As each key completed its turn a loud *crack* echoed from somewhere behind the fireback. As the fourth key completed its rotation, the surrounding room filled with a loud *crunch* followed by nothing.

Awash with curiosity and frustration, Stanley looked

around for any sign that something had moved, that the keys had unlocked something somewhere. There was nothing. Everything around them looked as it had.
'Why is nothing simple?' Stanley groaned as he turned towards the door leading back outside.

He managed a single step on the soft earth he had not disturbed before a second *crack* echoed from the floor beneath him. Turning to face the fireplace Hazel leapt back as the hearth she had uncovered shook and slid backwards, retracting into the fireplace, to reveal a concealed entrance leading deep underground.
'Whoa!' She exclaimed as a cloud of dust billowed from the retracting stone hearth. 'I never expected that.'

Against all of his better judgement, Stanley knew they would have to venture into the hole. Even without pressing more than his face into the opening he could see the top of a ladder leading down into the deep darkness.

Peering down, he recalled the moving piece of flesh that had been attached to the inside of the original Magnitudo. The thought of the skin moving and reacting sent of icy shiver down his spine as he sat back to think.
'Everything is saying we need to go down there,' he sighed. 'But everything inside me is saying not to.'
'I don't think we have a choice.' Hazel agreed as she moved to his side.
'We don't, and that's what I hate. Do you remember that piece of flesh at the Abbey?'
'How can I forget?'
'Well if that's just a sample of what we're up against, I dare not think what could wait for us down there.'
'The only saving grace is the fact this was created by one of the good guys. Someone trying to stop the thing that skin belonged to.'
'Good guys, bad guys. Hazel, I can't even understand

what a strange world we find ourselves in.'

Much to Stanley's surprise, she withdrew a torch from her bag and pointed it down the opening.

'I agree,' she declared with a false confidence. 'But we are in it now, we need to do something. Inspector Kelly is relying on us.'

Stanley watched as she swung her legs down the hole and descended the ladder into the darkness.

CHAPTER TWENTY-THREE

THE air was damp in the old tunnels beneath the Prior's house. As he descended the ladder after Hazel he felt the moss and growth on the battered rungs of the ladder. Keeping his gaze on the ladder, not daring to focus on the cobwebs and scuttling spiders that fled at their descent, Stanley made steady progress down.

Reaching the damp floor he found Hazel stood at the mouth of a tunnel that stretched off further than her torchlight could illuminate. In her hands she held the Magnitudo and flipped between two pages.
'What is this place?' Stanley quizzed as he wiped a clump of cobweb from his face and recoiled as a giant spider scurried across the back of his hand.
'I'd guess some mine from years ago. You can see bits of coal in the soil.'

Hazel panned the torchlight around and directed Stanley's attention to the tunnel walls. She was right. In the time it had taken him to follow her down through the open fireplace she had wasted no time getting familiar with their surroundings and trying to make sense of what faced them.

'Stand still.' She hushed.

'What is it?'

Stanley stood motionless as she scooped her hand above his head and removed an oversized spider with a bulbous body from the top of his head. Holding it out in her open palm, Stanley jumped back at the sight of the spider.

'Not a fan?' Hazel scoffed as she carried the spider to a wooden beam supporting the tunnel and waited for it to climb off her hand. 'So you can fight in a war but are scared of a little spider.'

'That is not little.' He shivered and watched as the spider moved into cover between the supporting beam and the earth above. 'Is there anything in there that will give us an idea what we're doing down here?'

'Beneath the earth the pathways lead, follow an honest path to salvation and seek the test.'

'Well that solves it, follow the tunnel and we will get there.'

'As long as there's only one tunnel.' Hazel corrected as she secured the book back in the bag.

'You had to say that, didn't you?' Stanley groaned as he moved to stand next to her. 'If we find a dozen different choices, I'm blaming you.'

Keeping the air between them light Hazel laughed and set off with Stanley close behind her. Traipsing deeper into the tunnel, it was not long before the dim light from the open fireplace disappeared. The only light came from the battered torch in Hazel's hand and even that did little to illuminate much ahead of them.

Pressing deeper, it became apparent that the tunnels had long been sealed and nobody had ventured into them for a long time. The denseness of the cobwebs was such that before long they were both moving with a trail of flickering silk behind them.

Whoever had constructed the tunnels had done so with care and expertise. The tunnel was high enough, just, to walk through without stooping and the supporting wooden beams were spaced apart to hold the earth ceiling in place. On several beams Stanley noticed Latin inscriptions but decided against loitering to make sense of what was written.

Deep beneath the ground it was impossible to say how long they walked and in which direction they were now faced. Much to their surprise there had been no adjoining tunnels, instead the solitary channel burrowed through the earth and they followed it until their legs ached from the unseen ascents and descents following the contours of the earth.

'There's something ahead.' Hazel declared as the torchlight caught on something out of place.

Slowing their pace, they edged with caution towards what appeared to be the end of the tunnel. Even before reaching the subterranean cave, they could hear the faint trickle of water in the distance. As the tunnel ended, they stepped into an enormous spring-water cave. Hazel's torchlight shimmered on the rippling surface of the crystal clear water as she panned around.

'Wow!' Stanley exclaimed as he looked up to the interwoven roots that covered almost every part of the cave's ceiling.

Unlike the tunnel, the cavern had been eroded through the rock from centuries of movement by the flowing water. Veins of black coal sat prominently amongst the lighter stone. Where the water had burrowed through the walls, there were narrow fissures and angled holes that led off in every direction.

'I wasn't expecting this.' Hazel hushed as she stepped to the edge of the rock and peered into the clear water.

'Don't touch it.' Stanley snapped as she reached down towards the glassy surface.

'What's wrong?'

'This could be his test, it could be poisoned or something.'

The thought had not crossed her mind and although she was unsure, Hazel stopped herself from touching the water and stood back up. Moving away from the edge, she took out the book and found the page that had mentioned the tunnel.

'Follow an honest path, what do you think it means?'

'No idea!'

Checking through the writing on the next few pages, Hazel found nothing that provided her an answer or direction. Heeding Stanley's warning about the water, she inched closer and stretched her arm out to tease the torchlight to the far wall of the cave. Moving the light from side to side, she found nothing helpful and rested the heavy torch on the rock at her feet and turned to face Stanley.

'We're blind down here but I say we carry on.'

'We have little choice.' Stanley agreed as he took the book and re-read the pages.

As they stood inspecting the images and words in the Magnitudo, the torch remained pointed out across the rippling water. The reflection of light off the shimmering surface sent the light dancing on the ceiling like a blanket of stars, adding to the mysterious feeling of their surroundings.

After a few moments, neither of them had discovered

anything that gave them a clue of what to do next. Frustrated again, Stanley snatched up the torch and moved the light to the wall beside their platform at the water's edge.

Hoping to find a narrow ledge around the edge of the cave, he found nothing but water beyond the outcrop of rock and sighed in annoyance. Watching Stanley, Hazel shared his frustration and turned to look across the mass of water. It drew her eyes to the opposing wall where the torch had been pointed as they had scoured the pages.
'Stanley, look.'

Turning around, he followed her gaze and pointed the torch towards the opposing wall.
'What is it?'
'Give that here,' she barked and snatched the torch from his grip. 'Just look.'

Extinguishing the torch it took a few seconds for their eyes to adjust, but straight away Stanley could see what Hazel was talking about. On the far side of the cave the light had reacted with a handful of placed stones that now shone a dull pearlescent blue. Someone had arranged the stones in the pattern of a crucifix, and beneath it the letters CDXII were visible.
'Well I'll be you sneaky bugger.' Stanley gasped as the crucifix and letters faded.
'I guess that's the way then.' Hazel proclaimed as she switched the torch back on.
'Just how do we get there?'
'You know what Stanley?' Not waiting for his reply she stepped to the edge and dropped to sit on the edge allowing her feet to slip into the icy water.
'Wait!'

No sooner had he spoken did Hazel let out a loud scream. Her legs had submerged to her knees and found the rock beneath, but it was the cold that had shocked her. Pulling her legs out she burst out laughing and rolled back onto the rock as she saw Stanley's terrified face, half expecting her to be in fits of agony.

'It's bloody cold!' She giggled as Stanley dropped to her side to help.

'What do you mean? Didn't it hurt?'

'No, it was just cold.'

'I thought you were in pain.' He barked and pushed her away as she rolled onto her side, still laughing.

'Nice of you to care.'

'Bugger off!'

'You are a sensitive one, aren't you?' She could not contain her laughter at the look on his face.

Standing up, she shook off her wet legs and moved to stand in front of him. Much like her brothers, sultry and moody Stanley turned away from her but she took hold of his shoulders and forced him to face her.

'It's nice that you cared. I'm sorry.'

In the mysterious cave, in a long abandoned tunnel beneath a ruined priory, the pair shared a smile. Unlike the train ride from London, there was nobody to disturb them now. Taking hold of Stanley's chin, she turned his head to face her and leaned herself closer. Not wanting to push, she poised herself close to his face. Seizing the moment, Stanley closed the gap and pressed his lips to hers.

Surrounded only by the sound of moving water, they shared a long overdue kiss.

'What about when all this is done we get to know each other without being arrested, shot at and traipsing through damp tunnels?' Stanley jibed as their tender moment ended.

'I'd like that.' Hazel sighed. 'Now what about we get our

backsides over there and find out what this test is we're supposed to be facing?'

Releasing one another, Stanley was grateful for the encompassing darkness of the cave as he felt the blood rush to his cheeks. Brushing the cobwebs from his shoulders, Stanley watched as Hazel lowered herself into the chilled water and waded out across to the far side of the cave.

'It's not too deep,' she shouted back as Stanley slid his feet into the ice-cold water.

Teeth chattering, they waded through the water as Stanley held the torch above his head to keep it dry. More than once he felt his feet slip on the smooth rock, but he stayed upright until they reached the far side of the cave where another outcrop awaited them at the mouth of the continuing tunnel.

Climbing from the pool, they both shivered as they charged the glowing rocks again to make sure they had reached the right place. Stepping into the tunnel, they did not need the guidance of the blue stones as they peered down the continuation corridor.

In the distance they could see light and fighting against the chill on their skin they moved along the tunnel towards it. Reaching the end of the tunnel, they emerged in a small circular room. Beams of light bore down from the surface through narrow holes spaced at equal distances in the ceiling above them.

Appearing as bars of light in the floating dust it illuminated a honeycomb patterned floor. Each hexagonal space appeared to be filled with a viscous liquid that frothed and bubbled. There was a familiar smell in the air, a mixture of moisture and rotting flesh.

'Something tells me this is the test.'

'I think you're right.'

Stanley pointed the torch across the circular room to the far wall where the same tree that had become a common sight had been carved into the stone on the far side. In the centre of the tree, in the carved trunk, a hole had been created and inside it they could see a small wooden box stood waiting for them.

'I don't like this.' Stanley warned as he bent to inspect the frothing liquid in the nearest of the honeycomb hexagons. 'Something's not right.'

As he peered at the reddish-brown liquid Hazel once again retrieved the book and started searching for a clue that would help them make sense of the strange room that stood before them.

CHAPTER TWENTY-FOUR

KELLY moved towards the magnificent home under the cover of darkness. The sky was filled with lumbering clouds that hid the moon and gave him an element of cover to approach across the lawn.

Taking cover in a large rhododendron bush, Kelly gathered himself. Heart racing and breaths ragged, he had made good time across the open grass but now needed to calm himself to move on. Dropping onto his backside, he peered through the gap in the bush towards the silhouetted house.

Once he had left Stanley and Hazel at the train station he had returned to Ealing Abbey where Jacob had been waiting for him. The old man's demeanour was more formal and colder with the young pair gone, and Kelly had sensed the change in the old man.

'It's as we thought, the same names from the past back to haunt us.' Jacob had intoned as he handed Kelly a piece of paper.

'What's this?'

'The name of the one we believe has the map.'

Jacob had left Kelly alone in the church's annex to read the familiar name on the paper. Eric Masters' name had been scrawled in elegant lettering and Kelly had felt his heart sink. He was more than familiar with the family name and had crossed paths with them many years before. Their last meeting had ended in tragedy with both Eric's parents being killed in an accident in Bangladesh, an accident that Kelly had been party to.

Although the address of the Masters' lavish home had been written beneath the name, Kelly did not need it. He knew the location all too well and had spent many hours observing from the shadows when Eric's parents had been close to discovering the location of Ad Firmamentum.

Without offering his farewells, Kelly had made his way from Ealing Abbey and travelled south to Dorchester. A day and a half after sending his newfound friends on their search for Alessandro's Test, he was now stepping onto familiar territory.

His arrival in the sleepy town needed to be unsuspecting and unnoticed as he knew Eric would have eyes and ears around the town. Because of this he had elected to wait for the nightfall before making his approach towards the vast estate.

Having caught his breath inside his camouflage, Kelly made one last check of the house and for any signs of movement. Although the elegant Rolls Royce stood proud in front of the main building there was no signs of life within the building. Although the blackout was in effect, he suspected such rules and expectations would be dismissed by Eric and yet the house stood dark.

Since getting his first view of the house, he had seen no

signs of movement or life. Making one last survey his surroundings, Kelly chanced his hand and emerged from the bush and moved towards the house.

The irony was not lost on him as he crept across the damp grass and up a set of stone steps towards the rear of the estate. Here he was, a reputable Inspector of the Metropolitan Police sneaking around like a common thief. Truth be told, he knew his credentials would mean nothing if he was found within the grounds of the house. He was here as a Brother of the Benedictine Order and not an officer of the law.

Reaching the top of the steps, he crouched low and allowed his eyes to scan the windows and double door in front of him. Still seeing nothing, his approach having been unnoticed, he stepped onto the raised terrace and moved towards a pair of panelled doors.

Not surprised to find them locked, Kelly removed a lock-pick from his pocket and set about at the locking mechanism securing the doors. He made light work of the lock and in less than a minute he heard the satisfying *click* as the lock opened and the handle dropped.

Wasting no time Kelly unlatched the door and snuck into the house, closing it behind him. Once inside the house the air was stuffy and warm unlike the chill in the air outside. Allowing his eyes to adjust to the darker interior, it relieved him to find the house was as silent as it looked.

Above the loud ticking of a grandfather clock somewhere deep inside the house there was no signs of life. Having entered a small reception room, he navigated his way through the house into the grand entrance. Through the stained glass of the front door he could make out the shape of the Rolls Royce and orientated himself in his head.

A dual staircase swept around either side of the entrance and led to a raised balcony high above. As he lifted his gaze Kelly froze on the spot as a figure emerged from the shadows to peer down at the front door.

More by luck than anything else, Kelly was obscured by a vast shadow. As the man leant on the banister of the balcony and looked down Kelly could not help but be filled with disbelief that the guard could not see him. Not daring to move, not wanting to give away his position, he held his breath and waited as the man lit a cigarette and smoked it while leaning against the handrail.

After a few moments the man turned around to lean against the balustrade facing back the way he had come. Out of his sight, Kelly scurried like a midnight mouse back deeper into the house. Knowing there was someone else in the house put him on edge all the more and each turn of the corner or movement into another room was done as tactical as he could.

Having cleared all the ground level for any other patrolling guards, he stood in the kitchen and took a moment to plan. The house itself was enormous. Room after room spreading the length and breadth of the house with so many areas to search he did not know where to start. In his mind the most logical place he could think of was Eric Master's bedroom or office and he suspected both of them would be on the first floor.

For the time being he would have to begin his search of the ground floor, hoping something would give him a clue as to Eric's whereabouts or else a safe or something where the map may be stored.

Standing in the middle of the kitchen, the clouds parted enough to allow the bright moonlight to pour in through the bay window. As it did, the moonlight illuminated the entire kitchen and the smoking man that had just stepped through the kitchen door.

Sensing the other man's presence, Kelly turned on the spot as the man lunged. Kelly stepped aside as the other man shoulder-barged into him, sending him smashing into the work surface beneath the bay window. Feeling the wood crash into his lower back Kelly thrashed out striking his attacker's back and shoulder to break free.

Pots, pans and crockery crashed around them as the two men struggled around the kitchen. Kelly felt more than one powerful blow slam into his ribs and stomach to break free to no avail. Gripping the man's collar, Kelly twisted it tight in his hands until he felt the stitched fabric pull around the other man's neck.

Releasing his grip to fight against the tightening material, the man threw a punch at Kelly that collided with the side of his head. Dazed by the cascade of stars that exploded in his vision, Kelly staggered backwards and the two men separated from one another. Shaking away the dancing light in his eyes, Kelly caught sight of the incoming attack and grabbed the handle of a pan that had scattered across the worktop.

Dragging the heavy metal pan through the air, Kelly felt the impact and the satisfying *crunch* of metal on flesh. The man was caught unawares by the blow, and he was diverted sideways by the sheer power of the attack.

Much to Kelly's surprise, the man crashed into a wooden shelf unit mounted to the wall and crashed through it. Plates fell and shattered on the floor but instead of the man coming to a rest against the brick wall beyond, he crashed through more wood and disappeared from view.

Moving to understand what had happened, Kelly stared at the shattered wooden door leading down a set of steps into the cellar. As the moonlight faded, he glimpsed the man's crumpled body at the base of the stairs. 'Weird place for a door.' Kelly mused as he replaced the pan on the worktop and stepped through the shattered plates and pottery.

As the kitchen was plunged into almost darkness again with the shrouding of the moon, Kelly was curious to see light in the cellar below. Awash with curiosity and confident the cellar was empty, he descended the steps and walked over the crumpled body of the other man. Much to his relief he could hear the laboured breaths of the man but suspected he had suffered more than one broken bone having bounced down the stone steps.

Looking into the cellar, Kelly delved further until he discovered the source of the flickering light. Much to his surprise someone had erected a wooden altar against the far wall and at least a dozen candles of varying sizes burned, casting their light on the walls and ceiling.

It was the intricate picture that stole Kelly's attention, much as it had Eric when he had first discovered the mural as a child. The crude image of the Iceman, painted in human blood, dominated the wall. Stepping closer Kelly had seen the image before in his study of the Magnitudo but seeing it in almost true-life size sent a chill down his spine.

Standing before the altar Kelly reached out to touch the lines of the image and recoiled when the blood was still wet to the touch. Looking down he saw a jagged dagger laid between the candles still wet with blood.

Kelly crossed himself as he examined the ritualistic altar and felt a sense of unease as he realised the magnitude of Eric's obsession. Taking a moment to steel himself, Kelly searched around the altar for the stolen pages but found nothing anywhere near the bloodied picture or array of flickering candles.

Returning his attention to the familiar image, he looked at the grotesque face of the Iceman and removed one candle from its mooring. Raising it up, he inspected the artwork and followed around the entire image until he found a solitary piece of paper pinned to the wall by a similar dagger to the one discarded on the altar.

Inspecting the sheet, it disappointed Kelly to see it was not one of the stolen pages but a part-burned map. Tugging at the corner, carefully so as not to destroy what remained of the burnt paper, he pulled it free of the blade to read what was left. All that remained was a range of mountains that could have been anywhere in the world.

Inspecting the map closer, Kelly could make out the names of two peaks marked on the map.
'Grawand,' he crudely pronounced as he read the first aloud. 'And, Simi, Similalum, Similaun. Just where are they in the world?'

Taking care not to damage the paper any more than it already was, Kelly folded it and placed it inside his notebook for safe keeping. As he was about to turn from the mural on the wall a second patch of blood on the wall stole his attention. Turning back around, he levelled the candle at the wall to find a single word painted on the rough stone.
'Otztal.'

Clueless as to its meaning, Kelly scribbled the word on the page and made his move to leave the cellar. Moving past the unconscious guard's body, he made quick work of searching the rest of the house but found nothing of use. Exiting the way he had entered, Kelly disappeared back into the night, leaving only the injured guard and scattered crockery in the kitchen as a sign he had been there.

As he vaulted the perimeter wall of the Masters' estate,

he cast one last look back at the vast house.

'At least I've got something to go on.' He mused as he dropped to the soft ground below.

CHAPTER TWENTY-FIVE

ERIC had deciphered the map as best he could and made his plans before the blooded image of the Iceman in the cellar. The two pages of scripture he had acquired contained a series of clues and a rough, hand-drawn sketch of a mountain range. On that image one particular area had been identified, a long crack in the mountain's face which he believed to be the Iceman's resting place.

The text on the accompanying page had been encrypted through a crude cipher that he had found easy to deconstruct. Very much within his comfort zone, Eric had admired the simplistic nature of the coding and located the resting place of the Iceman's tomb.

He had smeared the mountain range's name in the drying blood from the gash on his palm he had used to refresh the lines of the Iceman's image on the cellar wall. Ötztal had meant nothing to him at first. An entire page of cryptic text to reveal a single word had been more than a little frustrating.

It had been his friend, the nameless assassin who had offered him the solution. Producing the map from the library, Eric had taken it and stared at the mountain range his friend had identified. It showed the Ötztal Alps on the map as a dividing range of jagged peaks between Austria and Italy. The sketch of the mountaintops could have been anything along hundreds of miles of mountainous terrain and brought him no closer to discovering the mystical Iceman's tomb.

With nothing but antiquated maps and geographical textbooks, Eric had realised the only way to find his resting place would be to seek the mountains and those who were familiar with the terrain. The biggest problem, and a substantial one at that, was the raging war that occupied the world and embedded Austria deep within the Nazi regime.

Having paid no attention to the brewing global tensions, the matters and disagreements of nations mattered little to Eric in his mind; he had continued life ignoring the war. His family ties had long stretched around the world and yet, considering the place he intended to visit, he could only hope his influence remained.

'We leave for Austria.' He had declared much to the surprise of his friend.

'How will we be crossing Europe that is currently swamped with war and soldiers?'

'Leave that to me, I will plan to fly us there.'

That had been almost twenty-four hours earlier and now, teeth chattering against the Alpine air, Eric and his companion stood on the platform of an Austrian station facing three German soldiers.

'The matters of war are of no interest to me.' Eric
explained in fluent German. 'I am here as a businessman
and explorer.'
'You are a spy!' The ranking soldier spat. 'We will detain
you until...'
'I think not.' Eric countered, stunning the soldier into
silence. 'If you care to contact the name on that card you
will find I am allowed passage into the mountains.'

When they had been stopped exiting the carriage of the
train it had not been unexpected. Their presence on the
train had not gone unnoticed and Eric had felt the eyes of
other passengers watching them both with an air of
suspicion. Aside from his companion's accent, he
suspected they looked British and very much the enemy of
the occupying soldiers.

Prepared for the expected detention upon arrival at the
station he had produced his ace card at the opportune
moment. The name printed on the card referred to a high-
ranking German aristocrat with whom he had shared
many adventures in search of the Iceman. Although the
following that had built alongside his parents in previous
years there were very few who remained committed to his
cause. In fact aside from his companion there were no
others who had remained dedicated to the Iceman's
rediscovery.

That being said there were others he knew who
explored the same murky world of darkness, in search of
hidden treasures and truths in humanity's past that would
offer him support in his search. The name on the card was
one such man.
'Maybe I will, maybe I won't!' The soldier scoffed as he
struggled to regain his composure from Eric's abruptness.
'Perhaps time in the cells will give me time to decide.'
'I suppose you could do that,' Eric offered with a smirk.

'Remembering, if my friend discovers you have delayed a trusted friend he will be none too pleased. In fact I know Professor Fuchs has the ear of the local SS and Gestapo, maybe they will find a new posting for you.'

Eric's words may have been an idle threat, he wasn't confident Gabriel Fuchs would mix with the Nazi regime but the fear he saw in the soldier's expression was worth the gamble. Sensing the soldier's hostility waning, he stood confidently and waited for the young officer to decide.

'Do you think he will arrange passage?' His companion hushed in his ear as the three soldiers talked about the name on the card.

'I have no idea, we have spent many years mixing in the same circles. I expect he will understand why I am here.'

'Fine,' the soldier barked. 'Sit and I shall speak with Professor Fuchs.'

Leaving them under the watchful eye of the other two soldiers, Eric watched as the other stalked into an office at the station's rear. As the soldier snatched up a phone Eric took a seat on the bench at the side of the platform.

Doing his best to appear nonchalant and calm, Eric admired the scenery beyond the station. Jagged snow-capped peaks dominated the skyline with rolling hills of lush forestry stretched as far as the eye could see. Although the sky was bright, the spread of clouds allowed a slow flurry of snow to tumble down adding to the beauty of his view.

Under the watchful glare of the two soldiers, Eric sat back and admired the view. Although he sat silent, Eric could sense the rising displeasure in his companion and hoped he would keep his calm long enough to let his plan play out. After what felt like an age, the now red-faced soldier returned from the booth within the station.

'I am awaiting a return call from Professor Fuchs,' the soldier barked as he thrust the business card back at Eric. 'Until then you will remain here and wait.'

'I have no problem with that.' Eric replied with dismissal in his tone and folded his legs.

Two trains passed through the station, upon the sight of the gathered soldiers nobody disembarked the train once it had settled at the station. Amused by the general population's fear and wariness towards the soldiers, Eric remained calm and arrogant as he waited to hear the tremble of the bell on the phone.

At last the phone rang and the senior soldier sauntered to answer it. Infuriated by the man's ignorance, Eric soothed his rising frustration and smiled as he saw the solder's face flush red with frustration. Suspecting the content of the conversation, Eric tapped his friend and stood from the bench.

'Where do you think you're going?' One of the remaining guards snapped. 'You were told to wait here.'

'Young man,' Eric replied and took a step towards the nervous soldier. 'You may have the world trembling under the march of your boots, but I promise they mean nothing to me.'

'Watch your tone.'

'Step aside and let us past, I won't be delayed any longer by the likes of you.'

Eric could read the soldier's confusion at Eric's change in demeanour and open defiance. Compared to the people he interacted with day in day out, the soldier was used to docile obedience and fear. Reaching for the pistol at his waist Eric watched as the other man fumbled with how to respond.

'Enough!' A voice barked from the back of the station as the now red-faced soldier stalked towards them. 'They are to be allowed passage.'

'But, what about…'

'No questions.' Pushing his comrade aside, the soldier stood in Eric's path and made sure he had his attention. 'You would do well to remember the limits of your reach and connections in Austria, Herr Masters.'

'My reach is much greater than yours, now step aside and stop wasting my time.'

Not giving him the chance to retort, Eric pushed past the soldier and picked up his rucksack from the platform. Not offering a backwards glance Eric strolled along the platform and out of the main gates with his friend in tow until they were out of sight of the soldiers.

'That was close.' Eric sighed as they emerged onto a narrow lane behind the station.

'What do you mean?'

'The last time I saw Gabriel Fuchs it did not end on the best of terms.'

'So why did you use his name?'

'Because he will understand why we are here and why I would risk crossing Europe at a time like this.'

'You and your friends are a curious and dangerous bunch of people.'

'We are,' Eric mused with an arrogant smile. 'Today it has proven its worth and should we locate the tomb I'm certain Gabriel will re-evaluate his opinion of mine and my family's quest.'

'I don't like you gambling with our survival on whims and unreliable connections Eric,' it was the first time he had challenged Eric so clearly and it took him by surprise.

'You may not pay much credence to the war itself but if we cross the Germans, we can expect reprisals which I doubt your friends in high places will save us from.'

'I have no care for the war.'

'No, that's obvious. But I am aware of the wider world and the dangers and while ever I'm by your side I'd appreciate you at least having some consideration for me.'

The sudden defiance had stunned Eric and as he looked his friend in the eyes, he could read the same cold and calculating look he had seen many times before. That was one reason that Eric revered and respected him, not only his skills but also the coolness and callousness that came with him.

'I apologise,' Eric offered as he flagged down an approaching vehicle. 'We will find lodgings in Naturns and seek the right place to begin our search. Before deciding anything, I will make sure I consult your wealth of knowledge about the wider world.'

Careful to keep his words respectful and free from sarcasm, Eric waited to see if he had placated his companion enough. As the small car rumbled to a stop by the side of the road outside the platform, his companion offered a curt nod and opened the passenger door to speak with the driver.

Leaving him to negotiate the brief journey to Naturns with the unsuspecting Austrian, Eric looked towards the mountains and tried to brush aside the growing excitement, knowing he was closer than he had ever been to the Iceman.

'I know you're there, somewhere.' He hushed as he stared off towards the mountains, clambering towards the lumbering snow clouds.

In the middle distance he saw the impressive Juval Castle perched on the hilltop overlooking Naturns town. Even from their distance he could see the ornate medieval construction and could not help but admire it.

CHAPTER TWENTY-SIX

HAVING entered the curious room and stood bewildered for long enough, Stanley was the first to move. Looking around he found a thick root attached to the wall and prised it free. Snapping a section off, he moved to the nearest of the bubbling hexagonal pools on the floor and tapped the liquid with the root.

'What are you doing?' Hazel snapped as she moved to his side.

'Well, it's a fair stretch from this side of the room and I doubt this is something as simple as mud.'

The surface had a thin layer on top that broke as Stanley pressed the twisted root through. As the film pierced a puff of acrid smoke erupted and straight away, he could smell sulphur in the air. Fighting against his own gag reflex, he continued to press the stick down until he hit the bottom.

'What's in there?' Hazel pressed as she crouched beside

him.

'I'm not sure.' Stanley replied as he pulled the stick back out.

The twisted end of the root caught on something beneath the viscous surface of liquid. Tugging at it Stanley struggled to break free until suddenly a loud *crunch* sounded from the floor and the puddle of dark-brown liquid erupted upwards covering his upper body in the foul smelling gloop.

Recoiling Stanley stumbled backwards as he fought to wipe the liquid from his face, lips and mouth. Hazel could not hold back her laughter as Stanley spat and gagged at the sulphurous liquid on his face.

'Here.' She giggled and handed him a small canteen of water. 'Have a drink of that.'

Snatching the bottle, embarrassed and frustrated by Hazel's mocking laughter, he unscrewed the lid and washed away the bitter taste in his mouth.

'What was that?' He coughed as he swirled another mouthful of water around before spitting it onto the floor. 'Let's have a look.'

Moving to where they had been hunched, Hazel looked into the now empty hexagonal hole and tried to make sense of what had happened. Looking down the hole Hazel could see the root Stanley had been using standing proud, trapped between the jagged teeth of a triggered bear trap.

'That's brutal.' Hazel gasped as she stared at the activated trap.

Whatever the liquid had been, was blown from the hole with the force once the trap activated. All that remained was a shallow puddle in the very bottom of the hole. Having cleaned his mouth Stanley moved to her side and peered down the shaft.

'What are we supposed to do with that then?' Stanley mused as he handed her the bottle.

Looking across the expanse between them and the mural on the opposite wall, he suspected they would require precise balance and movements to not slip their feet into the wide hexagonal holes. It was clear they had designed the floor in such a way to make simple passage across somewhat of a challenge.

'Wait, what's this?' Stanley interrupted as he turned to look at the place he had pulled the root from the wall.

On the exposed stone he could see words etched into the stone. Moving back to the latticework of tree roots he started pulling them from the wall and in a matter of moments had exposed a large portion of decayed text etched into the stone.

'It's in English!' Hazel exclaimed.

'Here I stand safe in the knowledge only those true of faith and honest intention may cross my test and retrieve the sacred box. As the sky descends, there will be twelve chances to save yourself, but one wrong touch will end it all. The time has come to prove your worth and...'

'And what?' Hazel pressed.

'And it ends there.'

'What do you mean?' She huffed and pushed past him to read the text.

Seeing Stanley was right, the words having ended at a patch of rough stone that appeared to have faded over the years, she moved to the wall. Brushing her hand against the rough patch of stone it did not indicate what they had written there.

Feeling her frustration rising, she brushed harder against the rough stone until, quite without warning, the rock moved and dropped an inch into the wall.

'What did you do?' Stanley gasped, but Hazel had no time

to answer as the surrounding cave shook.

Without warning, the entrance through which they had disappeared. A solid stone, hidden in the roof, plummeted to the ground, sending a cloud of dust spilling into the room. As the dust settled, the rock had blocked their escape back the way they had come.

They could hear unseen mechanisms activating behind the walls all around them until they were plunged into darkness as all the holes in the ceiling were blocked all at once. Consumed by the darkness Stanley fumbled to find the torch.

'Don't move.' Hazel barked in the darkness, terrified to move for fear of stumbling into the vast honeycomb floor. 'We need the torch. We need light.' There was panic in Stanley's voice as he shuffled to find the torch he had left on the floor.

Moving with care, his foot crashed into the torch and they both heard the echo around them as it clattered across the floor. Both waited with bated breath as the torch tumbled end over end somewhere in front of them and then was replaced with a simple *plop*.

Both of them held their breath as they waited for something to happen. Seconds passed until the bear trap in another of the hexagonal holes activated and the bubbling liquid once again exploded into the chamber.

Unlike before, something else accompanied the explosion. Where all the lights had been extinguished in the ceiling, one by one a handful of them reappeared sending twelve distinct tunnels of light pouring in from the ceiling, illuminating twelve hexagons on the floor beneath them. The vibrations subsided and the neat columns of light offered them enough illumination to make out the rough details of the room.

'Well that's a pain.' Hazel sighed. 'But it could be worse.'

No sooner had the words left her mouth did the room shake again, this time focussing towards the ceiling. Looking towards the roof Stanley's heart sank as he saw the ceiling creep downwards and through the holes that were not illuminated he could make out the razor-sharp metal tips of spikes descending from above.

'You had to say something, didn't you.' Stanley snapped as his heart raced and he looked around the room in desperation.

'Oh, shut up.' Hazel snapped as she felt the rise of panic.

Looking across the room, the sunlight shimmered on the exposed spike tips as they descended, along with the ceiling. The movement eclipsed the entire roof and there was nowhere offering them any cover beside a narrow platform in front of the ornate tree carving.

'Over there.' Stanley groaned and pointed across to the far side of the room.

Not waiting for a reply from Stanley, Hazel snatched up one of the discarded roots they had torn from the wall and moved to the floor of honeycomb holes. Balancing as best she could across the narrow beams that made up the edges of the hexagonal pattern she moved across to the nearest of the illuminated pools.

Hazel knew they had designed the room to test anyone daring to enter, and every element had a reason or consequence. Fighting to remain poised in position, Hazel hoped her hunch was right as she pressed the root through the film on the surface of the puddle of liquid.

'What are you doing?' Stanley shrieked above the sound of crunching stone as the ceiling and spikes inched down towards them.

'Playing a hunch.'

Hazel knew if she was wrong, the chances were the pool would once again explode when the trap activated.

Steeling herself, she dropped low in the hope she would not stumble backwards and slip into one of the surrounding pools. In her mind there had to be a reason for the light, why twelve of pools out the hundred or more on the floor had been identified by the beams of sunlight.

From the solid ground, Stanley watched with bated breath as Hazel pushed the stick into the water. As the wood reached the bottom Hazel was poised and ready for the explosion, but it never came. Churning the viscous liquid around, she dragged the root around in circles to activate the trap but still nothing happened.
'What now?' Stanley groaned as his attention returned to the descending ceiling.

Hazel ignored him as she pulled the root free and rolled up her sleeve. Pressing her fingertips into the liquid, it surprised her how thick the water was. Pushing her hand deeper down, it was cold as it enveloped her hand and wrist. Reaching down into the channel, Hazel pushed her arm down until the surface of the water reached her shoulder and she could smell the acrid stench as her face hover above the bubbling liquid.
'There's something here.' She exclaimed.

Hazel could feel a lever of some sort attached to the bottom of the hole and wrapped her fingers around it. With enough of a grip on the slippery lever, she pulled upwards until the lever stood vertical beneath the surface.

With the rising of the lever the ceiling stopped moving and the room was filled with a sickening *ticking* sound as if a mechanism was counting down somewhere above them. Wiping her arm now it was free of the liquid Hazel counted the number of ticks and on the twelfth sound the ceiling once again began descending except this time it appeared to be doing so faster.
'Get yourself to the next one.' Hazel yelled as she looked

around for the nearest of the next illuminated pools.

Stanley stood gob smacked for a moment as the spikes dropped lower and the ceiling resumed its descent towards them. With ceiling's movement the air within the chamber felt more compressed and, although the spikes still afforded him room to move, Stanley started his precarious balancing act, stooping low as he moved.

Feeling the same wariness and revulsion as Hazel had, Stanley reached the first hole and pushed his hand through the surface of the liquid. Once the thin film was disturbed by his hand he was overcome with the putrid stench but continued.

'Wait.' Hazel hollered as Stanley took hold of the submerged lever.

'What?' Stanley groaned as his face hovered above the bubbling surface.

'If we pull them at the same time it might give us more time to move.'

Peeking upwards, Stanley saw the tip of the spikes were now about level with where his head would be if he was stood up.

'Get a move on then.' Stanley growled back and watched as Hazel pushed her own arm back into the water.

'Three…two…one.'

Together they pulled the levers and once again the ceiling stopped its descent. Counting the *clanking* sounds, it once again reached the twelfth and this time the ceiling resumed its descent even faster.

'We need to move.' Hazel gasped, and the pair scuttled their way across to the next pair of illuminated pools.

CHAPTER TWENTY-SEVEN

FEELING the pressure as the ceiling and spikes descended towards them, both Hazel and Stanley moved with as much speed as they dared. Having pulled three of the levers they stooped low to avoid the razor-sharp spikes as they balanced towards the centre of the honeycomb floor.

Stanley knew Hazel outmatched him when he watched her move with grace and speed while remaining balanced on the thin beams that made the hexagonal edges. Feeling less than graceful he struggled to find stable footing as his shoulder caught on the tip of the nearest spike.

The metal tip grazed through the material of his top with ease and he felt the sting against his flesh as the tip dragged through. Cursing, Stanley lowered himself down and moved as fast as he dared to the next illuminated hole.

'Ready?' Hazel huffed, already shoulder deep in the vile

fluid.

'Give me a second.' Stanley groaned as he dropped and pushed his arm downwards.

As he fumbled for the lever at the bottom he scanned around for the next pool of light. Much to his dismay he realised they had not made it halfway across the honeycomb floor and the ceiling felt it would crush them before they reached the far side.

'Got it.' He heaved and together they pulled the levers.

Not waiting for the rhythmic ticking behind the walls they both made a move as the ceiling paused in its position above them. Twisting himself between the vertical spikes Stanley made as best progress he could and felt his foot slip from its position and drop into the pool beside him.

Terrified of the impending activation of the submerged bear trap he grabbed for anything to stop his descent and wrapped his left hand around the shaft of the nearest spike. Straight away he regretted the decision as he felt the metal slice through his skin but it had done enough to stop him dropping into the hole and activating the trap.

Fighting against the searing pain across his palm Stanley pulled his sodden foot back through the tar-like puddle and regained his balance. As he released his grasp on the now bloodstained spike, the ceiling resumed its descent and he cast aside his concern for the jagged gash in his hand.

Hazel was once again dropping to pull the lever in the next hole.

'Pull it.' Stanley groaned. 'We might delay it enough to stop moving if we split the levers every time.'

'Are you ok?' Hazel gasped as she saw the blood oozing from his hand.

'I'm fine, just pull it.'

Feeling somewhat concerned for the steady flow of blood trickling down his arm, Stanley heard the ceiling mechanism grind to a halt and the sickening ticking begin once again. As Hazel pulled herself up Stanley felt his vision start to swim, the world around him fading in and out of focus as he struggled to keep his balance on the narrow ledges.

'Something's wrong.' He stammered, his tongue feeling too big for his mouth making his words sound slurred.

'What's wrong?' Hazel quizzed as she moved across to the next illuminated pool.

'I don't know, I don't feel…'

Stanley's left arm felt numb and hung limp by his side as the twelfth tick ended and the ceiling resumed its descent. Everything felt lethargic and slowed down. His limbs felt heavier than they ever had before and the mere thought of moving seemed a ridiculous notion.

'Spikes.' Stanley wheezed as he took a step and fell down with a *crash* landing face-up staring at the spikes. 'Poison, I can't feel my arm.'

Panic swallowed him with welcome arms as he stared at the ceiling closing in on him. Having landed on his back Stanley had managed not to activate any of the submerged traps. Laid there he knew, despite his fading senses, that to stay still would mean a certain death pinned between the ceiling and the honeycomb floor.

Much to his relief Hazel activated another of the levers somewhere behind him and the ceiling once again paused. Above the ringing in his ears, he heard Hazel shout something to him.

'Get moving, get to the other side, I'll sort the rest.'

Not in any position to argue Stanley fought against his lethargic muscles and rolled onto his front. Careful to keep himself from dropping an arm or leg into the holes he dragged himself towards the carved tree on the far side of the room.

Time passed slow as Stanley all but dragged himself across the expanse of the honeycomb floor. Every inch felt like a mile and the rhythmic *ticking* haunted him each time Hazel activated another of the levers. He had lost count how many she had done by the time he reached the far side of the room and pulled himself onto solid ground.

Clear of the descending ceiling Stanley rolled over to face back the way he had come and felt his heart sink. The ceiling had descended almost two thirds of the way down and he could see Hazel fighting to navigate the maze of jagged spikes to avoid the same lethargic state he was in. From where Hazel moved he could see two more columns of light between her and the platform his was now on.

Circumnavigating another spike she stooped down and lay on her side to press her hand into the next pool of liquid. Grasping the lever Stanley could see the struggle despite his swimming senses. As she pulled the lever the ceiling once again stopped moving and he watched as Hazel snaked her way on her stomach towards the final pool.

Even in his drunken state, he knew she would not make it. The path between the spikes forced her to flex and weave between them, taking her away from the pool before it moved her closer. From his position in the clearing, however, he had a clearer path.
'I'll thort it, thith ith eathy.' His words sounded ridiculous, but he knew what he meant to say.

Against Hazel's protests, he dropped and dragged himself back beneath the crushing ceiling and dragged himself back towards the final pool. As he pulled himself back onto the honeycomb floor of bubbling pools, the ticking ended and the ceiling began its final descent.

His progress was slow and laboured, forced to move himself only with his right arm, his left now hanging limp by his side, he huffed and heaved his way towards the pool. As the world bobbed and weaved in his vision Stanley reached the pool as he felt the heel of his foot graze against the stone roof.

Casting a glance upwards, he saw there was less than a foot of space between the top of his head and ceiling. Plunging his hand into the bubbling liquid, he found the lever and fought with his weakening muscles to pull the lever that slid between his fingers.

As the poison fought to weaken every part of his body, he struggled to find enough strength to pull the lever. Screaming with determination and frustration, his fingers slipped free from the smooth lever. Fighting against the sinking feeling of dread, he found the lever once again and tightened his grip as best he could.

The lever moved inch by inch until it was upright and the ceiling ground to a sickening stop. Expecting it to retract, Stanley felt sick as he heard the ticking begin once again.

'Move Stanley.' Haze screamed from behind him, having reached the safety of the platform behind him.

'It'th too late, I'm thtuck.'

Stanley raised his head enough to see the ceiling ready to press down the final few feet and crush him where he lay. Pushing his hand against the edge of the hexagonal hole he inched backwards at a snail's pace as he counted off the ticks in his head.

Peering back, he saw Hazel was fighting to find a way to him to help.

'Thtay where you are. It'th not worth it.' He spat.

Stanley was spent. Pushing himself back he counted the ninth *tick* and came to rest halfway between the final lever and the platform. He could no longer feel anything of his left arm and the numbness had spread up his neck towards his face. Giving up had attempted one last push before his arm collapsed and his face sank into the hole beneath his head.

Despite the foul smelling vapour from the pierced surface of the water, he did not try to pull his head free as he counted the tenth and eleventh tick. As the twelfth echoed around the chamber, the room was plunged into darkness and the sound of stone mechanisms grating once again sounded in the air.

In the darkness Hazel could not stand the sound and clamped her hands over her ears. Concentrating on the pounding of her heart, she closed her eyes and tried to block out of what was happening and how she could escape this frightful nightmare.

Beneath the stone ceiling and spikes, Stanley felt the pressure of the stone on his back as the ceiling descended. Unsure what to think in his last moments, he allowed himself a moment of sadness at the thought his parents would never know the truth and would always thing lesser of him than they should. As the ceiling pressed down the tip of the spikes activated the remaining bear traps within the hexagonal holes and simultaneously they all activated sending a wave of putrid water cascading in every direction.

Feeling the sudden spray of liquid, Hazel screamed at the thought it was blood and matter from Stanley being crushed beneath the tonnes of stone pressing down on him. As she recoiled back away from the crushing trap a hole appeared in the roof to her side allowing sunlight to pour into the chasm.

The harsh light burned her eyes, and it took her a second to adjust. Shielding her eyes, she watched in disbelief as the stone ceiling rose from where it had finished, less than a foot of space between the roof and the floor. Dreading what she would see, she waited with bated breath as the ceiling retracted to reveal the hexagonal floor once again.

With all the bear traps having been activated the mechanism had been reset allowing the cogs to drag the ceiling back into its original position. As it rose, she caught her first sight of Stanley's prone body face down, head pressed into a now empty hole, the activated trap sitting close to his face.

Stanley did not understand what had happened, feeling the pressure on his back he had expected to feel pain, but with the sudden rush of putrid liquid the movement had stopped. Pinned in position it was difficult to breathe and for a moment he feared he would die trapped and pinned in position forever unable to move.

When the ceiling had retracted he was overcome with relief and the effects of the poison coursing through his body. Doing the only thing that felt right he closed his eyes and let sleep take him, releasing a long sigh of relief as he did.

It was only when Stanley sighed did it snatch Hazel from where she was crouched. Moving with haste she dragged Stanley's unconscious body back to the relative safety of the platform and tried to rouse him from his slumber. With no luck, Hazel looked to the box in the wall surrounded by the familiar etching of the tree in the wall. Beside the box she saw three small vials, all marked with the same Roman numerals CDXII.

Acting on instinct, Hazel snatched one vial and popped the ages cork. Not considering the risks, she pressed the glass to Stanley's lips and poured the luminescent liquid into his mouth. With his head resting in her lap, she prayed that whatever she had given him would somehow bring him back to her.

CHAPTER TWENTY-EIGHT

HAZEL held her breath as she watched the luminescent liquid from the vial dribble down Stanley's cheek. She did not understand what made her believe she was right in feeding him the vial, but her instincts was all she had.

As the ceiling retracted back into its original position, she sat holding Stanley's head, cradling it in her lap.

'That tasted horrible.' Stanley groaned as he sat flexing his no longer lifeless left arm. 'How did you know that would work?'

'I didn't.' She confessed as Stanley moved to sit up facing her.

'Well, in that case I'm glad you did it, anyway.' Stanley toyed with the jagged cut on his hand as the feeling in his skin returned. 'That was a strange feeling.'

'Here let me bandage that up.'

Still somewhat dazed, Stanley sat back on his good arm

and watched as Hazel wrapped a tether of fabric around the cut on his hand. As the fogginess from the poison subsided, he could once again feel the fire across his palm where the metal spike and glided through his skin with ease. As she tied a knot on the back of his hand Stanley could not help but lean forward and once again place his lips to hers.

'Thank you.' He smiled and did his best to appear calmer than he felt.

For a moment they sat, out of breath and somewhat astounded they had made it through the Alessandro Test. Taking in their new surroundings, now bathed in the bright sunlight through the hole to their side, the room looked different.

The spikes had once again retracted into the ceiling and were replaced by the beams of light. The viscous liquid had flowed back into the honeycomb floor and most of the holes sat half full. Whatever intention Alessandro had when he designed the room, Stanley knew one factor was to push any who dared to cross to their very limit.

Looking up at the ceiling, he shuddered at the thought of the stone roof pinning him in place. He knew had they not activated all twelve of the switches, the test would have left him pinned in position until he took his dying breath. That thought along sent a wave of claustrophobia and panic through him.

'Where does that lead?' Stanley asked as his gaze fell to the hole in the ceiling to the side of the platform.

Although the hole was in the roof, they could see a set of steps leading up towards it. Even through the rough rectangle he could see lumbering clouds and a rich blue sky that looked more than welcoming compared to the darkness they had endured since descending the ladder from the Prior's House.

'I'm not sure,' Hazel confessed as she stood up and reached for the ornate wooden box resting in the wall at the centre of the tree. 'What do you say we get this and get out of here?'

'That sounds like the best plan we've had all day.'

Taking hold of the wooden box, Hazel paused for a moment as if she expected to activate a secondary trap. Testing the box, she found she could move it around the purpose built hole in the wall. With great care she lifted it from its resting place and felt relief when she found no secondary button or trigger beneath the box.

Not wanting to spend any more time than they had to in the deadly room, Hazel helped Stanley to his feet and they made their way towards the flight of stone steps. Glad to leave the subterranean room behind, Stanley cast one last glance back towards the honeycomb floor before staggering his way up the narrow flight of steps and into the fresh air.

It surprised them both to find the staircase led them up and out of a grave. Their way was initially blocked by a cracked stone slab but with a little effort they made enough space to climb out into the fresh air.

Reaching the surface, they stared at an impressive marble structure topped with an ornately carved cross. The shadow cast by the sun sent the shadow of the Celtic cross across the overgrown lawn behind the tombstone.

Checking they were alone in the graveyard, Hazel clambered free from the grave first and turned to help Stanley. Emerging into the quiet graveyard, they admired the view out across the rolling valley behind the impressive church building.

'Well this isn't where we started.' Stanley mused as he shuffled around the tombstone.

Much to his amusement, he brushed aside the ivy that

had attached to the fact of the marble tombstone and read the name hidden underneath.

'That makes sense.' He sighed as Hazel joined him. 'Here lies Alessandro Ramos.'

'There are no dates on the headstone.'

'Because he isn't here, is he?' Stanley quipped. 'It was just another clue along the way and I think if you check the map this will be the place of the second circle.'

Moving to a neighbouring headstone, Stanley perched himself on the crumbling stone and watched as Hazel removed the Magnitudo from her bag. Opening the folded map within, she realised Stanley was right. The second inked circle covered St Mary's Church beside the main road through Greasley.

'So,' Stanley began as he nursed his throbbing hand. 'What's in the box? What have we found that we almost died getting our hands on?'

Having forgotten all about the box, she retrieved it from the top of Alessandro's tombstone and moved to join Stanley. Admiring the craftsmanship, she brushed off a layer of dust from the top and exposed a trio of skulls etched in gold leaf on the lid. In the open mouth of each skull sat a symbol for wind, fire and water.

Grasping the lid, Hazel lifted it to expose the dusty contents. Inside the box, three similar vials of liquid had been laid on a soft blue satin material. On the inside of the lid, a piece of parchment had been folded and was held in place by two metal pins. Handing Stanley the box, Hazel removed the parchment and unfolded it with great care. 'What does it say?'

'Three elements are cast inside the glass, each must be combined within the element that gave the creature life. Only then will the process be halted, for there can be no death for the immortal.'

'Well that sounds ominous.' Stanley groaned as he inspected three glass tubes containing different coloured liquids.

'There's more.' Hazel interrupted as she scanned the rest of the page. 'The resting place of the hanged monk by the Hermit's Cave you will find the last element. In a stone wall deep beneath the ground you will find the chalice born of the earth, buried at the source.'

'More riddles and clues.' Stanley scoffed as he closed the lid of the box and stared out across the valley. 'It could be anywhere in the world, we're no closer to knowing what we have to do than we were before I almost got crushed to death.'

Hazel, who also felt an amount of deceit at the contents of the box shared Stanley's frustration. Neither of them knew what to expect from the discovery at the end of the Alessandro test but somehow they had expected more than this.

Dejected and frustrated they sat poised looking out at the picturesque valley view until a sudden sound disturbed their melancholy. The sound of a metal gate opening brought them back, and they turned to look towards the church a young couple emerged from the side of the building walking along the path towards them.

The man was in his later twenties and the woman a little younger. Arm in arm they walked along the snaking path between the gravestones and towards the two of them.

'Afternoon.' The man offered as they walked along the path behind where Hazel and Stanley were perched on the gravestone.

'Afternoon.' Stanley offered a polite reply.

Returning the greeting, the man paused in his tracks and stopped to look at Stanley with curiosity.

'Sorry but you're not from around here are you? London, I'd assume from the accent.'

'That's right.' Stanley was in no mood for pleasantries but feigned a smile at the young man and his partner.

'I'm a retained fire-fighter in London, back for a few days to visit my family.'

'I'm an Air Warden,' Hazel interjected, sensing Stanley's coldness.

'What brings you out here then?'

'A break from the city, from the bombings and all.' She answered, realising the honesty in her answer.

'Strange place for you to visit, in the middle of nowhere.' The man's partner interrupted, her expression far more sceptical than her companion's.

'My father used to come here when he was younger.' Hazel lied. 'I found his journal and wanted to see the places he used to visit as a boy.'

'That's nice.' The woman replied, unconvinced.

'Well, I would love to show you around, I know almost everything there is to know about the local history. It's a passion of mine.'

'Arthur!' The woman snapped. 'You're home for only a few days, it is not the time to be gallivanting around giving guided tours. I was hoping we could spend some time together, alone!'

Arthur flushed at the chastisement from his companion and dropped his gaze a little.

'We wouldn't want to interrupt that.' Stanley soothed. 'I'm sure we can find our way around without imposing.'

'There is one thing.' Hazel interrupted and felt the woman's glare as she spoke. 'I was trying to work out what my father wrote in his journal, a place that could be near here, perhaps?'

Hazel tried not to push as the other woman stared at

her. Arthur, on the other hand, seemed intrigued and all too eager to help.

'What did your father say?'

'He spoke of a hanged monk by the Hermit's Cave, I'm afraid we've drawn a blank.'

'Dale Abbey!' The young woman interrupted. 'It's not far. It's over towards Stanton.'

'Kathleen is right.' Arthur began. 'There's an old superstition that a monk from Dale Abbey haunts the caves, having hung himself at Hermit's Cave.'

Stanley noted the rising tension between the couple as Kathleen tugged at Arthur's arm as if to silence him. Sensing it was their time to make apologies and leave, Stanley moved from his seat on the headstone and offered their gratitude and apologies.

'Arthur is it?' Stanley disarmed with a forced smile.

'Thank you so much for your help but your good lady here is right, we shouldn't be keeping you when you're only home for a few days.'

'I don't mind.' Arthur pleaded, his offer once again accompanied by an indignant jab in the ribs.

'No my friend it's fine, you've been more than helpful. Maybe our paths will cross back in London and if they do, we can share some stories about local history.'

'That would be wonderful.'

Not wanting to delay their time together any longer, Kathleen pulled at Arthur's arm and they once again set off on their walk through the churchyard.

'Fortunate.' Hazel smirked.

'Just a little, here's hoping this place is the right one.'

'At least it's something to go on.' Hazel looked back at the map and found the tiny village of Stanton-By-Dale further to the south of where they were. 'Looks like this is the place. We should get your hand seen to before we do anything else, I say we head back to the pub and rest.'

Stanley was in no position to argue. His hand throbbed and his body felt like someone had thrown it over a cliff and he had tumbled end over end. Parts of his body ached in ways he had never felt before. The thought of a comfortable bend and a pint of beer seemed like the perfect remedy for what had been the most curious of experiences in the secret tunnels beneath the grave.

CHAPTER TWENTY-NINE

ERIC felt his hands shaking as he reached the small plateau atop the razor-edge cliffs. The view was beyond breathtaking as the Alpine mountains stretched in every direction. Snow-capped summits glistened in the bright sun against a crisp blue sky. The beauty almost melted away the chill in the air and bite against his exposed face.

'I would never have believed I would stand here.' He gasped, his breath clouding in front of him.

'It has been a challenge,' his stealthy companion agreed. 'I'm certain your parents would be proud.'

'They would be! They would also be happy knowing that those who turned away from our family's devotion were wrong.'

Eric removed the folded map from his jacket pocket and inspected the sketch. It had taken enough time to translate the location but now, he believed he had found it.

Holding the paper up he turned to face the mountain behind him and matched the sketch to their surroundings.

With the mountain silhouetted through the paper it made it easier to hold the sheet in the correct position. Once the jagged slopes, an almost perfect match for the physical mountain itself, were in place Eric found the mark and focussed on the snowy slope.

'There!' The excitement was barely contained as he pointed towards the spot marked on the sketch. 'Beneath the jagged crevasse, there's a fold of rock.'

His companion turned his gaze and followed Eric's description. Even from their distance, the identified area the rock had a unique colour to it. It was subtle, unnoticeable unless someone knew where to look.

'It's about an hour away.'

'Less!' Eric declared and set off across the snowy terrain towards the towering mountainside.

Eric had been right, before the hour had passed the pair reached the base of the jagged crevasse gasping for breath. Their altitude above sea level affected their physiology and, although fit, Eric leant himself against the copper-veined rock to catch his breath.

'We should rest.'

'No, not until I have found him, until I have seen him with my own eyes.' Eric growled and removed the rucksack from his back.

Heart pounding with a mix of oxygen deprivation and affects of altitude, Eric removed a crowbar and set about working to find a way behind the rock into the crevasse. Taking his cue, Eric's companion did the same, and the pair set about doing what they could to move the discoloured rock from their path.

Matching the surrounding rocks and stone the enormous slab was the same slate-grey colour. The bright sun caught on an intricate web of copper veins that traced through and across the surface. It had been those veins of darker colour that had made the slab stand out against its surroundings.

Try as they might the two men could do nothing to move the slab. Embedded in place for thousands of years the stone had withstood the onslaught of storms and extreme seasons. It soon became apparent that the will and strength of two men would do nothing to move it aside. 'Damn!' Eric yelled as he threw the crowbar at the rock.

The impact caused a spark before the crooked metal landed in the soft snow at his feet. His frustration boiled over as he looked up at the vertical face of rock that blocked his path.

'There must be another way.'

'Up?' Eric quizzed as he took a handful of steps back to inspect the magnitude of the rock.

The slab sat against a sheer face of jagged stone. The slab itself stood twelve feet tall and rested against the narrow base of the jagged fissure that Eric had seen from a distance.

'Perhaps if we get high enough that opening may lead inside?'

'I have to try, I haven't come this far to turn away now.'

'We could pay for help. Bring others with us to help remove the stone?' His friend offered. 'We could be back within the day.'

'I will not share this moment with anyone but you, I cannot risk it.'

His insatiable need to see the Iceman fuelled Eric. Despite the cold, he removed his coat and discarded as much as he could from the backpack he had brought with him. Dragging it over his shoulders, Eric, armed with a pair of ice axes, moved to stand at the foot of the rock.

Looking up the crack was too narrow for at least thirty feet. He would need to rise higher if he was to find any way inside the mountain.

Ignoring the protests of his companion, Eric decided and began his laboured climb up the rock and towards the beckoning crack in the slate-coloured stone. Although only a gentle breeze Eric soon regretted removing the warmth of his jacket as the sweat formed on his skin and the wind stole his body heat.

Teeth chattering and fingers struggling to maintain their grip, he fought through the searing pain and scrambled ever higher. After what felt like an age, his hand reached the narrow base of the zigzag crack and he pulled himself into a seated position.
'What can you see?'

The voice was hardly audible over the wind, and Eric chose not to answer. Looking into the crack he could see nothing at first. As he climbed higher he feared the crack had been a bluff. At last having climbed almost a hundred feet up the cliff, his hand pressed into the wide crack and he found no resistance.

The gap between the stone was wide enough to accept Eric as he climbed into the face of the mountain. He had made it a handful of steps along a narrow path filled with snow before the rucksack at his back caught on a jagged outcrop of rock. Detaching the bag, he fumbled inside and removed a battered miner's lamp and weatherproof matches.

Leaving the bag behind, Eric attached a scabbard and knife to his belt and lit the wick of the lamp. Hooking a coil of rope around his torso, he took a moment to steel himself.

As the flickering light burned through the darkness he cast one last glance back at the opening and the bright blue sky beyond before turning his attention to the tunnel. Moving with caution, Eric made slow progress into the mountain and felt relief as the tunnel led downwards.

It did not take long for the tunnel to spiral downwards and any light from the crack he had entered was gone. The only source of light now came from the miner's lamp in his hand as he followed the unknown path around and down, deeper into the mountain.

Eric did not know what to expect. He had dreamt of this moment for as long as he could remember and as he rounded the last corner, he did not know what was to come. Much to his horror and dismay, the last turn in the tunnel led to a dead end of polished rock.

Coming to a stop, Eric looked around the small chamber he now stood in and fought back the urge to scream. Everything he had done, everything he had worked for and obsessed over was so close and yet, it would seem, still impossible and out of reach.
'Why?' He asked the inanimate polished stone in front of him and dropped to his knees.

Placing the lamp on the floor, he stared at the smooth stone flooding with frustration. Mind racing, he tried to think back if he had missed a turn along the tunnel but knew he had not. The snaking path had been the only path inside the mountain, etched it would seem, to bring him to another blockage and dead end.

Eric slammed his hand onto the floor, sending a cloud of dust billowing in the surrounding air. As the particles of undisturbed dust settled in his throat, he coughed to clear the dryness. Standing up to distance himself from the dirt, the light from the lamp caught on a mark at the base of the polished rock in front of him.

Awash with curiosity, Eric scurried forward and dragged the lamp to his side to inspect what he had seen.

At first he could see nothing, and as he moved the surrounding light could make out a line of text carved into the face of stone.

'That's not possible!'

A string of text had been carefully carved into the stone but instead of being in the indiscernible language of the Iceman's era this was in Latin. Brushing aside the fine layer of dust, Eric uncovered the entire text and read it aloud in the small cave.

'We block the path, a protection against the raging darkness buried beneath. There shall be no resurrection of the beast, for my journey here ends yours. Brother Alessandro Ramos.'

Eric shook with rage. He knew the name all too well. The one man who had thwarted every attempt to discover the Iceman's ultimate resting place. Time and time again Eric had found Alessandro's actions blocking his path and now, so close, the spiteful Brother of Benedictine Order had once again thwarted him.

Unable to control his bubbling rage, Eric kicked out at the etched writing and solid rock. Frenzied and frustrated Eric smashed himself into the rock more for a cathartic relief than anything else until his hands throbbed with pain and he sank down the rock defeated and broken.

'I have come this far to be so close and yet unable to reach you.' Eric sighed as he buried his head into his hands.

He remained that way, subdued and frustrated, until the sound of laboured breathing and footsteps carried along the narrow tunnel. Raising his gaze, Eric felt a wave of relief as his companion edged around the corner.

'You needn't have bothered,' Eric groaned as he looked at his friend. 'This is it, another dead-end.'

'We can get help and try the main entrance again.'

'It will take weeks.'

'We needn't rush. We have come to this point.'

'I need to think.' Eric sighed as he rose. 'I need some air.'

Between them they squeezed their way back up the narrow incline until the outside world was once again in view. As Eric retrieved his bag, he slid the rope back inside and moved to blow out the flickering lamp. Holding it over the bag, his gaze fell to a handful of dynamite sticks they had packed for emergency.

Easing the bound candles of explosives from the bag, he knew the dangers of using them. His friend had insisted they bring them with the sole purpose of escaping an avalanche or cave-in once they were inside the mountain. Any other use would more than likely bring the mountain's fury tumbling down on top of them.

Turning around, his companion saw the explosives in his hands and recognised the look on Eric's face.

'Don't.'

Eric was having none of it, fuelled by his insatiable need to finish what he had started he snatched a single stick from the bound pile and tossed the rest into the bag. His friend was on him in a second and grabbed him firm by the wrist.

'Let me go.' Eric barked as he fought against the other man's vice-like grip.

'You are not thinking straight, we need to plan.'

'No, I need to finish this.'

'Eric.'

Eric slammed a fist into the other man's face breaking his nose with a sickening crunch. Staggering backwards, he released his grip on Eric's arm and fumbled for his bloodied face.

'I'm sorry my friend but we have come too far.'

Dropping the tip of the fuse into the glass jar of the lamp, the fuse caught and sparked. Not wasting a second,

Eric sprinted back along the tunnel and reached the dead-end cave as the fuse was almost halfway through burning. Tossing the stick into the darkness he turned and fled back towards the surface.

He had made it two-thirds of the way when the dynamite exploded and the searing shock wave threw him from his feet. Crashing into the wall, a fireball exploded over him and extinguished as fast as it had appeared. Coughing against the dust and debris, Eric took a moment to gather his thoughts. Outside the mountain rumbled and the sound of collapsing ice and snow echoed from the opening that remained out of sight.

CHAPTER THIRTY

RETURNING to the hospitality of the pub was a welcome change to the damp tunnels beneath the ruined priory. Seeking a local nurse, Stanley soon had his hand bandaged more appropriately, and they settled in for the evening. Devouring a plate of meat and vegetables, they couldn't help but allow the creature comforts of the local pub to swallow them.

Not wanting to overdo it, Stanley bought them both a drink and before the night had begun, they retired for the night. Stanley's body had been through the mill and no sooner had his head landed on the pillow did sleep swallow him and drag him into unconsciousness. His dreams were filled with the repeated feeling of being squashed and unable to move and although he slept through the night, he felt far from refreshed when the morning broke.

Having spoken to the friendly landlord it hadn't taken

them long to identify a local bus route that would take them as close as they could get to the ruins of Dale Abbey and, what they hoped, would be the final piece in the curious items secreted by Alessandro.

Boarding the bus they once again felt the curious glances from the locals, but nobody offered them any hostility. Fuelled more by their curiosity than anything else, Hazel and Stanley remained silent on the journey, content at being a source of amusement for the other passengers.

'This is your stop.' The driver announced to them as they pulled up outside a large pub. 'They Abbey's down there, can't miss it.'

The driver was a jolly man, his rotund face swamped by an unkempt brilliant-white beard. Peering over his glasses, he tipped his hat to them as they stepped onto the pavement and closed the door behind them.

'Let's get this over with.' Stanley announced as he looked along a side-road and towards a picturesque house on a hill in front of them.

Navigating the narrow street, they made their way along the roadway before meeting a path that passed alongside a thatched cottage. The cottage could not have been more perfect had it tried. Manicured lawns were surrounded by perfect trimmed hedges and in the field beyond, Stanley could see the crumbled ruins of what had once been a stained-glass window.

'Would you look at that?' He exclaimed as the sun burned through the void where the glass would have once been.

Following the path, Hazel spied a wooden sign at the top of the footpath and made her way towards it. As they reached the signpost, there were two arrows pointing in opposing directions, one being back where they had come from.

'Hermit's Cave!' She announced, pointing at the sign. 'That's where we're heading.'

Not giving Stanley a chance to say anything, she set off into the next field and followed a line of trees across the far side. The path was easy to follow across the dewy field as it crossed the width of the open land before meeting a more obvious path at the edge of the treeline. The chill of the morning air was more noticeable under the canopy of the woods as they left the sunlight behind.

Following the meandering path, the incline soon took its toll on their already tired legs and both were glad to see a wall of sandstone through the breaks in the trees. Having only glimpsed the rock face they steered themselves in that direction and soon found themselves stood looking at a row of cave openings carved into the sandstone.

Even though they were primitive additions to the landscape, the basic features were obvious as someone had crafted the holes to form doors and windows. The caves beyond had, at some point, offered shelter as makeshift homes and both of them had an odd feeling that they were not alone in the woods.

Unnerved, Stanley looked around but saw no sign that anyone had followed them into the trees. Glimpsing the abbey ruins in the distance, he orientated himself before returning his attention to the caves.

'What now?'

Hazel was already studying the various pieces of paper she carried in the satchel. In one hand she held the Magnitudo, and in the other the folded parchment she had recovered from the inside of the wooden box. Scanning the pages she tried to make sense of what had been written, hoping to understand what they needed to do next.

'Do you think this is what he meant?' Stanley pressed as

he scanned the written passage on the parchment. 'It doesn't strike me as being deep underground.'
'No and it's not made of stone either, is it?'

Stepping away from Hazel, Stanley moved to the opening to the nearest cave and stepped inside. Walking into the cave the air felt cold and damp. Sniffing up he was certain he could smell something other than damp earth and rotting wood. Looking around the small cave, there was nothing that showed anything like what the obscure passage talked about.

'This is like looking for a needle in a haystack.' Stanley complained, his voice dulled by the damp walls of the cave.

Hazel did not answer. Standing outside she had noticed a wooden information board nailed to a tree at the end of the row of caves. Reading the sign, Hazel realised it was an information board that gave a potted history of the Hermit's Cave and surrounding area. Taking the time to read it, her attention was drawn to the history of the site and a rough outline of the surrounding area.

The most interesting element was a small area that showed a well s way back along the path towards the old church building.

'Stanley, I've got something.'

Glad to emerge from the damp cave, he moved to join her at the temporary information board and looked at where she was pointing. Seeing the well on the map made perfect sense. Without a need for discussion, they orientated themselves and stalked through the undergrowth in search of the well.

After fifteen minutes of searching, they had found nothing hidden amongst the brambles. Kicking aside as much as they could, Stanley caught sight of something buried in a small divot in the ground.

Nature had reclaimed the small opening in the ground and it had only been by chance Stanley had noticed the piled stones beneath a thick growth of nettles and bracken. Dragging aside the entangled roots, it didn't take long to uncover the mouth of the old well.

Nine neat stones had been placed in an oval above the ground while they had placed a rectangular stone covering a third of the opening. Leaning against the moss-covered stones, Stanley peered into the well and was surprised to find the level of only just an arm's length from ground level.

'I've found it.' He shouted across to Hazel, who was busy searching another divot further along the path.

Reaching beneath the rectangular stone he felt his fingers break through cobwebs and sticky moss. Brushing the underside of the stone he found nothing of note and pressed himself further over the hole. At last his fingers brushed against something that did not feel right.

'It can't be that easy.' He huffed as he pushed both arms beneath the rock and fought to prise free what he had found.

Careful to not drop it into the stagnant water, Stanley pulled a much larger wooden box from a secret crevice on the far side of the well. Aided by Hazel keeping him from falling into the well, he pulled the box free.

The wooden box was of a similar design to the one they had retrieved from the Alessandro Test. Unlike that, however, this box was twice as big and had only a single skull carved onto the lid, this one with a symbol for earth carved into its open jaws.

'That was easy.' Hazel mused as Stanley reached to lift the lid.

'Almost too easy.'

Stanley winced as he opened the box, half expecting

something to happen. But the lid lifted free to reveal the same blue satin padding inside. An enormous spider scuttled across his hand as he dropped the lid down, revealing the curious wooden chalice that had long ago been laid inside. The chalice was carved into the shape of an upturned human skull with some bird etched into the base, its wings seeming to hold the skull in place.

Lifting the chalice with great care, Hazel admired the intricate craftsmanship of the cup. The bird sat perched on the base, and each feather on the wing had been painstakingly carved into the stained wood. The skull, balancing on the wingtips, could have been real had it not been for the fact it was stained the same way as the wooden carving that supported it.

'What's this got to do with anything?' Hazel gasped as she turned the ornate antique in her hand and admired it from every angle.

Stanley looked back at the box and saw the familiar pinned parchment on the inside of the lid. Reaching down, he retrieved the discoloured paper and unfolded it to read what was written. To his surprise again the text was written in English. Having known Alessandro's heritage from Spain and his native tongue most likely to have been Latin it was still surprising to find all his texts carved and written in English.

'There is no way to discover the sacred chalice without first proving your worth against my test at the Priory. There is no need to ask anything more of you than you have already proven in coming this far.' Hazel turned her attention to Stanley as he read the note aloud. 'Four elements of nature earth, air, fire and water are the only tools that may restrain the creature born of ice. My journey to its discovery has been long and arduous, and all I offer now is peace instead of darkness. The creature's sacrifice to the deity of earth cemented his immortality. There remains nothing on this earth, that I have discovered, that will take the life she gave him. Instead, what I offer here is a way to trap the creature in time, unable to achieve his final reclamation of his power and rendered once again restrained.'

'I don't like the sound of this.'

'All four elements must be combined and touch the creature's long dead heart. Only then will he be frozen, locked in time to remain imprisoned in his own immortal body. I trust to you the Magnitudo text that will tell you all that I have learned in my search for the creature of ice, may your path seek finality where mine has not.'

The note was ended with a flourished signature and a wax seal emblazoned with the all too familiar Benedictine medal. A sombre feeling hung in the air as they re-read the note and looked at the chalice held in Hazel's hands.

'All this for a cup and some potions?' Stanley sighed. 'Had we not been through what we have in the last few days I'd say it was fairy tales and superstition.'

'The scary thing is, it isn't.'

CHAPTER THIRTY-ONE

NOT daring to move, Eric pressed himself against the floor as the entire mountain shook. Feeling the vibrations as tonnes of snow tumbled from the slopes high above, he hoped and prayed he had made the right choice.
'Eric? Where are you?' Coughing against the acrid smoke, he saw his friend stagger towards him.
'I'm here,' he wheezed. 'I'm fine.'
'You bloody idiot!' There was unbridled anger in his voice and although the bleeding had subsided, his face was still mottled with blood.
'I know.'

The violence of the shaking and vibrations eased until all that remained was the distance *crack* and *echo* of the snow resettling somewhere outside. Doing his best to hold his composure, sensing his companion's frustration, Eric stood and dusted himself down.
'I know your obsession but acting like a spoilt child will

end only in disaster. I haven't come with you this far to die at the hands of a petulant child.'

Eric fought against his desire to strike him again. The fact his friend's words were filled with truth restrained him from lashing out and instead he turned away and stalked back along the smoky tunnel.

Having snatched the miner's lamp, Eric moved along the tunnel as the surrounding mountain shook one last time. Thrown into the wall, Eric felt his head collide with a jagged rock followed by a searing pain. Holding himself steady, he waited for the earthquake to pass before venturing back into the dead-end room.

Turning the corner, he felt a wave of excitement as the blast had destroyed the entire floor. Where Eric had been sat not moments before was now a vast chasm into a chamber below. Crawling to the crumbling edge of the gaping hole Eric peered into the darkness. The flicker of lamplight did nothing to pierce the darkness as Eric shuffled away from the precarious ledge.

'At least it wasn't for nothing.'

'He is in there,' Eric gasped as he stared into the void. 'I can almost feel him, I need the rope.'

Pushing past the stealthy assassin, Eric made quick work of retrieving their equipment and dragging it down to the edge of the chasm. Finding nothing to secure the rope, his frustration once again rose.

'Here,' his friend barked and pushed past Eric. 'We'll lower the light down, see if we can't find the bottom before we go exploring any deeper. For all we know this could be nothing more than a fissure in the mountain.'

'And if it is not?' Eric's excitement was hard to contain.

'If it isn't, then I'll lower you down myself.'

Not waiting for an answer, he secured the lamp to the end of the rope and set about lowering it into the void below. Peering over his friend's shoulder, Eric held his breath as the light lowered deeper into the space below.

At first the flickering beams of light met nothing but dancing dust, small particles of debris from the earthquake crossing the beams of firelight. As the rope moved lower a sudden shimmer caught both of their attention.

'There!' Eric gasped. 'I see something.'

Doing his best to position the lamp, the other man rotated the rope until the main beam cast around and settled on what had stole their attention. Even from their vantage point high above the curious item, it was easy to see the shimmer of light had been a reflection on an immense line of linked copper chain attached diagonally to the ceiling.

'Just give me a second I think I've…' No sooner had he spoken did the lamp slip free from the knotted rope and fall to the floor below.

Shattering on the rock, the paraffin in the lamps spread across the floor creating a pool of fire beneath them.

'At least we know there is a floor.' Eric offered as he shuffled around to retrieve the second lamp from the rucksack.

'I'm not sure. We should at least see what else we can see before going down.'

'I won't wait any longer.' Eric was defiant as he hoisted the now empty rope back up. 'I've waited too long for this.'

'At least let me go down first, if there's anything to be concerned about, you'll be safer that way.'

'I appreciate the gesture but this moment is mine, I've lived my entire life for this.'

The sudden softness in Eric's demeanour caught his friend off-guard. Having nothing else to argue, he set about tying the rope around Eric's waist and securing it with a variety of knots and ties to make sure he was secure.

'Hopefully a better knot than what you used on the lamp?' Eric scoffed as he lit the second lamp and dangled it from his waist, hanging it below his feet as he sat on the edge of the hole.

'I hope so too.' It was hard to read if his companion was joking or not. The man had little in the way of visible emotions other than a constant scowl on his face.

Shaking with a mix of nerves and excitement, Eric waited until his friend had taken the slack and edged himself over the crumbling ledge of jagged rock. With great care he tested his weight on the rope and felt it bite into the creases of his legs until he had no choice but to release the rock and hope for the best.

'It's now or never.' He hushed to himself and released his grip.

Eric slipped down a foot before the rope caught and his friend pulled tight to stop his descent. Hearing him struggle above, Eric chanced a glance and was relieved to see only his friend's feet wedge against the lip of the hole and both the rope and knots holding tight.

'I'll lower you down; shout if you need me to stop.'

Without waiting for an answer, Eric felt himself inch through the cold air and down into the darkness of the chamber below. Unable to control the descent, Eric rotated as he inched further down into the unknown until his light once again caught the diagonal chain connected to the ceiling.

Doing his best he tried to make sense of what he was seeing but the uncontrolled rotation stole what chance he could of making anything out. After what felt like an age, his feet met the floor as the last of the flames flickered out from the pool of now evaporated paraffin from the shattered lamp.

'I'm down.' He hollered and heard his own voice echo in all directions around him.

Freeing himself from the makeshift harness, he looked around for another source of light. Inching with great care, he panned the lamp around until a flicker of light caught his attention. Unlike the chains, this was at ground level and Eric maintained his focus on the source as he moved closer.

Reaching the far wall of the chamber, Eric found himself stood in front of a large stone bowl chiselled from the very rock itself. Above it, attached to the wall, was an enormous mirror of polished copper. Smoothed almost like glass, Eric could just about make out his own reflection in the polished surface.

Leaning over the bowl, he saw it was filled with what appeared to be water. Dipping his hand into the clear liquid, it surprised him to find it was not frozen despite the subzero temperatures of the chamber. Dipping his hand into the liquid, he raised it to his nose and noted the sweet smell of fermented fruit.

Wiping his hand on his trouser leg, he removed the matches from his pocket as he balanced the lamp on the uneven floor by his feet. Striking the match, he took a cautious step backwards and tossed the match into the bowl of liquid.

Even before the wooden match touched the surface of the liquid, the vapours ignited. The air was filled with a sickening *roar* as the stone bowl burst into flame. Feeling the heat on his skin, Eric backed away from the fire.

The angle and position of the polished sheet of copper cast the light of the fire in every direction around the cavern. Designed with the sole task of lighting the room,

Eric soon found himself bathed in an almost golden light that touched all corners of the vast space he was standing in. Mesmerised by the beauty and simplicity of the primitive lamp, he turned around to seek out the source of the chain he had seen on his descent.

What he found behind him was beyond anything he had expected. Two pieces of chain were attached to the high vaulted ceiling of the chamber and met in the middle with two similar lengths of chain attached to the floor. Connecting all four pieces, suspended in mid-air, was the figure of a partially decomposed human man.

Mummified by the cold, skin mottled and tight against the bones, the body of the Iceman hung suspended in mid-air. Entranced by what he saw, Eric moved to stand beneath the suspended body high above him.

Admiring the decomposing corpse, it was difficult to not feel revulsion at what he saw. The Iceman's skin had turned leathery and almost vacuum-formed against the muscles, sinew and bone beneath. What had once been his face was locked in a contorted visage of pain and discomfort from the bonds of his suspension.
'What did they do to you?' Eric sighed as he moved to admire the suspended body.

The clothing remaining on his torso, hung limp from his shrunken form. Hair and other features had long since been lost to the bitter cold. Laid on the floor, beneath the Iceman's corpse, sat a sheathed dagger in a leather scabbard.

Retrieving the weapon from the ground, Eric admired its craftsmanship in the dancing light of the fire. As the flames licked and flickered, he was sure the contorted face of the Iceman moved but as he watched. To his disappointment, it was only the movement of shadows in the hollows where his eyes would have once been.

'What have you found?'

'It's him,' Eric bellowed above the crackling fire. 'At last I'm standing before the man I have spent my life searching for.'

There was admiration and elation in his voice as he stepped back away from the links of the chain. Mesmerised by the dagger, the dancing light disguised the fact the suspended body held by the four lengths of chain now moved its head. Forever locked in a star position, arms and legs locked to the point of strain against the joints, the Iceman shivered.

A series of unintelligible words crackled from the corpse's throat as Eric dropped the dagger to stare up at the impossibility of what had happened. Peering up at the decomposing corpse, he gasped as the Iceman's head turned from its position and rotated to look at him.

CHAPTER THIRTY-TWO

STUNNED by the fact the suspended creature had spoken, Eric looked up as it moved its head as if surveying its surroundings. Although its eyes had long since decayed, the Iceman turned and fixed its attention on where Eric was standing. Fighting against the rising sense of fear, Eric moved forward and watched as the Iceman followed his movements.

'My name is Eric Masters, I have come to free you from the chains of your imprisonment.'

The creature tilted its head as if listening to Eric's proclamation, but its reply came in a language Eric could not understand. The words were guttural, the pronunciation sounding aggressive and filled with venom.

'I don't know what you're saying.' Eric pleaded as he moved closer.

Edging across the uneven floor, the Iceman fought against its restraints, tugging in all directions to break free from his bonds.

'Eric, what's happening?'

'Get down here, I've found him and he's...' the words sounded laughable as he said them. 'He's alive.'

Eric could guess his friend's expression poised high above, but paid it no mind. Moving to the nearest of the anchored chains, he inspected the solid hoop where it attached to the stone floor. Hearing the chains rattle as the rotten creature fought against his restraint, Eric peered closer for a weakness in the chain.

Whoever had designed the curious trap had done so with skill and expertise. The chains were solid, pulled as tight as possible, giving little slack or play. It surprised Eric to find the metal warm to the touch as he tugged at the chain.

The creature spoke again, the frustration clear in his voice but Eric could not understand what was being said. Sensing the rising anger in the creature, Eric moved to stand beneath the hole in the ceiling and looked up.

Much to his relief Eric found a second rope dangling through the hole and watched as his companion swung himself over the lip and began a controlled, yet speedy, descent towards him with both rucksacks dangling beneath his feet. Stepping aside, Eric watched as the rope burned through the other man's fingers and he landed with a *thud* on the uneven ground.

'I can't believe you've done it.'

'We have done nothing yet, they've trapped him in some strange device and I have no idea what to do.'

Eric guided his friend to the suspended creature and watched as he admired the craftsmanship of the restraints. 'It isn't what it seems,' his friend declared as he inspected the loop of copper anchored to the floor. 'There's something else beneath the ground. Look.'

Eric moved to where his friend was stood and inspected the ground around the anchor point. Looking again he now saw the anchor was a complete loop and had been wedged into the ground, beneath it there was a small hole, wide enough to see there was another void beneath the floor.

'What can we do?' Eric huffed as he looked around for a way down beneath the floor.

Standing, Eric moved to the furthest wall and began a desperate search along the wall for a staircase or tunnel that would lead him deeper into the heart of the mountain. Finding nothing, he pressed further along the wall until he felt his arm pass through a void and into thin air.

'Here, I've got something.'

An optical illusion disguised the passageway; someone had created the angles of the wall in such a way as to hide the entry from view. Even looking at the opening, Eric still could not see the way.

Looking back to the centre of the cavern, the creature had rotated its head around at a sickening angle to watch Eric's actions. Repulsed by the rotated head, he moved to the wall and stepped through the illusion of a wall.

Moving through, Eric descended a set of narrow steps that brought him back around underneath the floor of the main chamber. When he emerged in the room below he saw where the chains emerged from the floor and were held in place by massive boulders hanging over a crevasse wider than he could comprehend.

Each boulder attached to the four lengths of chain swung with the movement but were three times larger than the stone that had blocked the entrance into the tomb. Two of the suspended boulders were poised beneath the two chains Eric had seen anchored to the floor while the other two hung on the far ends of the room attached to the chains suspending the creature's arms.

'The craftsmanship is impossible to believe.' Eric jumped as his friend appeared from the staircase behind him.

'There's no way to free him, if we release them at different times they will tear him apart.' Eric mused as he looked at the lattice of chains.

'There must be a way.'

The tightness of the chain emphasised the tension against the underside of the floor. Despite the creature's continued struggling, the boulders barely moved. Eric moved to peer down the crevasse and could see nothing in the darkness beyond. Whatever lay beneath was far beyond the limit of the light reflected around the second chamber by more of the placed sheets of polished copper. 'Come on, we need to think of something.'

Eric stalked back up the staircase to the main chamber and ignored the rabid screams and groans from the Iceman. Having stared long enough at the suspended anchors of stone Eric had come up with a crude plan that could release the Iceman from his bonds.

'What are you going to do?'

'Anything I can to free him.' Eric replied as he reached the pair of rucksacks.

'Don't even think about it, not like that.' His friend warned and placed his hands on Eric's arms to stop him reaching into the nearest rucksack. 'We don't know the damage we've already done up there, we can't risk a cave-in.'

'It's our only option, anything else will tear him limb from limb.'

Eric looked at the Iceman as he thrashed and fought against the chains like an enraged animal. There was nothing human about what hung suspended between the chains other than the recognisable silhouette of a human being. The rest, skin, hair, eyes, features and behaviours had long since been decomposed by the chilled air of the cavern tomb.

'There must be another way.'

'Then suggest it and I will listen.' Eric snapped as he pulled his hand free and reached into the bag. 'If not then I must do all that I can to free him, my life has only ever led to this moment.'

'And if it costs you your life?'

'Then so be it, I didn't come here expecting anything less than sacrifices.'

Eric's reply silenced his companion, who could only watch as Eric retrieved the remaining sticks of dynamite and the coiled rope.

'Are you going to help me?' Eric snapped as he scooped up his ice-axe and moved back towards the disguised staircase.

'You know I will.' His companion groaned as he followed Eric back down to the sub-level of the chamber.

Eric moved with purpose as he rigged the rope around the ice-axe and ensured the knots were tight. The four suspended rocks were spaced above the crevasse in the floor. Satisfied that the rope was secure, he moved to the edge of the crevasse and swung the axe through the air.

'I'll do it.'

'No, this is mine to do.' Eric snapped and pushed his friend back.

Gaining enough momentum with the rotation of the axe he loosed it through the air and held his breath, waiting for it to land on the nearest of the suspended rocks. As the metal blade collided with stone it sparked but skimmed off to fall uselessly into the void. Cursing, Eric pulled the axe back up and prepared to make the throw again.

This time the axe and rope wrapped around the suspended chain and Eric pulled it backwards. As the axe skimmed across the surface of the rough stone he caught it right and the line pulled tight dragging the axe until it wedged in place pinned between the rope and chain. 'Give me the end, I'll tie it off.' His friend snatched the rope. 'Just know I think this is a terrible idea.'

Securing the rope to a rock, he tested its security and offered Eric a curt nod. Not bothering to say a word, Eric moved to the edge of the crevasse and took hold of the rope. Heart pounding in his ears, he hooked himself on the rope and shimmied as best he could up towards the suspended rock.

Hanging upside down, Eric fought against the desire to look down. Fighting to climb the shallow incline soon took its toll on his arms and legs that soon trembled in protest. Inching along the rope, his breath became ragged as he moved at a snail's pace towards the suspended boulder.

Reaching the stone Eric took a moment to find the safest way to transition from his rope to the rock. Finding the best hold he could, he hoisted himself onto the uneven surface of the rock and waited to see if it would take his weight.

'Stupid.' He hushed to himself, realising the stone had been suspended for centuries and the addition of his slight frame would make little difference.

Not wasting any time he set about pressing one of the dynamite sticks into the connecting loop between the chain and the stone. This was far from an exact science as Eric adjusted the length of detonation cord and set about preparing to make his leap along the row of stones.

The first jump went without issue, and soon Eric had set three of the four sticks of dynamite into position at what he hoped was the weakest point. Tucking the remaining explosive into his waistband, he took a step back and jumped to the last stone. Unlike the others, this rock moved as he landed.

The sudden addition of his weight affected the ballast of the stone and from above Eric heard the shrill scream of pain from the Iceman above. Feeling the rock shudder beneath him, he moved with haste to wedge the dynamite in place.

'I'll only have one chance at this.' Eric hollered across the cavern. 'When I light this, I must be quick.'

Lighting the long fuse, Eric waited for the cord to spark and then moved. Launching himself back to the previous rock, he cast a glance back as he dropped to his knees and fought to light the shorter cord on the next explosive. Not wasting a moment, he leapt to the third and repeated the lighting until he was back on the last rock.

Each length of cord had been shorter than the preceding one in the hope it would afford him enough time to get to safety. Lighting the final fuse, Eric didn't dare look at the cord on the furthest explosive and instead dropped to the rope and slid back down to the safety of the ground.

'Move!' He hollered as he crashed to the floor.

Both men ran towards the staircase as the first rock exploded, followed by the remaining three. As they sprinted up the stairs it filled the cavern with the sound of the explosions and chains crashing into the stones as they ran through the carved gulley and channels that had been used to suspend the Iceman in place.

A blood-curdling scream echoed through the air as they reached the top of the stairs and found the Iceman stood in the centre of the vast chamber, his body deformed yet very much alive.

'My lord.' Eric gasped and dropped to his knees.

CHAPTER THIRTY-THREE

LEAVING the rural towns behind, Hazel and Stanley made their way back to London. As they approached the capital, the scarring and damage from the war effort reminded them of the world they lived in. Having spent time in the peace and reasonably safe environment of the East Midlands, the stark contrast to London was not lost on them.

By the time the train had pulled into the station neither of them could believe how quick they had cast aside and forgotten what it was like.

'Maybe we should see our families now we're back.' Hazel suggested as they emerged into the bustling London street.

The thought had crossed Stanley's mind as he had glimpsed the familiar skyline of his neighbourhood in the distance. Knowing the mind-set he had left his father in from their last conversation, he didn't much like the idea of reinvigorating that disagreement.

'You can,' he answered after a long pause. 'I'd rather get this over and done with and not waste time repeating the same arguments with my old man.'

'I take it he's as stubborn as you then?'

'It has been said before, yes.'

Setting the notion aside, they returned to Ealing Abbey in the hope it would bring about a sooner end to their involvement in their curious adventure. After an uneventful bus journey they once again found themselves at the steps of Ealing Abbey looking up and the damaged roof against the gloomy grey sky.

'We've been hoping you'd be back soon.' Kelly's familiar voice announced as he walked along the pavement towards them.

'How d'you know we'd be here?' Stanley asked as the Inspector sauntered towards them.

'I didn't, I was just out getting food.' Kelly grinned as he took a bit from a packed roll in his hand. 'Perfect timing, shall we?'

Accepting his invitation, Kelly led them around the outside of the church and into a small secluded courtyard at the rear of the annex..

'They've returned.' Kelly announced, the excitement clear in his voice although he did his best to hide it.

'Excellent,' the old Friar looked up and placed the newspaper he had been reading on the bench at his side. 'I trust you succeeded?'

'You could say that.' Stanley smiled. 'It wasn't the easiest thing.'

'I would expect not.' The Friar sniggered. 'Alessandro was renowned for pushing the limits, both of himself and those around him.'

'He certainly did that.' Hazel retorted, grabbing Stanley's

bandaged hand and holding it for all to see. 'We're lucky that both of us stand here, it could easily have been a different story.'

The joviality evaporated with her words as her stern look remained focussed on the old Friar. Taking a moment to acknowledge the severity of Hazel's tone, the old man offered an apologetic nod and invited them to join him on the pews.

'Did you find anything more about who stole the pages in the first place?' Stanley quizzed as he sat.

'Less than I would have liked, but more than I had hoped.'

'I think we've had enough of convoluted answers and riddles.' Hazel interjected. 'Can we just speak plain to one another please?'

'Sorry,' Kelly looked taken aback at Hazel's sternness. 'I found a name amongst some of my informants on the streets that led me to Dorset and the home of a gentleman by the name of Eric Masters.'

'I've never heard of him.' Stanley interrupted.

'I would be surprised if you had Stanley. Masters is a member of the upper class, a businessman whose family has crossed the Brotherhood's before, more than once.'

'Did he have the pages?'

'I believe he has the pages, yes.'

'You believe?'

'When I got to his home it was already empty, guarded by a single member of staff but I could make sense of what he had discovered on the pages. It also means that now, more than ever, we will need to have received the secrets Alessandro buried.'

The conversation shifted to the pair of them and all eyes watched as Hazel removed the two wooden boxes from the bag around her body.

'Wait!' The Friar snapped, his voice echoing around the

empty courtyard. 'Have you opened them?'

'Yes we have.' Hazel snapped.

'May I?'

Holding out his trembling hands, the Friar waited for her to pass him the boxes. Placing the largest box on the seat, the old man inspected the faces of the box until he found what he was looking for. Pressing his index finger against the wood, he inspected his fingertip and held it out for his audience to see.

'Your blood I presume, Stanley?'

For a moment Stanley wasn't sure what the Friar was implying. It had been Hazel who had retrieved the box, but then he remembered the cut on his hand and how she had bandaged it with a tether of fabric before retrieving it. 'It must be.' He answered. 'It was Hazel who got it though, I expect she would have had my blood on it when she bandaged my hand.'

'Fortunate indeed.'

'Fortunate?' Hazel huffed. 'it poisoned Stanley, he almost died retrieving this box. Had it not been for him, neither of us would be sat here now.'

'That explains your mood.' Kelly scoffed. 'It's understandable but remember, this would never be easy.'

'But to the box.' The Friar continued, defusing the rising tension between Kelly and Hazel. 'Each box crafted by Alessandro is protected by ancient magic and can only be opened with the blood of an innocent with no desire to seek the creature with dark intent.'

'Is that why they murdered that man in the cemetery?' Stanley pressed.

'I believe that to be the case. 'Kelly nodded. 'Colin was an unfortunate victim of his own success it would seem.'

'What would have happened had I not got Stanley's blood on it?'

'Then it would never have opened. There are spells and magic beyond reason and comprehension that protect these things. Ancient magic the likes of which have been forgotten for centuries.'

Easing the lid open the Friar's eyes went wide as he admired the craftsmanship of the wooden chalice. Placing the box down, he opened the smaller of the two and removed one vial to inspect it in the dull light.

'What are they?' Hazel pressed as she watched the old man inspecting the glass vial. It was Kelly who offered an answer.

'The creature is bound to immortality from the sacrifice he made to the Forest Goddess, a deity of his time.' Kelly explained but Stanley's scoff interrupted him.

'Oh, come on. Gods giving men power, what's that all about? I mean, we know that God is just-' remembering his surroundings Stanley cut himself short and blushed. 'Know what?

'Well, you know,' Stanley fought for an answer.

'I think Stanley means he's sorry?' Hazel cast him a questioning glance and immediately he dropped his gaze to the box on the pew.

'I didn't mean anything by it, I just always struggled with religion.'

'Don't we all.' The Friar chuckled. 'Care to continue Brother?' Grateful for the redirection, Stanley returned his attention to Kelly.

'There is no way that, Alessandro could find, to reverse the dark curse that extends his life and empowers him. Instead, Alessandro sought the dark magic that could instead bind the Iceman in himself, a prisoner in his own body for all eternity.'

'The Iceman was bound in chains and buried to be forgotten from an inescapable prison. That tomb would be the cursed creature's resting place, not of isolation but hibernation. Where the creature would lie in wait until someone could release him from his bonds.'

'That's what this Eric Masters wants to do then?' Stanley pressed, engrossed in the account.

'The pages that were stolen show the Iceman's resting place and yes, Masters would seek to free the creature and unleash his untold power upon the world.'

'Thousands of years locked in chains, he will not be happy about it.' Hazel mused as she too hung on their every word.

'The creature, once freed will be at its weakest having been left to fester since the moment of his capture. It will take time for him to regenerate enough but with each passing moment he will increase in strength and power until he is reborn anew.'

'And these will do what you say? Trap him in his own body?'

'Yes, Alessandro confessed to having never discovered a way to slay the creature. Instead he revised his search for a way to imprison him, this appears to be that method.'

'Earth, air, fire and water,' Kelly continued 'each element alone will have no effect but combined, they will have the needed affect.'

'So, what happens now?' Hazel asked as she felt a splatter of rain from the heavy clouds.

'You have done what we asked of you, we will not ask more of you.'

'Sod that!' Stanley snapped. 'We've come this far, I'm not turning away now.'

'I won't ask that of you.' Kelly argued, looking to the old Friar for support.

'You're not asking.' Hazel corrected. 'We're offering.'

'There is no knowing what you will face. You have seen

the lengths an ally like Alessandro went to, to protect this, I cannot imagine what the creature will unleash towards anyone that threatens him.'

'We could all die.' Kelly finished.

Although the pair had faced death in the Alessandro Test and thrown themselves into a dark underworld of curses and magic, the possibility of certain death was something they had cast aside. Reading the expressions on both Kelly and the Friar's faces, they sensed that the new leg of their journey would be more dangerous than what they had faced until now.

'Sleep on it.' Kelly offered. 'If, in the morning, you still insist on accompanying me, then I will not refuse.'

'Shouldn't we be leaving now?' Stanley pressed.

'Masters has been travelling for two days already, a third will make little difference.'

'I thought you said the Iceman would get more powerful with every minute?'

'Just accept the offer of sleep, please!' Kelly groaned. 'I think I found the most stubborn pair in the whole of London. I appreciate your determination but please, take the time to discuss this and give me your answer in the morning.

Agreeing to Kelly's request, Hazel reached for the two boxes she had handed to the Friar. The old man gave her a curious look as he handed her the two items. Placing them under her arm, she waited for Stanley and they both made their way to the door leading into the church.

As Stanley opened the door, he allowed Hazel first passage into the damaged church and watched as she stepped through the wooden arch. As her foot passed over the threshold Hazel felt a physical force like a wall blocking her path into the church.

'What?' Stanley asked as he watched her stumble at the

threshold.

Pushing forward, Hazel could not cross the threshold into the church no matter how hard she tried. With one hand she tested the air in front of her, expecting to find glass blocking her path, but her hand passed with ease through the open doorway.

'What's going on?' Hazel snapped as she turned to look at the old Friar whose face still displayed the same curious smile.

'Ancient magic and dark curses my dear.' He chuckled. 'The darkness that helped construct these items prohibits them from the house of God.'

'That's not possible.' Hazel argued and once again tried to step through the door to no avail.

'Just because old magic is forgotten, does not mean it no longer exists. If you are to go with Damien, you will see things beyond what you believe is possible.'

'Lay them on the ground and step through the door.' Kelly proffered.

Awash with doubt, Hazel placed the boxes on the ground and was surprised to discover she could now pass through the door into the church. Looking down to the boxes, she watched as Stanley nudged them to the threshold with his toe and once again they could not pass into the deeper parts of the church.

'That is why we needed to speak in the courtyard, open to the air it is neutral ground.' The old Friar moved to pick up the boxes. 'Get rest, Brother Kelly and I will ensure these do not go astray in the meantime.'

Stanley followed Hazel into the church and paused for a moment before turning to face their hosts one last time. 'Don't think about leaving without us.' Stanley warned. 'You have my word.'

CHAPTER THIRTY-FOUR

WITH the scream still echoing around the room, Eric's sudden appearance at the top of the stairs silenced the fearsome Iceman. His skin was mottled and a sickly off-brown colour that clung to the bones where the muscle had long since decayed.

Fresh from the chained restraints Eric watched as the creature tested itself in the open space. Flexing each arm the upturned lip that exposed its top teeth flexed with curiosity. Despite the decay the creature's facial features were identifiable. Although the upper lip had misshapen and flexed into an almost cleft appearance.

Testing the strength of its legs the creature took a handful of tentative steps in Eric's direction as he remained perched on one knee at the top of the stairs.

There was something sickening and eerie about the way the Iceman moved. Aside the fact the creature was in a state of decay and its flesh discoloured there was

something unnatural about its movements.
'Kneel.' Eric hissed to his companion who remained
rooted to the spot looking on in disbelief.

Eric's words passed unheard as his companion stood
watching as the Iceman staggered towards them. The *click*
of its exposed heel bone echoed with every other step until
it had made it across the chasm to stand in front of the
pair.

Although the Iceman was shorter than Eric had
expected, the menace that radiated from the half-decayed
walking corpse was frightening. Despite his best
intentions Eric could not help but stare up at the Iceman.

Feeling the withered eyes staring back Eric tried to
speak but found his words catching in his throat.

Much to his relief the Iceman shifted its attention and
stared across at his companion who remained standing.
Eric's subservient position had somehow transcended
centuries of language and cultural barriers as a mark of
respect. His companion had not expressed the same
respectful position.

Eric watched in horror as the Iceman thrust out an arm
and wrapped its skeletal fingers around his companion's
neck.
'My Lord, he…' Eric was silenced by the terrifying glare
from the Iceman.

Pulling the other man closer Eric once again noted the
Iceman's small stature. That aside, his grip was tight and
unflinching as his fingers squeezed tight around the other
man's throat and neck. Speaking in a long-forgotten
language the creature muttered something as he held the
other man close to his face.

Grateful to not be the focus of his attention, Eric could
not help but feel overcome by the acidic odour emanating
from the decaying flesh. Unsure of what was being said

Eric looked up and watched as the Iceman snapped his companion's neck with a single movement.

The sound of bone cracking turned Eric's stomach, but the creature was not done. With the man's head twisted at an impossible angle the creature lowered its mouth to the other man's neck and pierced the skin with his jagged teeth.

Biting through the skin an arterial spray of crimson blood sprayed out soaking Eric's head and face before the Iceman's mouth stemmed the flow. Drinking from the rough wound on the man's neck the Iceman gulped on the oozing blood.

Releasing his rotten lips from the neck the Iceman allowed Eric's companion's twitching body to crash to the floor. Laid in front of Eric he could still see life in his friend's eyes. Paralysed on the floor the man blinked up, his eyes pleading with Eric who was powerless to offer help.

The Iceman was not finished as he dropped to his haunches beside the twitching body. Placing his hand against the other man's chest Eric watched in horror as the creature thrust his hand down and through the bone and flesh of his paralysed companion's chest.

The life left the other man's eyes as the Iceman ripped his heart from the centre of his chest. The permanent snarl from his deformed lip almost looked pleased as the creature raised the heart to his mouth and bit through the pulsating muscle. Mottled skin now discoloured and stained with blood the Iceman devoured the heart until there was nothing left in his bloodied hands.

Closing his eyes, as if savouring the taste of flesh, the creature took a handful of deep breaths before he returned his attention to Eric.

'Why have you come for me?'

The fact the Iceman now spoke in English astounded Eric as he looked up at the creature gob smacked.

'Speak!' The creature boomed.

'My family,' Eric stammered terrified. 'We have always searched to set you free.'

'Why?' The Iceman's words were slow and laboured, drawn out more than natural as he acquainted himself with his newfound language.

'We learned of what happened to you, the wrongs you faced and sought to set them right.'

'Your language is strange to me,' the Iceman mused as he looked around the cavern. 'His memories tell me of a world I do not recognise, what world is this you release me into?'

'It is nineteen-forty-one, the world differs greatly from what you will remember.' For all his desire to see this moment, Eric felt unprepared in his answers.

'How long have I been,' the Iceman struggled to find the word. 'Buried?'

'Too long.'

'How long?' Once again the coarse voice boomed and echoed around the vast room.

'Five-thousand years.'

Saying it aloud sounded even more ridiculous than Eric had intended, and it took a moment for it to register with the creature. Looking up, Eric dared not speak as he watched the Iceman mulling over a million and one thoughts that now raced through his mind.

'Was he your, friend?' The Iceman asked as he looked down to the body at his feet.

'Yes.' Eric sighed. 'That and more.'

'His sacrifice was necessary,' the creature continued. 'His life gives me understanding of your primitive language and the memories of his life.'

The Iceman looked distracted for a moment as he replayed the torrent of memories he had stolen from the dead man on the floor. Eyelids flickering, he saw a lifetime of events pass in a flurry of images.

'More indeed.' The Iceman smirked and looked down at Eric who despite his resolve felt a flush in his cheeks. 'You come to me to offer me my freedom but at what price?'

'Nothing.' Eric pleaded.

The Iceman stepped towards him and wrapped his fingers around his neck. Lifting Eric from his kneeling position, he could not help but shake with terror as the Iceman raised him until they were face-to-face.

Standing as close as he was to the creature he felt enveloped by the stench of death. Every detail of the deformed face was visible from the upturned curled top lip to the discoloured broken teeth in his mouth. What little hair was left on the skin was withered and greyed, but it was the lifeless cloudy eyes that were Eric's focus.

'What can I offer you in payment for my freedom? What does Eric Masters seek as a reward?'

Eric was once again stunned by the Iceman's knowledge but realised it was nothing more than a stolen memory from his friend.

'I ask for nothing.' Eric stuttered as the Iceman tightened his grip on Eric's throat as a warning. 'I only seek to right the wrongs of your past.'

The Iceman studied Eric, turning his head from side to side as he inspected every aspect of his face. After what felt like an age the Iceman appeared to have made his choice. Pulling Eric closer until their faces were almost touching the Iceman spoke in a hushed voice.

'I can offer you the gift of powers beyond your belief.'

'To what end?'

'Stand by my side, arise a loyal servant and you will see

powers and riches beyond your wildest dreams.'
'I swear my loyalty to you, regardless of power or wealth.
It has been my life's work to release you.'
'Then I give you this payment.'

To Eric's horror, the Iceman pushed Eric's head to one
side and sank his teeth into the side of his neck. The pain
was intense as the creature's jagged teeth pierced his flesh,
but unlike what the Iceman had done to his friend, Eric
did not feel the Iceman drinking in the pulsing blood that
coursed down his neck.

Instead he felt the warm breath of the creature as he
blew onto the exposed wound. What followed next took
the wind from Eric's chest as he felt a burning sensation
ripple beneath his skin, spreading from the wound.
'What have you done to me?' Eric gasped as he coughed a
mouthful of his own blood to the floor.
'Given you the gift of power.' The Iceman declared as he
stepped away from Eric to give him space. 'A new life to
replace your old one.'

As the words left his deformed lips, Eric double over in
agony. The underside of his skin felt ablaze, as if molten
fire burned through his veins. His mind swam as he tried
to comprehend what was happening to his body. In his
chest his heart beat at an impossible pace, feeling as if it
would burst from his chest at any moment.

Rolling onto his back, Eric clutched at his chest as the
feeling of fire spread towards his core.
'Help me.' He pleaded, but the Iceman stood over him and
watched.

To anyone watching it would look as if Eric was dying
an agonising and painful death. His muscles tensed and
bulged beneath the skin as his chest rose and fell at an
impossible pace. Unable to fill his lungs or calm his racing
heart Eric felt the world close in around him. Tears of

blood streamed down his face as he clawed at his own face to release the growing pressure and feeling of fire beneath his skin.

As his skins tore at the flesh of his cheeks he let out a blood-curdling scream before a last spasm raced through his body and he dropped motionless against the ground. Eyes wide, Eric looked up at the ceiling, his body now lifeless and unmoving on the stone floor of the cavern. 'Rise my son, my Torn servant.'

Although Eric no longer drew breath, his eyes moved to look around the cavern with a fresh perspective. Eric was dead, the life in his body consumed by whatever dark magic the Iceman had infected him with and yet he was still present. Sitting up, he felt different. Eric's body was somehow heavier and still he felt the shadow of the burning sensation beneath his skin.

'What am I?' Eric asked, his voice sounding unfamiliar to his own ears.

'You are my servant, sworn to remain by my side as a Torn soul.'

'What does that mean?'

'Your life is now my life, you shall not die unless I wish it so, upon the promise of your loyalty and obedience.'

Eric listened, but the words washed over him as he looked down at his forearm. Beneath the skin something shimmered. Awash with curiosity Eric placed his finger to the skin and pressed to see what was beneath his flesh. To his horror as Eric pressed harder against his arm the skin tore apart enough to reveal the bone and muscle beneath. It was no longer the colour of flesh and bone but laced with a hue of copper.

Recoiling at the sight Eric looked up at the creature who now smiled a crooked and menacing smile at the thing he had created.

CHAPTER THIRTY-FIVE

KELLY had kept his promise, and the pair found him waiting for them the following morning. Still insistent about their continued involvement, Kelly had agreed and allowed them to travel with him. Not that he would ever have confessed it to them, he was grateful for the company and the fact with three of them there would be a higher chance of success.

Not wanting to waste any more time than they had to, the three of them had packed their things and made their way back to the train station. They spent the next fifteen hours in less than ideal conditions, not least of which was in the back of a rumbling aircraft as it carried them above the English Channel.

'How did you get them to do this?' Stanley bellowed over the rumbling engine.

'The Brotherhood has many connections around the world, we consider ourselves to be the silent guardians.'

'That shows.' Hazel quipped as she looked around the empty cargo aircraft. 'How are we going to get into an occupied country?'

Looking out of the narrow window in the plane, Stanley glimpsed the French coastline as the clouds broke beneath them. In an instant he felt himself dragged back to the battlefield in his mind and felt his heart rate increase.

Staring down, it was impossible to make out any details on the ground below, but he knew they were there. Brothers and friends he had made in the army, fighting to repel an entire regime from conquering Europe. A sudden wave of guilt washed over him as he stared at the ground. There they were fighting and here he was gallivanting around the world in search of monsters and curses.

'What's wrong?' Hazel asked, having noticed his sudden sullen silence.

'It's nothing.'

'Come on Stanley, we've come this far together, I know when something's wrong.'

'Down there.' He huffed over the vibrations of the propeller engines. 'I should be down there, not messing around chasing monsters and stories.'

'Do you think the battle down there is more important than the one you are about to face?' Kelly asked from the opposite side of the hold.

'I didn't mean that,' Stanley countered in haste. 'I just mean that at least down there I knew what the enemy was and what I was fighting for, and...'

'And what?' Kelly pressed.

'And at least people recognise the fight. If I told people about this they'd laugh at me and think I was mad.'

'So war is what, something to boast about?'

'No, but-'

'But nothing!' Kelly was remarkably calm as he shuffled

over to sit by Stanley's side. 'Battles such as those on the ground down there are mankind's making. Conflicts built on opposing sides and their needs for power. What we move towards now is a battle against darkness where mankind's existence hangs in the balance.'

'It's just hard to feel right when I know my friends are down there fighting for our freedom.'

'And we will fight for theirs.' Kelly soothed. 'It may not feel it now, to either of you, but this is a far more dangerous journey with consequences that make the battle between us and the German's seem insignificant.'

'I know you're right.'

Stanley wanted to be left alone. Although he understood Kelly's point of view, it did not ease the guilt he felt. Standing up, he moved to the rear of the plane and sat himself against a broken crate near to the rear door. As Hazel was about to move to join him, Kelly grabbed her wrist to stop her.

'Leave him be.'

'He needs a friend.' Hazel argued and tried to pull herself from Kelly's grip

There was no menace in Kelly's words. The look on his face told Hazel he sympathised, and perhaps understood, what was going through Stanley's mind. With reluctance she took her seat back on the vibrating floor and cast a glance towards Stanley who was lost with his head buried in his hands.

'We will never know what he has experienced down there.' Kelly explained, sensing Hazel's worry for Stanley. 'War and conflict force young men to face things they should never have to see. I've seen it in the faces of many men who fought in the Great War, and we will continue to see it long after this war is over.'

'There has to be something we can do to help.'

'Being there and letting them know you're there when they need you to be. I know you have the best intentions but I can tell you from personal experience, right now Stanley needs time to himself.'

'He looks so sad.'

'He is hurting, he will hurt maybe for the rest of his life but those moments are fleeting. Memories will fade, but there will always be something that may trigger a moment of weakness. Right now he needs to face his own demons so he can move on. Leave him be.'

Releasing her wrist, Kelly watched as Hazel looked from him to Stanley and back again. Having faced many people in his career, he had become adept at reading emotions in people's faces. Since they had returned to Ealing the night before, Kelly had sensed a change between the two of them. Even without asking, he knew their friendship had grown into something more. The look in Hazel's eyes at that moment confirmed it to him.

'Where is the pilot going to take us?' Hazel changed the subject as she forced herself not to look at Stanley.

'I have arranged for passage to a remote airfield near to the Austrian border.'

'What about the Nazis? Surely we will be in danger of being caught.'

When Kelly had revealed their destination the added risks had been all too apparent to Hazel and Stanley. Not only would they be crossing a continent consumed with war, they would seek to find a way into an occupied country.

'The airfield is safe enough.'

'Safe enough?'

'The connection to the Brotherhood is well established, we will be afforded passage with a group that fights against the German invasion.'

'I thought you remained impartial in the wars of men?' Hazel pressed, amusing herself at Kelly's reaction as he stammered to argue the point. 'Sorry, I didn't mean to goad you, I understand why you would help.'
'It is the right thing to do, even though our Order exists to protect humanity from the darkness, sometimes that darkness can be manmade.'

As the journey continued Stanley remained isolated on his own while Kelly and Hazel discussed their plans upon arriving at the airfield. Kelly explained that a telegram had been sent and arrangements made for them to be transported from the airfield as close as possible to the Ötztal mountain range where the tomb of the Iceman was hidden.

Although the exact location remained a mystery to Kelly, the communications from his brothers in Austria had mentioned a pair of Englishmen venturing into the mountains. Under the watchful eyes of them, they believed they knew the rough location where the pair had been last seen.

It had surprised Hazel the reach that the Benedictine Brotherhood had and how well they had remained hidden. Not less than a week ago she had never even heard of their Order and yet now, because of them, they had arranged safe passage into another country having unearthed hidden crypts and buried secrets. Aside from the obvious feeling of admiration, Hazel also felt a level of concern that there was so much secrecy and hidden things that she did not know about.

With all of her questions answered, Hazel was grateful to feel the aircraft begin its descent. Having never flown before, it surprised her how comfortable she felt, but the longer they remained in the air, the stronger the feeling of nausea grew in her stomach. As the pilot banked the aircraft around to land, she longed to feel solid ground beneath her feet again.

Hazel gripped onto the cargo straps as the plane landed on the uneven runway. Jostled from side-to-side, her fingers ached as she gripped the webbing between her fingers. Hearing the engines die down her brow was damp with sweat and her eyes were wide as the plane came to a slow stop.

'You can let go now.' Kelly chuckled, no longer having to shout over the strange silence that filled the hold.

Embarrassed, Hazel massaged her hands once she had released the straps. A sudden gust of wind whipped through the cargo hold as the rear door was opened and two people stepped inside. For a moment Hazel froze, sensing the sudden change in Kelly's appearance as both the new arrival's faces were covered and their clothes looked military in design.

'Damien Kelly?' A woman's voice asked from beneath the head-covering.

'Who's asking?' Kelly replied, moving his hand to a knife that was sheathed at the small of his back.

'My name is Victoria, and this is Hans.' The woman removed the covering from her face and offered him a welcoming smile. 'We've been sent to escort you to the mountains and help you find the Iceman.'

Victoria wore her blonde hair in a tight plat and was in her early forties. Hans was however much older and sported a thick grey beard. He eyed Stanley with suspicion as he looked at each of them before speaking.

'I know these mountains,' he declared in broken English, his Austrian accent making it difficult to understand everything. 'I know you are not ready for them, dressed like that you will last half a day at most.'

'What Hans is trying to say is that we have clothes for you

all.' Victoria moved to stand in front of Kelly, whose hand remained at his back. 'May the dragon never be my overlord.'
'Let the devil not be my leader.'

Hazel's brow furrowed at the strange exchange of words but say the tension release from Kelly as he removed his hand from the handle of the knife. Whatever the curious exchange had meant had satisfied Kelly's suspicion about the two new arrivals. Hazel watched as Kelly moved to stand in front of Hans.

Hans dwarfed Kelly. He looked every inch a man of the mountains from his rugged and weathered skin to his untameable beard. As Kelly opened the top of his shirt to reveal the Benedictine medal tattooed to his chest, Hans returned the gesture by removing a glove and rolling up his sleeve.

The first thing that caught Hazel's attention was the fact Hand was missing two fingers on his left hand. Catching her staring, Hans offered a smile as he exposed the same tattoo on his inner forearm.
'Frostbite.' He grinned as he wiggled his remaining three fingers. 'I have spares, no worry for two missing.'

The two men covered their identifying tattoos, and they all collected their things to leave the plane. Stanley had observed the exchange from his position near the door and by the time they were ready to leave, he was back to his normal self and offered Hazel a look of thanks as he squeezed her hand.
'Feeling better?' She hushed as they moved towards the open door.
'A little.' Stanley grinned.

CHAPTER THIRTY-SIX

USHERED from the plane, Kelly, Stanley and Hazel moved across the vast expanse as a flurry of snow tumbled from the heavy clouds. The air was cold and Hans had been right as all three of them felt the stinging chill against their skin.

'Ten minutes and we will be there.' Victoria announced as they hurried over a fence at the airfield's perimeter. 'We will get you some more appropriate clothes.'

True to her word, they arrived at an isolated cabin nestled in a deep valley. Despite the falling snow, they could make out enough of the surrounding mountains to see how dwarfed the log cabin was. Pushing the door open they were all grateful for the warmth that washed over them from the open fire that heated the cabin.

'We will rest here,' Victoria announced as she removed her jacket and gloves. 'The weather is not on our side and there is no point walking the mountains in the dark.'

'The weather is not normally this way.' Hans complained as he too removed his outdoor clothing.

Seeing the evening pass, Hans and Victoria prepared a meal for their guests and as the snowstorm raged outside, they made preparations for their venture into the mountains the following morning. Glad to be inside, the storm raged outside as the wind rocked the cabin.
'I've not seen a storm like this for many years,' Hans declared as he looked out of the window watching the whipping wind and snow. 'The last time left its mark on me.'

They watched as Hans stared out at the raging storm and massaged the stumps where his missing fingers had once been. The older man's declaration brought a sombre atmosphere as the others remained silent. After a few tense moments, Hazel spoke to break the silence.
'Inspector Kelly said you might know where we need to look?'
'Inspector?' Victoria quizzed, looking across at Kelly.
'Yes, I work for the Metropolitan Police as a detective.'
'Are you not a Brother of the order?' Hans asked as he closed the curtains, blocking out the views of the storm.
'I am both an officer and a Brother. My role allows me to hide in plain sight and offer protection to some of our hidden secrets.'

The rest of the evening passed with Hazel and Stanley sat back listening to the discussions between Hans, Victoria and Kelly. Between them they discussed the likely location of the Iceman's tomb and the last time the two Englishmen they had mentioned were seen. They learned, from Hans' account, that what Kelly believed to be Eric Masters and whoever he travelled with had ventured high into the mountains a day earlier.

As tiredness crept in Stanley felt Hazel resting her head

against his shoulder. Looking down at her, she caught him looking, and he blushed.

'We should get some sleep.' She yawned and nestled her head in his lap. 'I think tomorrow will be difficult.'

It was not long before her breathing had become heavy and she had fallen into a light sleep. Placing his hand on her shoulder, Stanley felt his own eyes going heavy as he watched Hans pour a glass of something and hand it to Kelly.

'Care for one boy?' He boomed across to Stanley, who shook his head.

Sleep came, but Stanley's dreams were filled as always with memories and recollections of the war. By the time he was woken in the morning by Hans' gentle rocking, he had managed through another troubled night's sleep. Opening his eyes, it surprised him to see Hazel already up and about.

'The storm has lessened, but it is still unwise to venture into the mountains.' Hans declared as he offered Stanley a hand to stand up.

'We can't risk waiting for it to pass.' Kelly answered from across the cabin. 'Who knows what Eric Masters has already done, he is at least a day ahead of us.'

'If we are to venture out I suggest we eat and prepare.'

They shared a hearty breakfast of hot oats and Victoria presented each of them a selection of traditional cold-weather clothes. By the time they were ready to leave they were all dressed in similar clothing and each had their face covered to protect them from the biting wind.

Stepping out into the storm, there was even less to see than when they had arrived. The heavy clouds lumbered around the slopes of the surrounding mountains and the frenzy of snow whipped around them obscuring any view they had beyond a short distance in front of them.

'We should not go out in this.' Hans protested after an hour of trudging through the snow with little sign of progress.

'We have to continue,' Kelly argued as he moved to Hans' side. 'You said yourself the storm isn't as it should be, I believe it's because they have found the Iceman.'

The sombre declaration silenced any of Hans' further protests and against his better judgement Hans continued to lead them onwards and upwards.

Unfamiliar and unprepared for the arduous alpine trek, Stanley and Hazel soon lagged behind the three more agile members of the group. Fighting through the deep covering of snow, the incline took its toll on their calves as they trudged onwards and upwards in silence.

'Your friends are struggling.' Victoria sighed after another hour of trekking had passed. 'We should offer them rest.'

The snow had lessened and the occasional break in the clouds gave them a brief view of a jagged peak somewhere ahead of them.

'If we stop, we risk not moving again.' Hans argued as they all looked back at Stanley and Hazel.

'We should give them something, they're doing their best.'

'That may not be enough.' Hans snarled and continued on the path up the mountain.

Unaware of the disagreement between Kelly and their guides, Hazel caught her breath as Kelly handed her a bottle of water. Fighting to unscrew the lid with her gloved hands, she took a mouthful of what she had thought was water. As the alcohol burned her throat, she coughed and spluttered.

'It'll keep you warm.' Kelly chuckled as he lowered his buff and took a swig for himself. 'Stanley?'

Grateful for the offer, Stanley took the bottle and placed it to his lips.

'How much longer?' Hazel coughed as she replaced the fabric over her face. 'It feels like we've been walking forever.'

'Normally you would be absorbed in the beauty that surrounds you.' Victoria interrupted. 'But this storm has blocked everything from us.'

'This storm is not natural.' Hans added as he returned to the group. 'If we continue along this path much further, I fear it will lead to your deaths.'

'Take them back.' Kelly interrupted, the concern clear in his voice. 'This isn't your fight and I will not see you follow me in this storm, I will not be responsible for your deaths.'

'No!' Stanley barked above the howling wind. 'We're not going back, we are in this together.'

'You've already helped enough. Now give me the bag and go back with Victoria.'

Kelly held out his hand but neither Stanley nor Hazel made a move to hand him the satchel. Walking at a distance behind them they had expected this conversation and decided long before that they would not turn back and leave the group. Standing defiantly in the middle of the raging storm, they both shook their heads in defiance.

'You are a pair of fools!' Kelly groaned and turned to look at Hans. 'How much longer Hans?'

'Without this storm we would be there by now, with this storm I am reading the mountains with great difficulty. We have made terrible progress but another hour, maybe two and we should be there.'

'We can last that long.' Hazel declared and pushed past Kelly.

Hot on her heels, Kelly stopped Stanley and spoke to him in private as Hans and Victoria started off either side of Hazel.

'I appreciate what you're doing, Stanley. But if it comes to it, you must take her back, even if she protests.'

'Do you think I could make her listen to me?' Stanley scoffed.

'Promise me.' Kelly snapped, the joviality of Stanley's remark shot down with his harsh tone. 'I want you to promise me.'

'I promise.'

With nothing more to say, they set off behind the others and trudged further up the mountain. With Hans at the head of the troop, they trusted his guidance as the surrounding landscape remained nothing more than a whitewash of whipping snow.

The dangers that surrounded them was lost on all but Hans and Victoria, who knew all too well how easy it would be to slip into a crevasse or towards the unstable layers of snow beneath them. Even in the best of weathers a trek into the mountains was fraught with danger, but in the storm's blindness they risked death with every step.

Hans' unease was palpable in the air and as the time rolled on nobody dared to speak. Finding themselves approaching a jagged outcrop of rocks, Hans guided them into the shelter of a narrow fissure and took advantage of the quiet of the small opening. Sheltered from the wind, he removed his face covering and waited for the others to do the same.

Cramped within the confines of the rocks, Hans saw the sullen faces looking at him with expectation. Hazel's cheeks were red raw and her lips shivered with the cold. Stanley looked the same, and yet their resolve was obvious in their eyes. He admired their tenacity but could not shake the lingering fear that this would be too much for them.

'Where are we, Hans?' Kelly asked as he rubbed his

gloved hands together for warmth.

'These rocks mark a fork in the path between the mountains, I was hoping we would find them sooner than we have.'

'Where were the Englishmen last seen compared to where we are?' Kelly pressed.

'Half a mile up the mountain.' Hans replied. 'We shelter here, no arguments, and give time for the storm to lift.'

'I don't think it's going anywhere.' Stanley groaned as he found space to sit on the floor within the small fissure.

'That may be the case but these mountains are my home, I know when they are to be listened to and the winds tell me it is best to wait.'

Stanley was silenced from further protest by the grizzly mans glare. Huddled together in the narrow confines of the rocky fissure, they waited out the storm in the hope it would ease. Although Hans knew it was best to keep moving, there was something he had not told the group that was more the reason for him choosing to shelter them within the fissure.

As he had first caught sight of the rocks in the distance he had seen something else in the storm. The figure of a man had been stalking them since they had left the cabin. At first he had not been sure, dismissing the uneasy feeling as wariness at the dangers, but the longer they walked the more he had sensed eyes upon them.

When he had seen the rocks he had seen the man standing in the snow a distance from the fissure. As they reached them he had also noticed a bloodied handprint on the face of the stone. The blood was fresh, not yet frozen by the chilled air. They were not alone and something told him the shadowy spectre he had seen in the snow was not an omen of fortune but one of impending doom.

Keeping his concerns to himself, Hans moved to the

mouth of the fissure and looked out into the storm.

CHAPTER THIRTY-SEVEN

HANS remained at the mouth of the fissure, staring out as the others huddled together for warmth. Unnerved by what he had glimpsed within the storm, his eyes kept drifting back to the handprint of blood on the rock in front of him. There was something unnatural about the smeared blood and although it was not frozen, the blood was cold to the touch.

'I think we need to move.' Victoria huffed as she blew into her gloved hands for warmth. 'We will not get anything but colder if we stay here, Hans.'

Hans knew they were right but felt reluctant to move. Having shared nothing with the group, he knew how odd his sudden wariness would seem. Turning to face the group, he was about to speak when a look of pure terror appeared on Victoria's face.

The moment he had turned away from the whipping snow to look at the group, Eric Masters stepped around the edge of the rock and into the mouth of the tunnel. In any normal circumstances Victoria would have rushed to Eric's aid, concerned he was a lost mountaineer, but that was not the case.

Painted in the dim light, Victoria registered Eric's face and the clawed tethers of skin that hung from his cheeks. Even with the limited light, the interlaced copper beneath his skin shimmered. Dried blood stained his clothes around the top part of his shirt, and Eric's appearance was a confusing and terrifying sight.

'Hans!' Victoria shrieked, but it was too late.

As the larger man turned around, sensing Victoria's gaze having settled behind him, Eric attacked. Dragging his hand through the air, fingers held like a claw, he dragged his nails across the bearded old man's neck. Arterial spray splashed across the stone and Victoria's face as Hans' lifeless body dropped like a stone to the snow.

Frozen in position, they all looked on in horror as Eric grabbed Han's clothing and dragged him out of the fissure like a hunter claiming its prey. In a matter of seconds there was nothing but a trail of blood in the snow leading back out into the storm.

'What was that?' Stanley gasped as he looked around the group.

'I have no idea!' Kelly replied, still dumbstruck by what he had seen.

Victoria's head swam as she looked at the trail of blood staining the snow. For a moment she stared in disbelief, somehow expecting Hans to stagger back into the fissure, but as the moments passed her hope of that faded. Registering nothing of the surrounding conversation she took a handful of tentative steps to where Hans had stood and dropped to her knees. Fingering the snow, she clawed at the ground in shock.

'Victoria,' Kelly tried to grab her attention. 'Victoria, it could come back, get away from there. Hans is gone.'

The mention of Hans' name snatched her back as she turned to look at Kelly. The look on her face changed from shock to anger and instead of retreating from her vulnerable position, she turned and stalked back out into the storm.

'Where are you going?' Hazel gasped, but in an instant the storm swallowed Victoria.

'What do we do?' Stanley stammered as he looked at Kelly.

'We follow her.'

It was not the answer either of them had wanted to hear, but it was not a surprise. Wrapping the fabric back around their faces, they stepped back out of the fissure and searched around for any sign of Victoria.

Despite the buffeting wind and constant flurry of powdery snow, the path Eric had taken Hans was identifiable. It stained the brilliant white snow with blood stretching off away from the rocks. As they followed the trail Victoria's footprints had already been reclaimed by the falling snow.

The trail of blood in the snow lessened, and the storm had swallowed any sight of their previous shelter. Following the fading blood, the three of them huddled together and made slow progress until a shape caught their attention on the ground ahead of them.

Increasing their pace, it was Hazel who reached the motionless figure laid in the snow. A pool of fresh blood had spread beneath the figure's head and as she rolled it over Hazel recoiled at what she found.

Victoria lay shivering, her breaths short and ragged as her face was a mess of cuts and fresh wounds stretching from her scalp to her chin. In a state of shock her hands held her injured face as she lay in the snow.

'Try and lift her up with me.' Kelly barked at Stanley and between them they hooked her between them and continued on.

Victoria's body was limp and difficult to support as they sank deeper in the soft snow. Barely able to make out of the blood now, they blundered through the storm until the landscape changed in an instant.

Moving at the head of the group, Hazel stumbled and fell to the floor as her foot collided with a piece of stone part-buried beneath the snow. Landing on the floor, it knocked the wind from her. Releasing his support on Victoria, Stanley hurried to Hazel's side as the break in the storm gave them a view into the open mouth of a cave in the mountain's side.

Unbeknownst to the four of them this was the same entrance to the Iceman's tomb that Eric had looked at. Whereas before the solid slab of rock had blocked entry into the cave, it now stood open. A wide maw leading into the mountain with the heavy slab laid on the snow pushed out from the inside.

'Look, there.' Stanley yelled above the howling wind.

A smear of fresh blood was identifiable on the pale rock and told them whatever had taken Hans had come through this way. Moving back to help Kelly, they stepped out of the storm and into the entrance to the cave.

'Put me down.' Victoria hissed, her voice distorted with pain. 'Leave me here.'

'No.' Hazel protested as she moved to help tend Victoria's wounds. 'We will not leave you here, that thing could come back for you.'

'Just go, do what you have to.' Victoria snatched the bandage from Hazel and pressed it to her face. 'I'm as good as dead anyway.'

The declaration hit Hazel like a tonne of bricks, and she moved to argue with the injured woman when a sickening sound echoed from deep within the cave.

It was like nothing any of them had heard before and chilled each of them to the core. The sound was something akin to a blood-curdling shriek and set all of them on edge. As the scream reached its crescendo, the echo carried for a few seconds before it faded away to be replaced by the wind buffeting the mouth of the cave.

'The Iceman!' Kelly declared, his face drained of colour and eyes wide.

'What do we do now?' Stanley pressed as he moved to join Kelly and look along the length of the dark tunnel ahead of them.

'We finish this.' Kelly declared with grim determination and pulled the rucksack from his back. 'We must find a way to get him to swallow the combined ingredients.'

'Why?'

'Because the only way they can have their effect is if it touches his dead heart.' Kelly's reply was matter of fact.

'How do you suggest we do that?' Stanley pressed as Hazel moved to join them.

'You will find a way.' Kelly replied as he searched through the rucksack.

'And what will you do?' Hazel interrupted, sensing Kelly's intentions.

'I will provide you the chance to succeed, I will distract the creature long enough to give you time.'

Not waiting to hear the expected protests from his two companions, Kelly removed a pair of pistols from the bag and held one in each hand.

'Are they likely to do anything?' Hazel asked as Kelly checked the magazines in the weapons.

'I doubt it but we have to do something,' Kelly sighed. 'I

have to try. Take what you want from in there and find us a way to end this.'

Hazel and Stanley rummaged through the rucksack and divvied the remaining weapons between them. Stanley threw a bandolier of shotgun rounds over his head and racked as many rounds as he could into the Winchester shotgun. Hazel meanwhile had removed a revolver and fumbled with the various clips and knurling to check the rounds in the chamber.

'I've never used one of these.' She complained as Stanley watched her struggle.

'Here,' Stanley took the revolver and checked the seated rounds. 'Only use it if you have to, there's only six rounds, anyway. You focus on the chalice and ingredients, we will sort the rest.'

Hazel was about to protest as Stanley thrust the revolver back into her hands. Before she could speak he moved to her and kissed her on the lips. Stunned by the sudden courage and affection, Hazel embraced the moment and wrapped her arms around Stanley.

'I may never get to say this again,' he sighed as they released from their embrace. 'These past few days have been the worst of my life, but you've made everything worthwhile, I think-'

Hazel silenced him with a finger to his lip and smiled. 'Not here, not now. Save that last part for when we're done.'

Allowing them the tender moment, knowing it could be their last, Kelly interrupted them with a subtle cough. Sensing the meaning in the interruption, Hazel kissed Stanley one last time before the three of them turned their attention to the tunnel and what lay ahead of them.

Creeping in single file, they explored along the length of tunnel until a flicker of light appeared ahead of them.

Losing what light they had from the mouth of the tunnel, the only light now came from the flickering light at the end of the tunnel. As they neared the source, a second scream echoed through the air, once again sending the hairs on the back of their necks standing on end.

A little short of the tunnel's end, Kelly dropped low and signalled for the two of them to stop. Moving with caution so as not to reveal their position, the three of them crept to the opening in the tunnel and looked down into the vast cavern where the Iceman had been suspended in chains not days before.

The restraints now hung useless and swaying from their anchor points in the ceiling, but it was the sight in the room's centre that demanded their attention. Crouched over the remains of Hans' body was a creature none of them could have imagined. The Iceman, still in his state of partial decay, was hunched over the body tearing flesh from bone as he devoured Hans' remains.

The stench of rotting flesh and decay was heavy in the air, and Stanley fought to quell the sick that threatened to rise from his stomach. They looked on in horror and disbelief as the Iceman tore Hans' head from his shoulders and rose from the ground. As blood dripped from the tattered flesh around Hans' neck, the Iceman turned around allowing Stanley, Hazel and Kelly their first proper view of him.

The distorted lip, discoloured skin pulled tight against the sinew and bone beneath almost stole their breath. Had it not been for the fact they were seeing this with their own eyes, they would never have believed it. The Iceman was, for all intents and purposes, a walking undead corpse of rotten flesh that now moved awkwardly away from the decapitated corpse on the ground.

Still holding the head in his crooked hand, the Iceman

paused and looked up to where the three of them were hidden. Ducking down out of sight, all three of them held their breath as the eerie silence was filled with the sound of the Iceman *sniffing* the air.

'Do not hide in the shadows.' The Iceman's distorted and chilling voice declared. 'Stand before me so I can see what fools come to face me.'

Kelly looked to Hazel and Stanley while placing his finger to his lip to silence them. Before they could protest Kelly rose to his feet and stepped through onto the ledge overlooking the cavernous room below.

'Just the one fool I'm afraid.' Kelly declared with false bravado.

'Who and what might you be who thinks he can stand before me and offer resistance at my resurrection?' The Iceman's words were filled with mockery.

'My name is Damien Kelly of the Secret Order of the Benedictine Brotherhood, God has charged me to protect mankind from the Dark Curses that plague the shadows of which you are one.'

'You are a fool.' The Iceman scoffed as he dropped Hans' severed head to the floor. 'You face me as a mere mortal?'

'I face you as a Brother of God, sworn to protect humanity from the likes of you.'

'You are not worth my attention.'

Taking his cue from the Iceman's words, Eric launched at Kelly from the shadows.

CHAPTER THIRTY-EIGHT

ERIC'S movement caught Kelly's peripheral vision, and he turned in time to avoid a full blindside attack. Having been concealed in the shadows, Eric had waited for his master to give him word to attack. Pressed against the wall, he saw Kelly emerge from the tunnel and waited to pounce.

Sensing he had the upper hand Eric launched at Kelly but the man turned at the last minute. Still colliding with him, it was not enough to send Kelly tumbling over the edge of the platform. Instead, he was sent crashing to the floor, landing at the top of a set of stone steps that stretched down to the cavern's floor below.

Still concealed within the shadows, Stanley and Hazel watched in horror as Eric launched a second attack at Kelly. This time there was little in the way of movement and Kelly had to take the brunt of the attack full force as Eric threw himself at him. A single gunshot reverberated around the room as Eric and Kelly tumbled head over heels down the length of the stairs until they crashed onto the solid floor below.

Both pistols tumbled from Kelly's hands as he smashed into the floor, cracking his head. Stars danced in his vision as he struggled to locate the guns as Eric rose to his feet. As sickening as it was to see, Kelly watched as Eric's right arm hung limp by his side, having dislocated from his shoulder and was now facing the wrong direction.

Taking a step towards Kelly, the curious movement of his limp arm stopped Eric in his tracks. Taking hold of the injured arm, he tugged it down and rotated it in a swift and sickening motion. With a loud *crunch,* the bone returned into the socket and he returned his attention to Kelly.

The momentary delay had been enough for Kelly to wrap the grip of the nearest pistol in his hand and pull the gun up on aim. Firing a second shot, he watched with dismay as the round slammed into Eric's chest and did nothing to stop the man's relentless drive towards him.

Firing another round, Eric saw this one ricochet off Eric's injured cheeks as it collided with the strange mesh of copper exposed beneath his skin. Not knowing what to do, Kelly dropped the gun and propelled himself up to meet Eric head on.

The two men crashed into one another and fought. Their attacks and blocks moved them towards the room's centre as the Iceman watched from beside the enormous burning bowl of liquid that helped paint the room in the flickering light. Amused by the desperate attempts to hold back the attacks of his Torn servant, the Iceman grinned as Kelly's attempts were easily cast aside.

Occupied by the furious battle between Kelly and the Torn Eric, the Iceman did not see Stanley and Hazel creep through the tunnel entrance. Chancing a glance to the ground, they watched from their vantage point as Eric pushed Kelly back towards the burning pool of fire and the watching Iceman.

'What do we do?' Hazel hushed as they looked around for an alternative path down to the lower level of the chasm.

Using the stairs, they knew it would bring them into the eye-line of the Iceman. Looking around, they fixed their attention on a narrow ledge that fed around the width of the room. Across from them, on the far wall, they could see a pile of crumbled rocks resting against the wall that would offer them the chance to sneak around the Iceman out of his line of sight.

'We can climb around to that pile of rocks.' Stanley suggested as they scanned the ledge. 'But once we are there, I have no idea.'

'We need him to drink the mixture.' Hazel said as she moved to test the strength of the narrow ledge.

'Just how do you suppose we do that? Somehow I think a five-thousand year old monster might be suspicious if we walk up and offer him a drink!' Stanley failed in hiding the sarcasm in his voice.

'We will think of something.' Hazel hissed as she pressed her foot on the ledge.

The narrow rock took Hazel's weight, and she started her shimmy around towards the pile of rocks that rested against the far wall. Careful to keep her back pressed to the wall, she faced out towards the main room and watched the furious fight beneath then as she moved.

Shrouded by the deep shadows cast by the dancing firelight, Stanley and Hazel made slow progress around the width of the room. All eyes in the room below were focussed on the fight between Eric and Kelly.

Eric sensed where they were but could not see them,

instead his focus remained on Eric who once again thrust out and sent him crashing to the floor. Kelly's body groaned from the onslaught and he caught sight of the Iceman's devilish upturned lip as he watched from beside the fire.

Leaping into the air Eric landed on all fours straddling Kelly, pinning him into place on the floor. Face-to-face Kelly saw the damage on Eric's face and the strange meshed copper exposed through the jagged wounds across his cheeks.

'What's happened to you?' Kelly gasped as he threw a flurry of punches up towards Eric.

Eric's eyes were lifeless. Although he acted alive, being this close Kelly could see there was no life behind them. As Eric, enraged with frustration, pinned him to the floor he appeared more animal than man. Gnashing his teeth together it took all of Kelly's might to keep the frenzied man from crushing his neck between his crunching teeth.

'I have created him in my own image.' The Iceman mocked in answer to Kelly's question. 'It is in my power to gift those that would serve me.'

'What is he?' Kelly heaved as he rolled Eric from on top of him and scurried away.

Looking around for one of his discarded weapons, the barrel of a pistol caught the light and he sprinted towards it.

'He has become my Torn, a soldier by my side, impervious to your meagre weapons.'

Rolling across the uneven floor, Kelly snatched up the pistol and once again opened fire at Eric. Each of the rounds found their mark but made no effect on his movement as Eric once again barrelled towards him.

Prepared for the attack Kelly snatched the sheathed dagger from the small of his back and timed his attack for the right moment. As Eric was about to launch himself at him, Kelly sliced the blade diagonally through the air and felt resistance as the blade cut through Eric's clothes and scraped across his chest.

Recoiling from the surprise attack, Eric tumbled to the floor and clawed at the jagged gash across his chest. Peeling the tattered fabric from his torso, Kelly once again saw the same mesh pattern of copper beneath Eric's skin. As he watched Eric's curious exploration of the fresh wound, Kelly stole the time to see what it was beneath his skin.

Even keeping his distance it looked as if he had grown a fine weave of shimmering metal beneath his skin, making him impervious to every attack Kelly had thrown at him so far. Satisfied the injury had done nothing to him other than break through the dead flesh on his chest, Eric returned his gaze to Kelly.

'Stop.' The Iceman commanded and Eric froze in position, ready to strike.

Still gripping dagger in one hand and the pistol in the other, Kelly watched as the Iceman stalked his way across the cavernous room.

'I can't let you leave this place.' Kelly declared in defiance.

'Why?' The Iceman pressed as he stopped by Eric's side.

'For what reason do you seek to stop me?'

'It is my duty.'

'A ridiculous notion, born from fear of the unknown.'

'I know what you are.'

'Do you?' The Iceman raised his withered hands and held them out in front of him. 'You have no idea of what I am or what I am capable of.'

To show his power, Kelly watched as the Iceman manifested a ball of swirling ice and snow in the space between his hands. As the swirling ball rotated in his hands the Iceman glared across at Kelly.

'The storm outside is but a demonstration of my power,' launching the ball of rotating ice, Kelly dived to the side to avoid it. 'What makes you think a man of your God can do anything to stop me?'

The frost ball exploded on the ground at Kelly's side, and he covered his face from the shards of ice that exploded from the impact. Overpowered and at a loss, Kelly looked around for anything he could use to help him but saw nothing.

As his gaze wandered along the walls, he caught sight of Hazel and Stanley silhouetted against the wall on the far side of the room behind the Iceman. They had almost reached the pile of rocks, and Kelly knew he needed to buy them all the time he could.

'Witchcraft and gifts of the devil.' Kelly spat as he righted himself and once again stood defiant, keeping the Iceman's attention on him.

'Nothing of the sort.' The Iceman cackled. 'I am a God amongst men.'

With a nonchalant wave of his hand he once again released Eric, who bore down on Kelly with renewed ferocity. As Kelly dodged to the side to avoid Eric's attack he felt himself launched through the air by a violent gust of icy wind. The wind had come from nowhere and propelled him the full length of the room to smash into the solid wall.

Winded and gasping for breath, Kelly crumbled to the floor as the Iceman's manic laugh echoed around him. Eric charged across the room towards him as the Iceman raised his deformed fingers to the sky and in response the roof of the cave came alive with a pulsating electrical storm.

Mesmerised by the dance of electricity from the manifested storm cloud that rolled across the ceiling, Kelly was caught unawares by Eric's attack. Feeling the sting against his skin, he recoiled back as Eric dragged his fingers across Kelly's back, tearing his skin with his nails as he moved.

Yelping in pain, Kelly recoiled away as a bolt of lightning crashed into the rock at the side of his head. Feeling the crackle of electricity against his face his vision was lost for a moment as the bright flash from the lightning blinded him.

Seizing on the advantage Eric dragged Kelly to the ground sending the weapons he held tumbling away. Unable to see what was happening, Kelly thrashed around to keep the crazed Torn Eric from silencing him. Fighting in desperation to stay alive, Kelly's vision returned and he could see Eric's glaring down at him.

Feeling the sting as Eric hooked his fingers around Kelly's shoulder blades, Kelly knew he was done for. Eric was like a predator trapping its prey, there was no escape as his sharp fingers bit into Kelly's skin and all he could do was growl to hold back from screaming in pain. Using Kelly's own body against him, Eric used every ounce of his newfound strength to pull himself inch by inch closer to Kelly.

'I've devoted my life to releasing him from his bonds and he rewards me with power the likes of which you will never understand.' Eric's words were all but snarled through his gritted teeth.

As his head moved to sink his teeth into Kelly's neck a new sound stopped him dead in his tracks. It was a scream of surprise and terror, but not of human lips. Pinned on the floor, Kelly chanced a glance towards the Iceman and saw Stanley had hooked his arms beneath the Iceman's and now held him in some primitive wrestling move with his legs hooked around his body and one arm tight around his neck.

Behind Stanley he brimmed with pride as he saw Hazel move forward with the steaming chalice gripped in both her hands.

CHAPTER THIRTY-NINE

REACHING the pile of rocks, Stanley had descended first as the Iceman had showed his powers. Navigating the pile of stones with great care, he had reached the base and looked up to see Hazel following the same route he had used. Looking around, he kept to the shadows but was grateful to see all attention fixed on Kelly.

Helping Hazel the last part of the way, they looked around and saw an altar filled with curious items to the side of the rock pile. The altar was bathed in the dancing firelight and they brushed aside the array of weapons from a long-forgotten period to prepare the concoction of liquids they had recovered from the Alessandro Test. 'How are we going to do this?' Hazel asked as she removed both boxes and extracted the ornate wooden chalice.

'I'll grab hold of him and pin him to the ground, you just

need to pour it into his mouth.'

'Is that going to work?'

'Who knows?'

Stanley kept one eye on the frenzied battle between Eric and Kelly as the Iceman continued to showcase his power. Much to Stanley's surprise, a storm now raged beneath the ceiling of the cavern and bolts of lightning crackled between the forming clouds.

'We need to hurry.' He groaned as he directed Hazel's attention to the forming storm.

'I'm going as fast as I can.'

Hazel opened the first vial and poured the orange-red liquid into the cup. Feeling the heat against her face it surprised her to see the viscous liquid move as she would expect lava to move in a volcano. Having no time to admire the fluid, she opened the next container and watched in disbelief as the grey fluid floated down from the vial into the cup as if made of air itself.

The final vial was filled with crystal blue water that reacted upon contact with the lava-like liquid. The contents of the chalice hissed and frothed, emitting an eerie pink glow. Stepping away from the chalice, they both watched as the mix of items frothed and foamed over the lip of the cup.

As a crack of lighting illuminated the room, colliding with the wall beside Kelly's head, they returned to the chalice to see it filled with an oily liquid that moved of its own accord.

'Is that it?' Stanley quizzed as he looked at the fluid.

'I hope so.'

Not wanting to waste any more time he turned in time to see Eric drag Kelly to the ground and pin him into position against the floor. Even from across the room Stanley could see Kelly's face contorted with pain as Eric pulled himself closer to the other man he had pinned beneath him.

'Let's go.' Hazel declared and snatched the chalice from the table of discarded copper age weapons.

Stanley moved as fast as he dared while remaining out of the Iceman's sight. The stench of rotten flesh and decay was overwhelming as he moved nearer to the creature. When he was within striking distance, he turned to check Hazel was still with him. Taking his cue from her nod he made his move.

Acting on instinct, Stanley jumped onto the Iceman's back as he once again raised his hands towards the roof of the cavern to call down another bolt of lightning. Caught by surprise, the creature released a guttural scream of anger and surprise as Stanley wrapped his legs around the Iceman's waist and trapped his rotten head between his arms.

Thrashing to break free of the surprise attack the Iceman bellowed as he fell backwards to the floor crushing Stanley beneath him. Scrambling to break free from Stanley's chokehold, he glimpsed Hazel as she hurried towards them.

'Do it now!' Stanley screamed as he fought to hold himself tight around the Iceman's throat.

The creature knew their intention, not through any recognition of the chalice but from the smell of the steaming liquid that filled it. The acrid smell was repulsive to him and he knew their intention.

Rolling from side-to-side, Stanley fought hard to maintain his grip but felt the creature slipping free from him. Desperate for Hazel to complete their attack he closed his eyes and clenched his jaw to exert every iota of effort he could despite the frenzied struggling of the impossibly strong creature.

As Hazel closed down Eric released his grip on Kelly and moved to assist his master. Detaching from his prey he made to move but Kelly took hold of him and dragged him back to afford Stanley and Hazel the time they needed.

With one arm trapped out to his side, the Iceman fought to brings his hands together and call back the raging storm that had rumbled at the cave's roof. Struggling to hold him back, Stanley felt himself moving as the Iceman brought his hands together.
'HAZEL!' He bellowed, but no sooner had the words left his mouth did the creature call the lightning to his hands.

Catching the crackling bolt of electricity between his poised hands, neither Stanley nor Hazel reacted. Clapping his crooked hands together, the lightning exploded in a blinding light and shock wave that sent Hazel flying and detached Stanley from the Iceman's neck.

As Hazel crashed into the altar where she had prepared the frothing chalice the oily contents spilled out across her, the altar and the collection of items that covered it. Her back throbbed where she had landed on the stone table, and she rolled to her side to see the Iceman lift Stanley from the floor.

Feeling his muscle twitching from the explosion of electricity, Stanley could do very little to fight against the Iceman as he lifted him from the floor. Feeling the creature's wiry fingers wrapping around his neck, he clawed at his hand to break free.
'You seek to imprison me, why?' The Iceman growled as he suspended Stanley in the air. 'None of you are worthy.'

Throwing Stanley through the air, the young man crashed to the floor and had no time to react as his body became pinned in place by a stream of electricity called down from the rumbling clouds above.

Controlling the storm, the Iceman fed the flow of electricity down from the clouds and through Stanley's body as he laid on the floor a conduit for the flow of current. Unable to move, his muscles in a state of spasm, Stanley could do nothing but scream in response to the immense pain that coursed through his body.

'Let him go!' Hazel screamed from the altar as she stumbled to her knees, having rolled off the tabletop.

The Iceman responded by calling a second bolt of lightning from the clouds and directing it in Hazel's direction. Having expected the attack, Hazel did her best to roll clear of the attack as the lightning bolt exploded onto the stone where she had been crouched.

Keeping his attention on Stanley, the Iceman redirected a second bolt down onto Stanley's convulsing body. Above the screams of pain that echoed around the room, Hazel could not help but cry as she favoured her broken ribs that throbbed with every intake of breath.

Powerless to do anything she could only watch as the Iceman continued to torture Stanley with wave after wave of electricity.

'Stanley,' she groaned as she struggled to crawl towards him. 'Please.'

Kelly could see everything that was happening and felt sick as the Iceman tortured Stanley. As Eric had tried to scramble free to assist his master, Kelly had made his move to stop him. Lifting a rock from the floor Kelly had slammed it into Eric's head sending him sprawling to the ground. Now, as wave after wave of lighting pulsated down from the ceiling, he slammed the rock down onto Eric's head until Eric could only twitch beneath him.

Bruised, battered and bleeding, Kelly staggered to his feet and ran across to help Stanley. Fighting the desire to scream in defiance Kelly reached the Iceman and kicked out at the side of his head sending him crashing to the floor.

As soon as the Iceman had lost his connection with the storm, the torrent of electricity ended and Stanley's body could relax. His body steamed from the constant flow of electricity and he could do nothing but groan on the floor. His body and muscles screaming in response to the pain. 'Stanley.' Kelly's voice was filled with concern as he raced to his friend's side.

Stanley was hot to the touch and his clothes smouldered where the electricity had danced through him. Relieved to see Stanley still alive, he saw the young man roll his head to look at him.
'Sorry.' Stanley heaved between his chapped lips.

Kelly had no time to respond. As he moved his lips to speak he sprang to his feet with a look of pure terror on his face. Trying to register what was happening, Stanley looked up in time as Kelly's chest exploded outwards in a spray of crimson blood.

Protruding from the centre of Kelly's chest was a spear of solid ice that transformed into a human hand before his eyes. In a state of extreme shock Kelly looked down at the icy spear that now protruded from his chest, he raised his hands as if testing if what he was seeing was real. Feeling the cold ice against his skin, terror consumed him as the ice transformed into the mottled flesh of the Iceman's arm.

From across the room Hazel watched in disbelief as the Iceman thrust his right arm out towards Kelly who knelt at Stanley's side. The creature's hand launched through the air and extended into a piece of pointed ice that flew through the air and impaled Kelly from behind. Lifting him to his feet, the Iceman casually walked towards Kelly as his arm of ice returned to its decaying form. As he arrived at Kelly's back the Inspector was suspended in the air with the Iceman's arm passing through his chest. 'Your God has seen fit to challenge me with nothing more than fools.' The Iceman mocked as he ripped his arm back through Kelly's chest, allowing him to fall to the floor.

Kelly slumped lifeless to the floor beside Stanley, who looked on in horror as the Iceman gripped Kelly's heart in his bloodstained hand. Looking at his companion, Stanley could see nothing in Kelly's lifeless eyes that stared up at him.

'Foolish,' the Iceman goaded as he raised the heart to his mouth. 'But his courage will feed me and help me grow. His death will serve my purpose now and afford me the strength to reclaim the power stolen from me.'

Still fighting to regain control over his muscles, Stanley could only watch in horror as the creature bit into Kelly's heart. As thick blood oozed down his chin Stanley felt repulsed by what he was being forced to watch.

From the other side of the room, Hazel fought against the pain in her ribs and moved to the altar. Looking through the antique weapons, she grasped a bound bow and knocked an arrow against the string. Having fired such a weapon only once before, she drew the string back and closed one eye to take aim. As he prepared to take his second bite of Kelly's heart she fired the arrow at the Iceman.

Sensing the attack, the creature stopped short of biting the heart and moved with impossible speed to catch the flying arrow in his hand. Turning, he scowled at Hazel as he held the arrow in mid-flight. The creature was about to speak but let out a shriek of surprise as the arrow in his hand smouldered against his skin sending a burst of blue flames from his hand forcing him to drop the arrow.

Staggering back in surprise, eyes wide and face filled with fear, he stepped away from the arrow trying to make sense of what had happened. Bending down to inspect the wooden shaft and stone arrowhead he noticed it shimmered in the firelight. The arrow was slick and wet where the contents of the chalice had spilled over it. Recoiling back he looked around in search of Eric but there was no longer any sign of him anywhere in the cavern.

Nursing his burned hand the Iceman turned and ran towards the cave entrance leaving Hazel and Stanley alone in the tomb.

CHAPTER FORTY

CLUTCHING at her side, Hazel staggered across the cavernous tomb to Stanley's side. As she neared him the acrid smell of burnt flesh invaded her nostrils and she fought back the desire to gag. Nursing her own injuries, she dropped to the floor and shook Stanley, surprised to find his clothes still warm to the touch. 'Stanley, please wake up.' Tears streamed down her face as she looked down at him.

Stanley groaned as he rolled his head to face her. His face was bruised and a jagged welt had formed across the side of his head above his ear. Where the electricity had scorched the skin he had lost a jagged track of his hair. 'What happened?' He groaned, his voice dry and crackling. 'Where's it gone?'
'He ran off,' Hazel explained as she checked him over. 'Something happened when I shot an arrow at him.'

Stanley was trying to listen over the ringing in his ears

and the strange sensations of pain that still pulsed through his body. With tremendous trepidation and effort, Stanley sat himself up onto his elbows and felt a wave of sickness flow over him.

'Give me a second.' He coughed as the world span around him. 'I feel like I've just, well, I'm not sure how I feel.'

'Can you walk?' Hazel pressed, aware that the creature had left them but uneasy at the fact they no longer knew where he was.

'Let's try.'

Helping him to his feet, Hazel hooked herself beneath Stanley's arm and winced as he put his weight on her. The pain in her ribs caused her to struggle for breath, and she was grateful when Stanley moved his weight off her.

'We need to find him, we've still got to stop this.'

'Where's Kelly?'

No sooner had the words left his lips did his gaze fall to the lifeless corpse a few feet away from him. Kelly's dead eyes stared up towards the ceiling of the tomb and the icy floor was stained with his blood. The hole left by the Iceman in Kelly's back was rough and turned Stanley's stomach as he could see a mass of blood and internal organs through the gaping hole. In a heartbeat the foggy memories of Kelly's death came flooding back.

'He died trying to save you,' Hazel explained as she realised Stanley did not understand what had happened while the Iceman had rained down the bolts of lightning at him.

'What happened to you?' Stanley lifted his attention from Kelly's corpse and looked to Hazel's battered appearance.

'When we tried to attack it, he threw me across the room.' She wheezed between sentences. 'I think I broke something when I landed on the table.'

Hazel pointed back to the stone altar and Stanley saw

the mess on the tabletop. He also noticed the upturned chalice and the oily contents swimming across the surface and dripping off the edge.

'What do we do now?'

'This seemed to hurt him.' Hazel explained as she lifted the discarded arrow she had fired. 'There has to be something about it, something that we can use to stop him.'

Stanley took the arrow from her and admired the stone tip and wooden shaft. There was nothing distinguishing about the arrow, nothing that could identify why it had influenced the Iceman. Turning the arrow between his fingers Stanley was about to speak when the cavern shook, almost knocking them from their feet.

'We should move.' Stanley declared and retrieved one of Kelly's pistols from the floor as they made their way out of the cavernous tomb.

The ground continued to shake as they evacuated the tomb. Clouds of dust and stone tumbled from the high ceiling as they moved and threatened to come down on them at any moment. Although they both longed to escape the tomb, there was little they could do to make speedy progress as their injuries forced them to move at an agonising pace.

Struggling up the lengthy staircase, they found themselves back on familiar ground as the entrance tunnel stretched out ahead of them. Hearing the enormous chains that had once held the Iceman rattling behind them, they moved with renewed purpose as another tremor rocked the mountain.

Supporting one another, they arrived at the tunnel's opening and gasped as they saw the storm that had been raging and hampered their progress had gone. Outside the cave entrance they could see the vast expanses of snow-tipped peaks stretching off into the distance. Brilliant untouched snow and patches of dark stone were illuminated by the bright sun and framed against a crystal-blue sky.

Astounded by the sudden change in weather, they turned to see any sign of the Iceman, but there was nothing. Scanning the ground, it was Hazel who noticed the uneven footprints in the fresh snow that led off away from the way they had come and further up the mountain. 'We have to stop him.' She declared and forced herself, against the pain, to follow the fresh tracks in the snow.

With little in the way of argument, Stanley stuffed Kelly's pistol into his trousers and followed Hazel as she staggered through the snow in search of the Iceman.

Had it not been for their reason for being there, they would have been swallowed by the picturesque scenery that surrounded them. As it was, as they clambered up the steep slope their surroundings were lost on them. Fuelled by grim determination, the pair followed the tracks until they reached a blind summit. Cresting the bluff their view opened up onto a wide plateau of snow and in the centre of it they caught sight of the Iceman.

Against the backdrop of the mountains, the creature looked frail and insignificant. Had it not been for the creature's display of immense power in the tomb, they would have been fooled by his appearance. Drawing the pistol from his trousers, Stanley took aim and prepared to fire.

As his finger tensed on the trigger Hazel pressed on the barrel and lowered it from Stanley's eye line.
'What are you doing?' Stanley growled as he pulled the gun free.
'You think that will kill him?' Hazel hissed as the creature continued to limp through the snow, his focus on the path

ahead.

'What do you suggest?'

'We have to try this.' Hazel snatched the arrow from him and held it out. 'It's the only thing that has had any effect on him.'

Stanley looked unconvinced as he brought the pistol up on aim. Feeling Hazel's glare, he shifted his attention to her and lowered the gun.

'What are we going to do then?'

'It burned him when he held it, we need to hurt him with it.'

'Kelly said the potion, or whatever it was, has to touch his heart, we should do the same with that.'

'It's worth a try.'

'Is it?'

Hazel answered with a curt nod and stalked off through the snow in pursuit of the decaying creature.

The Iceman was unaware of them as they pushed to close the gap between them. The terrain on the plateau was uneven, with outcrops of rocks half-buried beneath the snow. As they halved the distance between them and the Iceman, the creature stopped and sniffed the air.

Moving to take cover behind a pile of snow-capped rocks, Stanley dragged Hazel with him just in time as the Iceman turned to face back the way he had come. Peeking between the rocks, Stanley realised how gruesome the creature looked in the sunlight, his tight skin pulled across his face and mouth deformed into an upturned scowl.

Stanley watched with bated breath as the creature scanned the landscape, knowing or sensing someone was there but seeing nothing. Finding himself holding his breath, Stanley's hand flexed on the pistol grip as they remained hidden behind the rocks.

After what felt like an age the Iceman returned his

attention in the opposite direction but did not move. Instead, he raised his arms out to either side and spoke. From their position neither of them could make out what the creature was saying and as they watched a cloud passed in front of the sun blocking out the sun's warmth.

Turning to look at what had blocked out the sun, Hazel saw a layer of growing cloud forming in the sky as if conjured by the creature. As the clouds spread, the air grew colder and Hazel felt the chill once again against her skin. Looking back to where they had come from she could not help but scream.

The snow behind them, only showing the disturbance from their footprints, shudder and moved as something rose from the snow. Taking a human shape, whatever it was devoid of eyes or features but knew where they were. As the snow-person lunged towards them Stanley turned around and threw a punch into the thing's face.

As his blow collided with what appeared to be a head, the snow-figure disintegrated into a cloud of dusty snow. No sooner had the first snow-figure disappeared another appeared in its place, and another, and another.
'Bring them to me!' The Iceman's voice echoed from the other side of the rocks.

Acknowledging their master's instruction, the half a dozen figures of snow turned their attention to the pair of them. Grabbing her, Stanley pulled Hazel behind him and pressed towards the side of their cover.
'Get to him, do what you can, I'll keep these things busy.'
'I'm not leaving you.' Hazel argued.

Stanley ignored the protest and lunged forward as the nearest of the snow-figures lunged towards him. Driving himself forward, he hoped to give Hazel the time she would need to put an end to the craziness that surrounded them.

Hazel emerged from the rocks and found herself face-to-face with another of the snow-figures. Taken aback, she thrust the arrow in her hand out towards where she imagined an eye would be. It surprised her how her hand passed through the figure, as if the interior was hollow and the snow had morphed into a humanesque shell.

As the snow disintegrated she caught sight of the Iceman who remained poised with his back towards her. Steeling her resolve, fighting through the pain, she stalked through the snow as the Iceman continued to conjure up whatever demonic event he had planned.

The clouds continued to build and obscure the sunlight as the world grew darker around her. Hazel almost reached the Iceman when he turned to face her. What she saw chilled her to her core as the creature had taken shape into something different.

The ground around the Iceman appeared to be flowing towards him and inch by inch she could see the ice and snow fusing with his skin, giving it shape and colour as if regenerating his decaying flesh. The grotesque upturned lip had healed and a pair of vibrant emerald green eyes stared at her where there had been nothing before.

His newfound flesh seemed to ripple and move as if alive. It was this movement of flesh and sinew regenerating that chilled her. The sight in front of her defied everything she had ever believed.

'There is still time for you to absolve yourself of the ridiculous charge of your dead friend.' The Iceman snarled as he stared at her. 'Why fight the inevitability of my power?'

'Because nobody is supposed to have that power, everyone dies.'

'Not me.'

The Iceman lunged towards her but Hazel had

expected the attack. Dropping to the snow, she rolled away and regretted her action as the pain in her side coursed through her. The Iceman was relentless and stamped his bare foot into the snow beside her. Still grasping the arrow she dragged it across his calf and he screamed in pain.

The same pearlescent blue flames spat from the point where the tip had scraped across the new flesh, making the Iceman recoil away. Eyes wide, the creature screamed and launched another attack.

Doing her best to keep the Iceman at bay, he rained down blow after blow at Hazel until she had nowhere to go. Feeling his solid knuckle smash into her face she dropped back to the snow and let the arrow fall from her grasp.

'This world of yours will become mine,' the Iceman goaded as he lifted her from the snow and held her near his face.

The Iceman's skin moved like a million insects as it regenerated his face into something less deformed and decayed as the creature that had been imprisoned in the tomb. Held so close to his face Hazel fought to pull herself away but could not break his grip on her clothes.

'You're a monster.' She spat in defiance.

'Are you afraid of death?' The Iceman mused as he hovered his face close to her neck.

'Yes.' Hazel confessed. 'But I welcome it if it means I get to be away from things like you.'

'Are you not tempted by immortality? The chance to live by my side and save yourself from the pain of death?'

'No!'

'So be it.'

The Iceman stood tall, dragging Hazel up with him. Opening his mouth he forced Hazel's head back at an awkward angle and drove his face down to the flesh of her exposed neck.

CHAPTER FORTY-ONE

A single gunshot echoed in the air. Having closed her eyes, Hazel had expected to feel the Iceman's bite at her neck but instead tumbled to the ground. Released from his grasp, Hazel looked up to see the Iceman, face contorted with rage, turn to look back to where she had come from.

Stanley stood atop the rocks they had been hiding behind and kept a flow of snow-figures at bay beneath him. Still aiming the pistol towards the creature, Stanley kicked out and kept the figures from reaching up towards him.

'How dare you!' The Iceman roared as he turned to face Stanley. 'Your weapons cannot hurt me.'

The Iceman raised his hands to the heavens in defiance as Stanley loosed another two rounds that passed through the Iceman to bury in the snow behind him. Laughing at Stanley's futile attempts to kill him, the Iceman screamed at the clambering snow-figures that clawed at Stanley's feet.

'Kill him!'

Time seemed to move in slow motion as Hazel looked up at the Iceman and then across at Stanley. Balancing on the snowy rocks, Stanley appeared confident and defiant. She realised how far they had come together, having only just met. Two innocent young souls, surrounded by war and conflict, who had become embroiled in something so impossible to comprehend.

Seeing him stood there, she realised how much she cared for Stanley, how their ordeals and adventures had drawn them together. Where she had first seen him as a rebellious young man, hiding from the war, she now saw him in a very different light.

As Stanley fired another round the echo of the gunshot brought her back to reality. Desperate to do something, Hazel looked around and found the discarded arrow laid on the snow. Acting without thought, she ripped the arrow from the snow and looked at the glistening stone arrowhead.

The Iceman dropped his arms to the side and raised them again, and in response the floor erupted in a shower of stone and snow. Ripping the floor apart, Hazel watched as a gaping chasm appeared in the floor and stretched out towards Stanley. With nothing else at hand, Hazel rose to her knees and thrust the arrow upwards towards the Iceman's outstretched arms.

As the stone tip, still glistening with the spilled liquid from the altar, pierced the Iceman's flesh, a brilliant flash of blue flame erupted from his skin. Recoiling back Hazel released the arrow and dropped back to the snow and watched as the creature screeched and staggered backwards in the snow.

The surprise attack had stopped the jagged chasm from reaching the outcrop of rock where Stanley was balanced. Watching from his vantage point he sensed what Hazel was doing and took aim again as the Iceman fought to rip the arrow from his armpit. To Stanley's dismay the arrow had done nothing to end the Iceman, instead it had only offered them a distraction.

Taking aim for what it was worth, Stanley pulled the trigger to hear only a *click* as the magazine had run empty. Beyond frustrated and knowing their time was ending, Stanley launched the pistol at the nearest of the clambering snow-figures and leapt over them from his precarious place atop the rocks.

Flying, Stanley landed in the snow and ran as fast as he could towards the flailing creature. Catching sight of his attack, the Iceman fought against the searing pain in his side and thrust his right arm out towards Stanley. Much the same as it had when the creature had murdered Kelly. His hand transformed into a spear of ice and propelled out towards Stanley.

Expecting the attack Stanley dropped to the snow allowing the spear of ice to fly past him brushing across his shoulder. Crashing into the soft snow, Stanley fought to claw himself up but had rolled too far and felt his lower body skid towards the edge of the exposed chasm the creature had created.

The distraction was enough for Hazel as she launched up towards the Iceman and threw her bodyweight onto the arrow. Driving it deeper into the creature, the wooden shaft snapped under her weight as the Iceman launched her through the air away from him.

'You have nothing to bring against me.' The Iceman roared and turned on her.

Knowing they had done all they could, there was

nothing left for them to fight with, Hazel prepared herself for death. Looking up at the enraged Iceman, she saw his expression change as the clouds blocking out the sun broke.

A look of confusion painted across the creature's face as he raised his now quivering hand to the skies to conjure the clouds. The sun continued to burn away the heavy storm clouds and as Hazel watched, the creature's flesh once again returned to its decayed and discoloured appearance.

'What is this?' The Iceman coughed.

As he coughed, the creature spewed out a mouthful of the same oily liquid that had filled the chalice. As the creature clutched at its chest, he staggered backwards in the snow. Staring wide-eyed at Hazel, he fought to find the broken arrow in his armpit as another flurry of blue flames erupted from the ragged wound.

'Hazel!' Stanley's voice carried in the air as he fought to keep his position balanced over the gaping chasm.

Snatching her attention from the Iceman, Hazel moved to Stanley's aid and pulled him back from the ledge. Once they were both on safer ground, they turned their attention to the creature.

Before their eyes, they saw him return to his half-decayed form. Dehydrated flesh once again tightened around his bones and the curled upper lip returned. Anything that had appeared alive with the creature once again was replaced by the rotten decay of near-death.

'You cannot kill me. I cannot die.' The Iceman staggered in the snow, the panic clear on his face. 'You delay the inevitable.'

The creature's grasp on the English language faded, and he delivered his final words in his native tongue. Neither Stanley nor Hazel could understand the words, but saw their meaning painted on the Iceman's face.

As if exposed to a bolt of electricity, the Iceman went rigid with both arms outstretched to one side. His lifeless eyes stared at them as his body went rigid, as if frozen by the ice he himself had commanded. The creature remained in that position, standing in the snow, frozen in place, for a moment before he tumbled back and disappeared over the edge of the mountain.

Helping one another up, Hazel and Stanley staggered across the plateau of snow and moved to the mountain's edge. As the sun once again dispersed the eerie storm clouds, the world around them was bathed in light. Peering over the precarious edge, they could see down to the jagged valley far below.

Peering at a landscape of uneven rocks and snow, there was no sign of the Iceman, no indentation in the snow or signs that his body had landed anywhere. All they could see hundreds of feet below was the uneven slopes of the mountain and the landscape of snow stretching as far as they could see.

'Is it over?' Hazel quizzed as she watched Stanley scouring the landscape for signs of the creature.

'I think it is,' Stanley sighed as he stepped back from the edge. 'For now.'

Bruised, battered and struggling for breath, the pair dropped to the snow and sat on the cliff edge to admire the view. Bathed in the glorious sunshine, they huddled together as Hazel rested her head on Stanley's shoulder. 'Who would have thought it?' She mused as she felt safe for the first time in a long time. 'Me and you, two strangers a little over a week ago, would have gone through all of this?'

'I know, it's almost too unbelievable to be true.'

'Imagine telling anybody,' Hazel laughed and held her

side at the pain of her ribs moving. 'They would say we were mad.'

'We should get moving, it's a long way back and I don't know how much daylight we've got left.'

'Not yet.' Hazel pleaded. 'Let's just admire the view for a while, I want to remember this moment.'

She was tired, they both were, and thought of moving didn't appeal to either of them. Feeling more exhausted than ever before, Stanley wrapped his arm around Hazel and pulled her closer. Feeling her warmth against his own, he savoured the view and looked out across the Ötztal Alpine mountains.

Before long their exhaustion had swallowed them both and they sat, perched on the precarious cliff edge with their eyes closed. Exposed to the elements it was a dangerous place to stay, but they were beyond caring. Surrounded by the picturesque beauty of the mountains seemed the right place for their journey to end.

'Hazel? Stanley?' The voice was soft and sounded distant at first. As they repeated their names Stanley was the first to open his eyes.

Much to his surprise, the sun was dipping behind the mountains and a handful of the snow-capped summits glowed almost golden in the dying sun's light. Rousing Hazel from her slumber, he turned to seek the source of the voice.

'What happened here?' The soft voice pressed as Stanley turned to find Victoria knelt in the snow behind them.

She had bandaged the wounds on her face so that a third of her head was wrapped in bloodstained cloth. Only able to see out of one eye, the other obscured beneath her makeshift dressing, Victoria shook Hazel to being her around. The air was colder, the warming rays of the sun no longer touching them.

'We should move if you want to survive.' Victoria warned as she helped them to their feet. 'You'll die of exposure and frostbite if you stay out here any longer.'

'I don't know if I can make it.' Hazel coughed, wincing at the pain of her broken ribs and battered body.

'We will.' Victoria answered.

The surviving trio made their way down the mountain by the light of a waxing moon. The sight of the cabin in the distance had been a welcome vision and spurred them on for the last leg of their journey. Unlike before, they could now see the beauty of the valley that surrounded the isolated log cabin. The Iceman's storm had obscured the magnificent landscape but now, bathed in moonlight, it was almost perfect.

Reaching the cabin, the three of them were beyond exhausted. Their injuries had hampered them but in the relative safety of the cabin they had survived the trek and could, at last, relax. Before he allowed himself to sleep, Stanley redressed Victoria's injuries and helped lower Hazel into the comfort of her bed.

Alone in the living room, Stanley found Hans' drinks cabinet and poured himself a glass of scotch from an almost empty bottle. Sliding into an empty chair, Stanley savoured the heat of the drink in his throat and allowed himself to drift into an uneasy sleep.

CHAPTER FORTY-TWO

DAYS had passed while the trio had not only recovered from their ordeal but also allowed Victoria to plan for their return home. Journeying into the local village, Victoria had contacted Hans' connections and secured them passage once again from the isolated airfield.

With farewells concluded and thanks shared, Stanley and Hazel had been reluctant to bid farewell to their picturesque surroundings. Returning to London seemed to mark the end of their shared adventure and a return to a world that would never appreciate or understand what they had been through together.

Their flight back had been quiet, leant against one another, they had spoken little and both been consumed by their thoughts of what awaited them upon their return. Although Stanley had faced a mythical creature and helped protect humanity, the thought of returning home to face his father filled him with trepidation. He knew he could never explain the truth and, as ridiculous as it seemed, he feared his parents would always believe him a criminal.

Much to their surprise, when they had disembarked the train at Paddington, Brother Jacob was waiting for them. Standing on the platform the old friar looked out of place but his warm greeting was a welcome relief than finding their parents waiting for them, not that they would be.

'Your companion warned me of your return,' Jacob announced as they joined him on the platform. 'She explained of Brother Kelly's death and of your success in defeating the creature.'

'I don't know how we can call that a success, we have no idea where he is or if he's dead.' Stanley replied as Jacob encouraged them to follow him out of the station.

'He is not dead, surely Brother Kelly explained that to you before his end?'

'Then what did we achieve?'

'You returned the Iceman to the only prison that can contain him.' Jacob smiled. 'Such a place is inescapable, I think you of all people would understand that Stanley.'

The answer caught Stanley by surprise. The old man's meaning was lost on him.

'I'm not sure what you mean.'

'His own mind, trapped inside a world of his own memories and hurt, an inescapable world of relived pain.'

Stanley blushed as he realised what Jacob referred to. Nodding in agreement, he sensed Hazel's curiosity but was grateful she did not press him further for an explanation. The knowing look on Jacob's face told him the old man understood the torment and self-torture that haunted Stanley from his time in France. Thinking of the pain and memories that would haunt such a creature as the Iceman, the certainty of that mental imprisonment was a satisfying conclusion in Stanley's mind.

'I expect you are eager to return to your families?' Jacob pressed as they emerged onto the street.

To their surprise, a police car was waiting for them outside the station and Jacob guided them towards it. Awash with concern, Stanley stepped in front of Hazel and stopped in their tracks.

'What's going on?' Stanley defended as the uniformed constable that had stopped them in the churchyard moved to open the door.

'This fine officer is aware of your adventure.'

'Damien Kelly was good friend of mine, both in the service and outside of it within the Brotherhood.' The constable opened his collar to reveal the same black inked tattoo of the Benedictine medal on his chest. 'I know he trusted you, I know we offer you our thanks.'

'You'll be relieved to know the constable has assured your parents of your innocence in the crimes you were arrested for. When you return home, it will be to relief and open arms.'

'Thank you.' Stanley felt overwhelmed as they followed Jacob into the rear of the waiting police car.

'Do they know what we have done?' Hazel asked as she shuffled closer to Stanley.

'No, and it must stay that way.' Jacob answered as the car pulled away from the curb.

'So where do they think we've been all this time?'

'It has been explained you have helped with the investigation and are to be commended for your help.' The constable added from the front of the car as he drove. 'Your reputations are restored.'

'Good.' Stanley bit with more frustrated than he had

intended.

'Where are we going then?' hazel interjected, giving Stanley a moment to calm his frustration.

'Victoria tells me she retrieved the artefacts from the tomb before finding you?'

'Yes.' Hazel answered and opened the rucksack that contained the ornate wooden boxes and what remained of their contents.

'I would seek to return the Magnitudo and these items into The Vault. I would be honoured if you would replace them.'

'You're going to keep them all together?' Hazel pressed as she looked across at Stanley.

'You can, if you wish, seek to return them to their original resting place?' Jacob's wry smile caught Hazel by surprise. 'Although I expect you're in no rush to seek passage through Alessandro's tests again?'

'Not at all!'

'Then would you honour us in replacing them in The Vault?'

Neither answered with words, they nodded, both knowing this would mark the end of their journey. They made the remainder of the short drive in silence. All the while Stanley looked out of the window and realised how dark and dismal London now looked. Although it had changed little in their absence, the world outside felt different and less alive.

Lost in his own thoughts and melancholy, Stanley was surprised when the police car pulled up outside St Margaret's Church. Snapping back to the moment, they exited the car and walked to the large doors of the church. 'I will wait here, my place is not within Ad Firmamentum.' The policeman announced as he opened the door to allow them entry into the church.

Relieved to find the church empty, Stanley and Hazel admired the grand arches and ornate decoration of the church's interior. A stark contrast to the damaged interior of Ealing Abbey, the church seemed untouched by the war that raged around it. Following in silence, they moved along the length of the church and followed Jacob as he guided them to a small door devoid of a handle or lock on the far side of the altar.

Placing his hand against a hidden button, Hazel and Stanley watched as the door shifted back and slid aside. Much to their surprise they looked down at a narrow staircase and before they could move a figure appeared at the bottom and walked up towards them.

'I wasn't aware you were here.' Jacob announced to the man who walked with confidence up towards them.

The man was in his forties and sported a well-worn Panama hat atop his head. Hearing the voice the man smiled and removed the hat out of respect. As he emerged from the door, he nodded to Hazel and Stanley then offered his greeting to Jacob.

'My apologies, I had hoped to be done before you arrived.' The man offered and shook Jacob's wrinkled hand.

'I trust you were satisfied the items remain in our protection?'

'Very much so, I can only thank you for your assistance in all of this. I had hoped my death would have ended my involvement, but alas it appears that may never be the case.'

The curious conversation stole Stanley's attention as he took in the man. There was something about him that stood him apart from Jacob and the constable, whereas the two men of the Brotherhood seemed serious and somehow at the mercy of their beliefs, this man was different.

'You must be Jacob's latest heroes?' The man enquired as

he replaced his hat onto his head. 'If I can offer you one piece of advice?'

'What's that?' Hazel hushed.

'No matter what they offer you, don't become one of their Brotherhood, keep yourselves free of all of that, help them by all means but keep your freedom.'

'Archy, please.'

'Jacob, you can't expect me to let you steal these two into subservience. I see the same fire in them I had in myself in my youth.'

'Who are you?' Stanley asked as the man made to take his leave.

'My name is Archibald Skevington, well it was before they forced me to assume a new name.' Archy offered a knowing smile to the two of them. 'I've heard what you've faced and know the toll it takes.'

'You've seen the same?'

'Oh no, dear boy! Our paths cross on our journeys towards different dark curses, yours was the creature of ice and mine is something entirely different.' Archy moved closer to whisper to them out of Jacob's earshot. 'Keep yourselves free and if the need ever arises seek me out. Perhaps one day we can sit and compare adventures.'

Archy slid a business card into Stanley's hand and offered him a crafty wink. Slipping the card into his pocket, Stanley and Hazel watched as Archy offered his farewells and disappeared out of the church.

'I won't ask what he said.' Jacob groaned as he led them down the staircase. 'Archy's path has cost him more than we could ever appreciate.'

'How's that?' Hazel pressed as they walked.

'He had a family once, a wife and children.' Jacob's voice was filled with sadness.

'What happened to them?'

'To them, nothing. But to secure their safety, Archy had to sacrifice his life with them. Now he hides himself under a new name and ensures his sacrifice keeps them safe.'

'What was he doing here if he's not one of your Order?' Stanley asked as they passed along the familiar subterranean corridor where all this had started.

'We help him on his quest to rid the world of a different evil.'

'Different? There's more than just the Iceman?'

'Much more my friends, Ad Firmamentum is the tip of the iceberg and is one of many places where we keep those secrets as safe as we can.'

Removing a key from around his neck, Jacob unlocked the wooden door and pushed it open. Stanley recognised the organised chaos of The Vault. Unlike before, the room was bright and lit and he could take in the vast array of artefacts, scrolls and items stacked on every shelf. The room was filled with curiosities and once again his attention fell to the curious skull sealed within the glass box.

'I think it is time for you to relieve yourselves of your burden.' Jacob encouraged as he guided them to a table where a large wooden box stood empty and open.

Hazel removed the bag from her back and one by one removed the ornately carved boxes from within. Checking the contents, the three empty vials in one and the chalice in the other, she handed them to Jacob.

'Should the need ever arise for these artefacts again, you will know where they are.'

Jacob placed each of the boxes inside the larger box and closed the lid. A small key with a chain looped through the head sat in the lock, and Jacob twisted it to secure the crate. With a resounding *click,* the box was locked and Jacob removed the key. Turning, he held out chain and let the key hang in the air.

'The Brotherhood offers these secrets protection, but they are yours now.'

For a moment neither of them moved until at last Hazel reached out and took the key from the old man.

'Brother Kelly was once the sworn protector of the Magnitudo of the Iceman, now that honour falls to you.'

'Does that mean you expect him to come back?'

'It means we do not know but must always be prepared in case he does. This is now your legacy to continue as you see fit.' Jacob looked around them room, admiring the collection of antiquities. 'This place is a treasure trove of secrets, each item links to some part of human history. I have spent my life protecting this world and yet it is two strangers to my Brotherhood that I owe my thanks to.'

'We didn't mean to be a problem.' Hazel apologised.

'My dear Hazel, it is my belief God sent you when it was needed. Without you, without either of you, the world would be a darker place, haunted by a creature of immeasurable power. It is you and you alone that have saved us all for an eternity of danger and death.'

They remained in The Vault for some time before Jacob led them back into the church. As they moved towards the doors leading back out into the street, he stopped them for a moment.

'This place and any other linked to the Brotherhood are open to you if ever you need them. We owe you our gratitude and I offer you my friendship.'

'Thank you,' Stanley felt a lump in his throat as he shook the old man's hand. 'I'm sorry about Inspector Kelly.'

'Brother Kelly sacrificed himself in protection of humanity, he is an honourable man and will be remembered.'

Stanley and Hazel made their farewells and left the church hand-in-hand. Having first met in the ruined churchyard as two complete strangers, they now left it very much in a different place. As London continued to move around them, they shared a kiss before offering one last look back at the church.

The doors were closed and neither Jacob nor the policeman was anywhere to be seen.

'I think it's time we went home.' Hazel sighed as they turned and left the churchyard and their adventure behind them.

EPILOGUE
1991

THE small cottage overlooked the ruins of
Beauvale Priory and had become Stanley and Hazel's
family home. When the war had ended they had moved
from London and settled into a life far away from the
capital. Marrying soon after they had travelled the world
and had many more adventures, but soon settled to have a
family.

Stood on the small patio, looking out across the rolling
landscape with the ruins in view, Stanley, now in his
senior years, smiled at the memories. Holding a mug in his
hand he took a sip as he remembered the first time they
had visited the ruins.

With both their children having families of their own,
Stanley and Hazel had settled into their solitude. Age had
caught up with them and although Stanley still sported
the rough scar above his ear, there was little to show for
their journey into the world of the Iceman and his dark
curse. Alone on the patio, he admired the view and felt a
swell of pride in what they had achieved in their lives.

'Stanley,' Hazel's voice yelled from inside the house.
'What is it?'
'Come here, quick.'

There was something in her tone that worried him. Hazel's health had been failing of late and she was often to be found sat wrapped in a blanket in their bed watching television. Snatching up his cane, Stanley made his way back into the house and moved through to their bedroom.

They had adorned the walls with photographs of their adventures around the world, each picture giving a snapshot of their journey around the world. Above the bed, sealed inside an ornate frame, was the key that Jacob had handed Haze inside The Vault. Looking down from the key Stanley saw Hazel sat up in bed, her eyes wide. 'What is it my love?' Stanley asked as he perched on the edge of the bed.
'Look, the news.'

Stanley turned his attention to a news report that played on the small television set mounted on the wall. Turning up the volume, Stanley listened as the reporter spoke.

'The young couple found the remains in the Ötztal Alps almost a week ago. Believing it to be the body of a mountaineer they called for help and it was soon discovered that the body, trapped in the ice, was that of an almost perfect preserved man thousands of years old.'

Stanley rose from the bed and moved to stand in front of the television. Turning the dial, he raised the volume until it was almost deafening.
'This can't be possible.' Stanley hushed as he stared at the news report.

The reports showed a young couple posing for photographs next to a corpse half submerged in the ice. Although face down the body's position and the familiar discolouration of the skin was all too familiar to them. 'Authorities have recovered the body, and it is the source of debate because of the mummified remains' location as it sits close to the border of Italy and Austria. We have exclusive images of what experts believe may be the oldest naturally preserved human remains in history.'

The screen was filled with a photograph of the recovered body's face. Stanley staggered back from the television and sat back on the bed as the Iceman's deformed face filled the screen. The upturned lip, hollow eyes and mottled skin were like a nightmarish memory. Feeling his heart beating in his chest, Stanley turned to look at Hazel.

Placing her hand onto his, she looked up to the key in the frame above the bed.
'I think we need to make a phone call,' she hushed as the news report ended and she muted it with the remote control. 'If they don't know already, we should warn them.'

Sat in their bedroom, the freedom they had felt since defeating the Iceman melted away. Alone in the cottage, the two of them took a moment to overcome the sickening feeling of despair before Stanley rose to make a phone call. As he reached for the receiver he pulled Archy's business card from underneath the phone.
'Let's just hope he stays that way and they don't wake him up.' Stanley sighed as he dialled the number written on the back of the card.

*   *   *

The mummified remains of the Iceman remain preserved in South Tyrol to this day. Dubbed Ötzi the Iceman, the corpse remains the focus of much debate and research. For the time being, the Brotherhood of the Benedictine Order watch and wait in the hope the creature remains trapped within the prison of its own mind.

Should the day arise that its Dark Curse is once again released upon the earth, there are those who are prepared to protect humanity from its evil.

Let us hope that day does not come.

GET A FREE BESTSELLER (AND FIVE ADDITIONAL STORIES)

Building trust and a relationship with my readers is one of the best things about being a writer. Knowing I have created something you want to be part of fills me with pride. I occasionally (when I remember and am not trying to write something new) send out newsletters, offers and inside "behind the scenes" titbits relating to my books. I'd love to see you on my mailing list so you can see the exclusive secrets but also be the first to know about new and exciting adventures I want to take you on.

If you sign up to the mailing list I'll make sure you get:

- A FREE copy of **Origins Of The Magdon: Anthology**. This includes the bestselling novelette "Vercovicium" and the four extra novelettes that complete the series all in one handy anthology of adventures.

- Exclusive "behind the scenes" information about the Timothy Scott Series and future projects including never before seen original sketches and plans.

- Exclusive discounts and offers to do with my catalogue of projects and more.

SUBSCRIBE NOW AT TOBEY-ALEXANDER.COM

ENJOY THIS BOOK? YOU CAN MAKE A HUGE DIFFERENCE...

Reviews are the most powerful tool in helping me build trust in my stories and creativity. When it comes to getting attention for my books, there is nothing better than an honest word from someone who has entered my world and enjoyed the story I have told.

At the moment I don't have the power behind me to advertise on billboards or in newspapers (trust me, I'm working on it) but I do have something the big advertising agencies don't have and that's YOU!

An honest review shared, no matter how short, catches the attention of other readers and help give my books validity.

If you have enjoyed this book I would be more grateful than you can imagine if you would spend just a few moments leaving a review on the book's Amazon Page.

Thank you so very much for your time and I look forward to inviting you back for another adventure soon.

ABOUT THE AUTHOR

Tobey Alexander, the author of Timothy Scott and
many other stories has his online home at
www.tobey-alexander.com. You can connect with
him on Facebook at
www.Facebook.com/TobeyAlexanderAuthor or else
on Instagram at
www.instagram.com/tobey_alexander_author and
should you want to contact him via email at
TobeyAlexanderAuthor@GMail.com it would make
his day to hear your thoughts on his adventures.

ALSO BY TOBEY ALEXANDER

Have your read them all?

In the Magdon Series

Origins Of The Magdon: Five Novelette Anthology

In 1911 a teenage Archibald Skevington travels to Vercovicium, a Roman Fort on the border of Scotland, to satisfy his interest in history. An accidental discovery of a subterranean crypt thrusts him onto a path that will consume his life. Following Archy's adventures from five key events in his life he uncovers a terrifying monster, forgotten from history, that slumbers in the darkness. What secrets lay in the shadows and how far will some go to see it unleashed upon the earth?

FREE to download

Into The Dark

Picking up decades after Archy's death, an unsuspecting family are dragged into the same world of the fabled mythical creature. When his wife is kidnapped and held to ransom, Gabe and his two children must research their long-dead ancestor's obsession if they hope to save her.

The family must come together as a secret cult hell-bent on resurrecting the beast holds everything they hold dear on a knife's edge. When the time comes, they must make an impossible choice, save the one they love or save the world?

Available now

From The Dark

With his family shaken by their encounter with the Magdon and cultist Veks, Gabe once again finds himself in their crosshairs. Dragged once again into a world of secrets, Gabe and his daughter must seek the help of others allied to the protection of humanity. Despite their actions, the world remains at risk as the Veks have discovered a new way to recall the beast from the shadows.

Dragging you once again into a world of shadows and monsters, Gabe and his allies must search through their family history and seek help from a most unexpected ally in this twisting mystery adventure.

Available now

In the Timothy Scott Adventure Series

Timothy Scott: Shadow Island

Meet twelve-year-old Timothy Scott as he discovers a hidden world behind an antique mirror. Plagued by bullies, ostracised by his peers and seeking solace in his only friend who is invisible. Thrust into this new world he must learn to overcome his own self-doubt in an epic coming-of-age fantasy adventure.

Born from the style of adventure in Harry Potter and the Chronicles Of Narnia, be prepared to enter a whole world of adventure for all ages.

Available now

Timothy Scott: The Torn Mountains

Timothy must return through the mirror to help save his younger sister. When a familiar voices beckons from the shadows, Timothy must steel himself to return except this time he will not be alone. Mielikuvitus has changed, the foreboding shadow of the Darkness has started to lift but Timothy knows there is something else at play.

Travelling once again through the mirror we join Timothy and a most unexpected ally as they venture to the mythical Torn Mountains in the hope of saving his sister from the hands of a sinister creature.

Available now

In the Blackout Series

Blackout

Michael Swann is a man haunted by his past. After the untimely death of his son, he has withdrawn from his family and seeks a life of danger and solitude. After an uneventful free-climb Michael crosses paths with a mysterious woman that sees him dragged from modern-day Greece to the battlefields of the First World War. Somehow, Michael has travelled back in time.

Waking in a cold and sterile military facility, Michael finds himself recruited into the Tempus Project, a secret project researching movement through time. All is not as it seems as Michael soon discovers more to the secrets behind Tempus and its intentions. Through his journey Michael will not only question his world, his beliefs but also his sexuality.

Available now

Collapse: A Blackout Time Travel Novel

Michael Swann is back. Having turned his back on Tempus and the clandestine military project he now lives on the run with his partner Adrian. When a surprising face from his past drags him back, Michael must unravel a series of seemingly unconnected events if he is to piece together the world that is crumbling around him.

Spanning even more epic locations throughout history, Michael will need guidance and help from those who understand the ability of time Leaps if he is to secure leverage to restore his life and save his newfound family.

Available now

Aaron Raven Series

Gridlock

What connects a retired Metropolitan Police detective, a chemical attack on a train and the unsolved murder of an Eastern European mob boss twelve years ago?

Aaron Raven must piece together the interlaced events if he is to help prove the innocence of his hospitalised sister who is the prime suspect in the chemical attack. Be prepared for a heart-racing thriller spanning Europe as Aaron skirts the line between right and wrong as he fights to save his reputation and family.

Available now

Printed in Great Britain
by Amazon